DWELLINGS

DWELLINGS

A PETE BARROW MYSTERY

KEN LINN

For Judi, with thanks for all the quiet time.

Chapter One

Strangers don't usually show up here unannounced. My place isn't along the way to anywhere. Unless your intended destination is the Potomac River. The road ends at the water, where remnants of a long-gone boat ramp, cracked and broken chunks of green-slimed concrete, appear and vanish with the changing tides. Turn right just before the river, and you're soon into a cluster of houses known as Tusker's Beach. Turn left, and you're in my driveway.

It was the Saturday after Memorial Day, the weekend before exams, six days until graduation. All my schoolwork was done. There were no more homework papers left to grade. No more quizzes or tests to construct. All my mathematics exams were copied, stapled, and stacked, ready to go. Nothing to do until the impending exams were taken.

Once the exams were graded, final grades calculated, closing faculty meetings concluded, my time would be my own. I wasn't teaching summer school that year. My Virginia state certification was up to date. No need to take a class, as I'd been required to do so many summers in the past. These days, I wondered how much longer I would keep going. Retirement was calling, but so far I'd declined to answer. Others who had answered the call kept telling me I'd know when the time was right. Though they never said just *how* I'd know. Like it was some kind of secret Zen thing. Some teachers are such know-it-all assholes.

I was out on my deck in the late afternoon sun, seated at the picnic table, wrestling with a windblown copy of the latest edition of The Potomac County News, the local weekly newspaper. I was dressed in a plain red t-shirt and khaki cargo shorts, with black Nike athletic shoes sporting a swish that matched my shirt. That's about as fashionable as I get.

The weather was perfect for early June. Not too hot, a stiff breeze blowing in off the river, kicking up waves more than a foot high. Far out on the water, a variety of sailboats glided and bobbed. Speedboats were thumping and buzzing around, closer to shore. Nearly seven miles across the water, the Maryland shoreline was a distant gray blur. The stifling heat and humidity would be arriving any day now, settling in for the long season here on the Northern Neck Peninsula.

While scanning the paper, looking for something of interest, I was thinking about how to spend the coming Sunday. Maybe a little fishing. Catch up on some reading. Put out a couple of baited crab pots off the pier. Take a nap or two.

When my phone buzzed, I picked it up off the table and read a text message from my friend, Potomac County Sheriff Oscar Murphy, asking me if I was at home. I answered with a simple *yes* and waited for a response that didn't come.

Returning to the newspaper, I was surprised to see no one I knew, directly or otherwise, listed in the week's obituaries. I read through every detail of the yard sale notices, though I'd never attended one, and had no inclination to rummage through other people's castoffs. I had plenty of my own stuff that needed to go. The events calendar included notices of an antique boat show at an inlet marina off the Rappahannock River over in Dominion County and a horse show scheduled for mid-July at the 4-H arena outside of Weston. The police and court report sections took up half a page. Rural Potomac County isn't exactly a hotbed of crime, but we have our share of the usual: traffic violations and accidents, minor thefts, DUIs, bar brawls, domestic disturbances, and drug busts. But little of the major mayhem that goes on in the cities.

I turned the page, spotted an article titled *Body Found in River Remains Unidentified*, and started to read. *'Maryland authorities continue to seek help from the public in identifying the body of a woman found floating in the Potomac River, off the Maryland shore, two months ago.'*

When I heard the crunching sound of a vehicle pulling onto my crushed oyster-shell driveway, I expected it to be Murphy. It wasn't.

My visitor arrived looking like he'd spent a lifetime in the shade. His pale face in sharp contrast with the dark clothes he wore. His loose-fitting suit, slightly frayed at the lapel and sleeves, had seen better days. He wore a skinny black tie that matched his physique. By the time he'd climbed the three steps to the deck, he was out of breath. He took off his sunglasses, struggled out of his jacket, and draped it across his arm. His worn, translucent, white shirt revealed the form of a sleeveless t-shirt underneath. What some people call a wife-beater. A name that didn't seem to come close to matching the man standing there, holding himself up by leaning his hip against the porch railing.

I folded up my newspaper, waiting for him to speak. We teachers are a patient lot. If Murphy had sent him, there would be a worthwhile reason. I noticed a small, circular object like an over-sized bottlecap protruding beneath his shirt, up high on his left chest. When he caught his breath, he moved slowly toward the picnic table. I rose, still waiting for him to tell me why he was there.

"Mr. Barrow?" he said, his voice low and raspy. "Mr. Peter Barrow?"

"Yes," I said, reaching out to shake his hand, his firm grip a surprise. "Please, just call me Pete. And you are...?"

"Ben Skoville. Nice to meet you, sir. Sheriff Murphy told me where to find you. Sort of an out-of-the-way place you've got here. But a beautiful spot on the river, indeed."

"Yes. Yes, it is," I said, motioning at the bench. "Please, take a seat. I was about to get a bottle of water. Would you care for one? Or something else to drink?"

"Water will be fine," he said, easing himself onto the bench.

I went inside to the fridge. When I came back out, some of the color had returned to his face, and his breathing seemed less labored. He gulped down a third of the bottle and replaced the cap. I sat and waited. I was pretty sure he wasn't there seeking help with his algebra.

Chapter Two

"Sheriff Murphy tells me," Ben Skoville said, "that in addition to being a high school math teacher, you're also a licensed private investigator."

"That's right," I said.

"Sort of an odd combination, isn't it? Math teacher and private investigator."

"I've never thought so. Both jobs require logical thinking and attention to detail."

"Indeed, they do," he said. "Been doing it for quite a while, I understand."

"More years than I'd care to admit. But it beats the hell out of scraping barnacles off boats in the heat all summer."

"You've done that also, have you?"

"In my youth. For a couple of summers. It was a learning experience. Taught me what a pain in the ass owning a boat would be."

"Ha! What's the old definition of a boat? A hole in the water..."

"...into which you pour money," I finished.

"Sounds like you don't have much idle time on your hands."

"I like to keep busy. I take time for myself when I need to."

"Well, good. Good for you."

"So, you're looking to hire me?" I said. "As an investigator."

"I am, indeed," he said. "I need someone who knows this area. Someone with local contacts. Someone who might be able to obtain information that an outsider could not. The sheriff recommended I speak with you. Says you're the only P.I. in the county."

"It's a small county. Might be hard to find another one on the whole

Northern Neck."

Shifting his weight on the hard wooden bench, he reached into the pocket of his jacket, stretched out across the table. He pulled out a bifold leather wallet, opened it, and handed it to me. Inside was his identification. In the photo, he looked much heavier and younger. I didn't get the impression that his dramatic weight loss was the result of an overzealous dedication to the Keto diet.

"As you can see from my license, Mr. Barrow, I am a private investigator, as well. My office is in Fredericksburg. May I ask if you are currently engaged in an investigation that would prevent you from devoting some time to another matter?"

"Most of the investigative work I get is from a local law firm. Wadsworth, Wadsworth, and Keys. As far as I know, there's nothing they need me for right now, or anytime soon. But of course, there *is* my day job. We still have exams this week. Graduation on Friday evening. Closing meetings and check-out on the following Monday and Tuesday. But I might be able squeeze in a few hours to poke around. Provided it's something I'd be interested in taking on."

"I don't think that would be a problem. I doubt what I have in mind would take up much of your time."

"That would be a plus," I said. "What's this all about?"

"It's a possible missing person case," he said.

"Possible? Either someone is missing, or they're not."

"I suppose that's true, Mr. Barrow. But there is a distinction between being missing and not wanting to be found. So far, I haven't been able to discern the difference in this case."

"And who is it that might be missing?"

"A young woman from Fredericksburg, named Melissa Adamson. Maiden name Carney."

"So she's married. Husband the one looking for her?"

"Well, he may indeed be looking for her, but he's not the one who hired me to find her. My client is a close personal friend of Mrs. Adamson. Her name is Kasey Dylan."

"So why isn't the husband involved?"

"The couple had recently…uncoupled. There were some, shall we say, allegations of abuse."

"Made to the police?"

"No. As far as I can tell, no one has taken the matter to the authorities. I believe she has only confided in her friend, Kasey Dylan. Perhaps others."

"And no one has reported her missing to the cops?"

"No, sir. They have not."

"Including the husband?"

"I don't believe so," he said, pausing to take another sip of water.

"And what is it that brings you down here to Potomac County?"

"The last message my client received from Mrs. Adamson stated that she was here, in your county. Staying with an acquaintance."

"And you, being an outsider, don't want to approach this person, who might not trust someone like you. You're afraid they'll think it's the husband looking for her? Whereas I'm local. Might even know the acquaintance. Or know someone who knows them. Thereby being less of a threat."

"Indeed, that is one reason I wish to hire your services," he said, struggling again to catch his breath. His lips moved without voice, as if he'd chosen his words but they'd resisted coming out at first. "But I'm sorry to say there is a much more pressing issue, of a personal nature, that must be dealt with immediately. It doesn't take a professional investigator to see that I am not a well man. Cancer. Second time around. In fact, I'm due at the hospital in Fredericksburg tomorrow afternoon. More surgery on Monday. Another intense round of chemotherapy. I'm sure you've noticed the chemo port here on my chest. I won't be up to pursuing this case, or any other for that matter, for quite some time. If ever."

Indeed.

Chapter Three

By the time Skoville finished talking, he was visibly exhausted. His hands were trembling, and he was breathing hard again. I offered to let him stay for a while. To rest before the forty-mile drive back to Fredericksburg. He thanked me, but politely declined in his southern gentleman sort of way.

I agreed to do what I could for him in locating Melissa Adamson. He understood that my free time was limited over the next week or so. When I walked him to his car, he pulled a manila folder from a leather bag and handed it to me. He said the file contained everything he'd told me about the case, and more.

When he drove off, I felt guilty, wondering if someone in his condition should be driving at all. Thinking he might be a danger to himself or others. I felt about as bad as I would have if I'd allowed someone to drive drunk.

There had been something familiar about the man that I couldn't put my finger on. Something that reminded me of someone else. I thought about it for a while after he left, but gave up, knowing it would come to me later. Hopefully, not when I was trying to sleep.

I spent half an hour or so, inside my cabin, up in the loft area where I like to read, perusing the sparse contents of the file Skoville had left with me. Clipped to the inside of the folder was a candid photograph of a woman sitting on a front porch swing. The name *Melissa* was written in cursive on the back. It was a summer picture. She wore denim short-shorts with a tight-fitting top, cut off to reveal her midriff. Her hair was long, straight, and dark. She wore little makeup. No need for it. She was a natural beauty.

Her faint smile seemed forced, as if feigning contentment for the camera.

The file contained names, addresses, and phone numbers for some of the people with whom Melissa Adamson had been associated. But not many. Some came with fuzzy-looking printouts of photos. There were printed pages of an exchange of text messages between Melissa Adamson and her friend Kasey Dylan. The last message from Melissa said she was safe and staying in Potomac County with someone she'd met named Tammy Tydiss. There was no address. I did a Google search on my laptop. Nothing. Maybe the spelling of Tydiss was wrong.

When I finished, I went downstairs and made a quick sandwich. After eating, I went out for a short walk along the beach, still trying to figure out what it was about Ben Skoville that had reminded me of someone else. While I was walking, I made a phone call.

When I got back, Wendi Wynston's white Toyota SUV was parked in the driveway.

Inside, she'd made herself at home, curled up on the sofa, sipping from a bottle of beer, leafing through a recent copy of *The New Yorker* searching for a short story to read. She was, as she had always been, petite and slim. Her shoulder-length hair was a dark shade of brown, highlighted with a streak of natural gray here and there.

At our age, the term *girlfriend* doesn't seem to be an accurate identifier. But until some clever wordsmith invents a better description, we'll have to stick with that one.

The two of us have a long and winding history. Together and apart. Back in the day, during our first year of teaching here in Potomac County, we became a couple in a matter of days, after meeting at a new teacher gathering out at the state park, along the river. The event was a Teacher's Association-sponsored crab feast. Wendi had never eaten crabs before. Being the gentleman I was, I picked out some meat and fed it to her. She moaned with pleasure at the taste and giggled between bites. Under my expert tutelage, she learned the proper way to pick a crab. She was a quick learner, soon feeding herself. And things moved pretty fast with us after that.

But close to the end of the school year, things began to change between us. I was preoccupied with coaching track that spring. On weekends, she'd been going off on her own to spend time with her college roommate and friends. Every time she came back, she seemed a little more distant. When I proposed, she made me wait for an answer, then turned me down two days later. At the end of the school year, she surprised everyone, especially me, when she left for a job in the Maryland suburbs of D.C.

By the middle of the next year, she was married to the guy she'd dated in her senior year of college. A cheapskate accountant named Devin. I got married two years later. After a few years of raising a family with her former college sweetheart, the relationship soured. We kept in touch through mutual friends for a while, then started writing letters, talking on the phone more and more. We shared stories of life events. Complained about school. Talked about how our kids were growing up too fast. We sent funny holiday cards back and forth, vented about life's problems on email, and caught up with each other for a platonic lunch in D.C. every couple of years. She advised and coached me through my own divorce years later.

Three years ago, without telling me of her plans in advance, she moved back here to Potomac County, taking on a new job as an elementary school psychologist. She just showed up smiling at my door one day. She always did like to surprise people. As a couple, we sort of naturally picked up where we'd left off all those years ago.

"You're back," she said. "Out looking for driftwood again?"

"Not this time. Just needed a walk. To decompress."

"Hard day's labor out on the deck? Struggling with the urge to nap?"

"It *is* hard work. But I did manage to resist. And I had a visitor, which required me to remain alert."

"And who was that?" she said, sitting up, taking another sip of her beer.

I told her all I knew about Ben Skoville and what he'd asked me to do.

"So this Melissa is staying around here somewhere with this Tammy Tydiss person?" Wendi said when I'd finished. "Never heard of her. How old is Tammy?"

"No clue," I said. "All I have is her name."

"And you have time for this?" she said. "With exams this week?"

"I have all day tomorrow. Only one exam on Monday, in the morning. So I might have a little time in the evening to make some calls. See if anyone has ever heard of her. After that, little or no time for a couple of days."

"You should consider making your exams multiple choice. You could grade them in no time."

"Math exams? Multiple choice? Like the AP tests and SATs? I know people have done that. But constructing good distractor choices takes a lot of time, too. And no matter how well you do it, there's always the chance that someone's just a good guesser."

"I know you feel sorry for him," she said, changing the subject again. "But do you think you can trust this Skoville man? I mean, he *could* really be working for the woman's husband."

"I'm not sure. Don't know enough to trust anyone at this point. That's why we're going to Fredericksburg tomorrow afternoon. To talk to my client, Melissa's friend, Kasey Dylan."

"I thought Skoville was your client. That he'd sort of subcontracted the job to you."

"I don't work that way. I prefer to work directly with people. Know exactly what I'm getting into."

"And you said '*we*' were going to Fredericksburg. What if I'm busy?"

"Well, if you're *not* busy, there's a new restaurant we could try out while we're there. A block off Caroline Street. Near where the old Colonial Theatre used to be. I hear the crab cakes are scrumptious."

"Hmm. I'll have to check my calendar."

Chapter Four

"I talked with Mr. Skoville after you called yesterday," Kasey Dylan said. "He confirmed that you'd be taking over the case for him. I understand he's not at all well."

It was early afternoon. We were sitting in cushioned chairs out on the front porch of her white, clapboard Cape Cod home on Hawke Street in Fredericksburg. A couple of blocks from some of the town's historical sites, like Kenmore, the home of George Washington's sister, Betty Washington Lewis, and her husband, Fielding Lewis. Kasey's home looked historical itself and was well-maintained. The functional wooden shutters were painted a dark shade of blue. The porch was bordered with an abundance of spring flowers. If you breathed in deep you could smell the boxwoods that lined the walkway in from the street. I wondered what the inside of the house looked like. We hadn't been invited in for a tour.

We'd been expected, and she'd been waiting out front when we arrived. Sitting in her chair, a purse beside her on the floor. Like she was waiting to get this over with so she could go somewhere. She was a plain-looking woman with short dark hair, wearing trendy pink-framed glasses and a lot of makeup, dressed in pink slacks and a white silk blouse, accessorized with white open-toed shoes, revealing painted nails that matched the color of her slacks. I'd introduced Wendi as my associate, though I hadn't explained our association.

"No, he's not well," I said. "Unfortunately, he expects to be out of commission for the foreseeable future. My own availability is somewhat limited over the next week or so, but I'll do what I can to continue the search for your friend."

I told her what little I'd learned from Skoville and his file, then asked if there was anything else she could add that might help. I felt like Wendi's presence might make Kasey feel more relaxed and forthcoming. Wendi was a good listener and had an encouraging smile. Her smile had encouraged me often. Especially at night.

Kasey Dylan folded her hands in her lap and told us about her relationship with Melissa Carney Adamson. The two had been classmates back in middle school for a while. They became fast friends, despite the fact that their lives had little in common. Kasey's family was comfortable, financially and socially. Melissa, on the other hand, had a troubled family life. Her father's employment, when he was sober, was intermittent at best. His relationship with Melissa and her mother was volatile. Her parents were both involved with drugs. The family moved around a lot. But even when Melissa was forced to change schools, she and Kasey managed to stay in touch. Melissa often spent the night with Kasey in her welcoming, stable, family home. Neither Kasey nor Melissa had siblings. In the early years, the pair felt like sisters.

After high school, they'd kept in touch less and less. Kasey attended Mary Washington University, there in Fredericksburg. Melissa bounced around town from one job to another. Eking out a living, working in bars and restaurants. The kind of establishments Kasey was not likely to patronize. Both women, now twenty-seven, had married in their early twenties. Kasey, to a lawyer with a promising future. Melissa, to a tattoo-covered biker who made a lot of promises *about* the future. None of which he kept.

About six months ago, Kasey and Melissa had a chance meeting, downtown at the Women's Christian Unity Crisis Center. Kasey had been volunteering there in her spare time away from her job as an investment advisor. Melissa was a new resident. Melissa confided that her husband, Greg Adamson, had been knocking her around. She showed Kasey some of the bruises. Kasey offered her a job as a live-in maid. A chance to hide out from her abusive husband. Save up some money. Try to get her life back on track.

But about six weeks ago, Melissa's husband found out where she was living and started to harass her. Kasey said she and her husband, Fordy, wanted to get the police involved. Melissa didn't want that and decided it would be best for everyone if she left town. She said a woman named Flo at the Crisis Center had given her a number to call if she ever needed to get away. Kasey didn't know Flo's last name and had never met her.

"When she left, I gave her some money," Kasey said. "Just the cash I had on hand. Around two hundred dollars. She had some of her own that she'd saved. And I gave her something else. I'm sure Mr. Skoville must have mentioned it to you."

"No," I said. "I don't think so. What was that?"

She picked up the purse from the floor next to her chair and placed it on her lap. It had a wooden base and handles, with sides made of a thick, flower-patterned fabric.

"I have a friend who's very crafty," she said. "I mean, she's really good at making things. She made a few of these for me. To give to some of the women at the Crisis Center."

She pulled out a piece of cardboard covered in green felt from the inside bottom of the purse, then held it up to show us. The wooden bottom had a hollowed-out rectangular space in the middle.

"It's to hide a phone," she said. "Melissa had her own phone. But I gave her another one I bought for her. A smartphone, but one of those cheap ones you can buy at the drugstore. What are they called?"

"A burner phone," Wendi said.

"Yes. I told her to hide it in there and use it to call me if she needed help. I put my number and my husband's number in the contacts. That's the phone she sent her last message on."

Chapter Five

Before we left, we discussed my fee. Kasey Dylan didn't seem concerned with my hourly rate and didn't bother to complain that she'd already paid Skoville. It was nice to have a client who could afford me. I always felt bad when I knew someone desperate was spending money they couldn't spare. She gave me her business card and one of her husband's, with all their various contact information.

Back in the car, Wendi read from the husband's card like an overwrought actor. "Rutherford Anderton Dylan, III."

"That's a mouthful," I said.

"She called him Fordy. Short for Rutherford?"

"A playful nickname. Maybe he drives a Ford."

"Easier to call out in the heat of passion," she said.

"In the back seat of his Ford?"

"No," she said. "Too classy for that."

* * *

After a nice crab cake dinner at the new restaurant off Caroline Street, we swung by the Crisis Center. It was located in an old storefront on William Street. Wendi opted to wait in the car.

The hairy guy at the front desk was tall and wide, with a large red nose and an acne-scarred face. A tall red-haired woman, who looked like she could have been his wife or his sister, came over and stood beside him when she heard me asking questions. She didn't offer to introduce herself. Neither did the hairy guy.

"I'm looking for a woman named Flo," I said. "She might have been a resident. Or worked here?"

"We don't give out information to strangers," she said.

"I understand," I said, handing her my business card. "I'm trying to help a client locate a woman she's concerned about. I just have a question or two that I'm hoping Flo might be able to help me with."

"How do I know you're not working for someone's boyfriend or husband?"

"You don't. But I'm not. I'd appreciate your giving me a call if you could connect me with Flo."

"She don't work here no more," the woman said. "Don't know where she is now. Ain't none of my business."

Back in the car, I let out a long sigh. Wendi could tell I was disappointed.

"No Flo?" she said.

"Well, she did work there. But no more. The people were not very forthcoming with information. Maybe they don't like private investigators. Do I look suspicious?"

"Mmm. Sometimes. Were they tall people?"

"They were."

"Maybe they don't trust short people. Some tall people are suspicious of our kind."

"Some of our best friends are tall people."

"I didn't say *all* tall people. But it's probably best that I didn't go in. They might have been twice as suspicious."

"Good thing I didn't confess to being a math teacher," I said. "You know how some people feel about that."

Chapter Six

While trying to go to sleep that night, I finally realized what it was about Ben Skoville that had reminded me of someone else. It was the shape of his mouth and the look of his teeth. It bothered me that it had taken so long to figure it out. Those features had reminded me of my late grandfather, though nothing else about the man came anywhere close to resembling Pax Barrow.

My grandfather, Paxton Isaac Barrow, was tall. One of the few physical attributes I did not inherit from him. Growing up, I'd been told time and again by many people how much I resembled him. Same nose. Same eyes. Same chin. We shared the same middle name.

As a young kid, I had a difficult time trying to figure out why he and my father didn't get along very well. My mother and father, Susan and Brent, and I lived in the small town of Riverport, Pennsylvania, where my father had been raised. My grandfather no longer resided there. When I was born, he lived in North Carolina, where he worked as a small-town cop. When I was around five years old, he retired and moved to Virginia.

His best friend in Carolina had been a Black guy he worked with on the police force. The man owned a piece of riverfront land in Virginia he'd inherited from an uncle. He told my grandfather that some wealthy real estate people in Virginia were pressuring him to sell them the property for an amount much less than it was worth. After driving up to Virginia to have a look at the property, my grandfather offered to buy the place from his friend at a fair price. And that's how my grandfather ended up here in Potomac County.

Pax Barrow was also a skilled carpenter. A talent I did not inherit. With some hired help, he built this cabin here on the river, where I've lived off and on throughout my adult life.

My grandfather would come to visit us in Pennsylvania twice a year. Once in the fall, around the time when the leaves in the mountains were turning color. And again at Christmas time. He never stayed for more than three days or so. He and my mother seemed to enjoy each other's company. He was always kind and thoughtful where she was concerned.

I was the only child of his only child. He gave me a lot of attention, and I idolized him. He was the only grandparent I ever knew. The others had died before I was born, or soon after. My father spent a lot of time working at his job, delivering heating oil to homes and businesses. It was physically demanding work. He was always tired at the end of a long day's labor. Most evenings, after dinner, he seemed refreshed and eager to talk and spend time with me and my mother. But when my grandfather was there for a visit, my father never had much to say.

Every summer, starting from the age of nine, I was invited to spend three weeks with my grandfather at his cabin on the Potomac. At first, I remember having a tough time understanding that the Potomac was, in fact, at nearly seven miles wide, just a river. Back home, rivers weren't much wider than a four-lane divided highway in most places. And the only waves came from the wake of the power boats buzzing up and down the waterways. There were no tides in the Susquehanna where it wound its way down between the mountains.

We spent those weeks having fun and doing chores. Mostly fun. We devoted a lot of time to fishing and catching crabs in his home-made, chicken-wire pots. He took me to historical sites like George Washington's Birthplace National Park and Stratford Hall Plantation over in Westmoreland County. Some years, when I was older, we'd make the two-hour drive for a long day trip to Colonial Williamsburg.

When I was about twelve, my grandfather started to keep two horses at the nearby farm of a friend. He taught me how to ride, western style, and how to groom and care for the horses.

Sometimes we would ride on the trails in the state park, all the way to the river, where we would trot the horses through the shallow water along the shore.

My grandfather, Pax Barrow, had been a great influence in my life. He'd been gone now for more than four decades. All these years later, thinking about the sudden way he passed still stirred feelings of overwhelming sadness, anger, and regret.

When I gave up on trying to sleep, I got up and read for a while.

Chapter Seven

On Monday morning, I stopped by the sheriff's office in Weston. It was 7:15. Exams didn't start until 9:00. The high school was three minutes away. I had plenty of time.

The deputy at the front desk was a Black woman named Adele Carter. Her maiden name was Smithborne. Her husband, also a deputy, had been killed five years before when responding to a domestic dispute. I'd been her math teacher for most of her high school years and had taught all but one of her four siblings. She was in her mid-thirties now. A smart and efficient deputy. If she'd pursued a city career in law enforcement, she would most likely have been a detective by now. But after two years in Washington, D.C., she'd made the choice to return to Potomac County, to serve and protect the people she knew best. She'd once told me she didn't care much for city life. Found it to be "Too much loud and hustle. Not enough quiet and slow."

"Sheriff Murphy will be here in a few minutes, Mr. Barrow," she said. "You can go on back and wait in his office. It's open. I'd offer you coffee, but I know you don't drink the stuff."

"Still resisting taking up the habit," I said. "Maybe I'll try some next week. I hear they've decided it's good for your health."

"That's this week. Next week they'll be reporting it's gonna kill us all."

I went back to the office, settled into the comfortable chair behind the sheriff's desk, and waited. You can never practice the art of patience too much.

* * *

One day, back when I was here for one of my annual visits, my grandfather took me to the clean white, sandy beach at the state park. At the age of twelve, I guess I was too naïve to realize that the beach, in those days, was still segregated. If not still by law, then by tradition and intimidation. The Black section was strategically situated downstream from the White people.

There were very few Black people in the town where I grew up. But even at that age, I was conscious of the civil rights movement. I watched the news. Our teachers at school kept us informed. My parents never spoke a bigoted word. I wasn't raised to judge anyone by the color of their skin, the way they looked, or the way they talked. Only by what they said and did, and how they treated others. Sadly, I can't say that everyone in my hometown felt that way. Even as a kid, I could never understand how some of them could throw hateful names at a whole group of people who'd never done anything to them, or how it was possible to judge a whole race by the actions of some. I wondered how it was possible to hate someone you'd never talked to, or even met. I saw no logic in bigotry.

My grandfather had gone off to the park office to chat with a friend who was a ranger. I'd been out swimming and splashing around in the water for a while, trying to avoid the jellyfish. A big, muscular, tanned kid with sunglasses and a blond crew cut stood at the edge of the water, watching me with a twisted smirk on his face.

Awhile later, I was lying on my beach towel with my eyes closed, enjoying the feel of the sun on my skin. When a football landed at my feet, I heard a voice yell, "Sorry!" and looked up to see a group of Black kids standing there. They asked if I wanted to join them. So I did.

At that age, I was not only small, but scrawny. Most of the kids were around my size, but probably younger than me. We had fun for a while, tossing the ball around, trying to emulate the motions of the quarterbacks we'd seen on TV.

After a few minutes, the big kid with the crew cut swaggered over and stood next to me.

"What the hell you doing, kid? You blind or something? Don't you know them's colored boys you messing with? You need to get back over to the side where you belong."

"What of it?" I said. "Mind your own business."

"Aw," Crew Cut said. "I can tell by the way you talk. You a *Yankee*, ain't you, boy?"

"So what," I said. "Just get out of here and leave us alone. We're not bothering you."

Without warning, he picked me up and slammed me to the ground. The thick layer of loose sand kept it from hurting too much. Spitting sand from my mouth, I got up and charged him. It must have looked like a Chihuahua going after a German Shepherd. He slugged me hard with his fist, and I went down face-first in the sand again. When I turned to get up, my nose was bleeding, and there was a large Black kid standing between me and my assailant. I hadn't noticed him before. He'd seemed to come from nowhere. He was taller and even more muscular than Crew Cut guy.

"Leave the kid alone," he said.

"Or what?" Crew Cut said.

"You wanna take the chance to find out?"

"I got friends, you know."

"I don't see anybody."

"They ain't here. But I can sure go get 'em."

"You do that. If you think it's worth it. But I know who your daddy is. And I know for a fact he's not the kind of person who'd be happy to hear about what you're trying to stir up here. So why don't you just go on and enjoy the rest of your day and leave the little guy alone."

Crew Cut looked scared. He didn't say anything. Just put his head down, turned, and walked away.

"Thanks," I said. "My name's Pete."

"Oscar," he said. "He gives you any more shit, you let me know."

* * *

Oscar and I didn't cross paths again for another ten years. I was fresh out of college, three weeks into my first year of teaching at Potomac County High

School. On my way home one afternoon, near the entrance to the state park, I got pulled over by a county deputy. There was something familiar about the man requesting my driver's license and registration. The way he stood. The way he moved. His voice, deeper now, but somehow familiar. The brass name tag pinned to his uniform shirt identified him as Deputy Oscar Murphy.

"You know how fast you were going, Mr. Barrow?" he said, scrutinizing my license.

"No, sir," I said.

"You were doing sixty. Limit's posted as fifty here. I see your driver's license and registration are for Pennsylvania. Do you live around here, sir?"

"Just moved here a few weeks ago. I'm a new teacher at the high school."

"I'm going to issue you a warning today for the speeding, Mr. Barrow. And I need to advise you that Virginia law requires new residents to the state to change their vehicle registration within thirty days. You're cutting it a might close. You have sixty days to obtain a Virginia driver's license."

"Okay, thanks," I said, nervously jamming my license back into my wallet. "I appreciate the warning."

"Just remember to watch your speed in the future. And you might want to help out any of your colleagues who've also moved here from out of state, by advising them to take care of their obligations as well. I have some colleagues of my own who like to cruise the school's faculty parking lots, looking for out-of-state plates. You enjoy the rest of your day, Mr. Barrow."

He gave no sign that day of recognizing me from the incident on the beach ten years earlier. I'd certainly changed a lot. So had he. We would meet many times in the years to come. Professionally and socially. Sometimes at odds over my extracurricular occupation. I taught both of his kids. Thank God he never had to arrest either of mine. He was elected sheriff more than twenty years ago. Few challengers have ever come close to unseating him. If I called him my best friend, he'd accuse me of sentimental exaggeration.

In all the years we've known each other, we've never discussed that day on the beach.

Chapter Eight

"You're in my chair," Sheriff Oscar Murphy said. "If one of your students did that to you, you'd be pissed as hell."

"They do it all the time," I said. "I think it makes them feel powerful and mature."

"That explains why you're sitting in *my* seat. Now get up and let me park my ass where it belongs."

I went over to my proper side of the desk and sat down.

We spent a few minutes talking about the weather and the current high price of crabs. There was talk about us taking some time in the summer to sneak off for a day at a Nationals' game in D.C. He was looking at the team schedule on his laptop when a deputy named Runyon Pugh came in and put a takeout box on his desk.

"Scrambled eggs and toast, sir," he said.

"No bacon?" Murphy said.

"No, sir. Your wife said no more bacon, sir."

"Since when does my wife order my breakfast? You taking orders from her now?"

"Only food orders, sir," Pugh said. "She outranks you in that regard."

"Since when?"

"Since last week. When she told us all, no more bacon for you."

"Well, you can tell her…"

"I ain't gettin' in the middle of y'all's business, sir," he said, escaping to the outer office.

Pugh was a good deputy and smart enough to do what Elnora Murphy told him. He'd spent a couple of years as a deputy over in Dominion County before coming back home to work for Murphy last year. I don't think he cared much for me. He seldom spoke to me when I was around the office. I'd taught him algebra a dozen years ago. He'd struggled with the concept of adding and subtracting positive and negative numbers. As a result, he'd failed to earn more than a C-minus on any evaluation. I think he blamed me. Some kids are like that. They hold a grudge forever. Even into adulthood.

Murphy pulled a Heinz ketchup bottle from the mini fridge behind him and proceeded to pour it on until the yellow of his eggs was barely visible beneath the thick layer of red. To Oscar Murphy, ketchup was as necessary to his survival as water. He put it on nearly everything he ate. Except crab meat. If he ever committed that sin, our friendship was over.

We talked about Ben Skoville while he ate.

"He told me he was looking for a girl named—"

"Melissa Adamson," I said.

"Yeah. That's it. Said she was rumored to be staying around here somewhere with a woman named Tammy—"

"Tydiss," I said. "Ever heard of either of them?"

"Nope," he said. "Told him if there was no missing person report filed, I couldn't do anything officially, but I could ask around some. He said he'd rather not have anyone in law enforcement asking questions about them. Afraid it might scare them. He didn't explain why. In fact, he didn't even volunteer to say why he was looking for the Adamson girl. Wanted to know if there was a competent local private investigator he could use to help him. I told him *no*, but there was you."

"Very funny," I said. "What was your impression of Skoville?"

"Seemed straightforward. But some of those city boys in his line of work can be right slick talkers. Not a healthy man, though."

"No. Not at all. Cancer. Can't work the case. Asked me to take over."

Murphy looked at his watch and wiped ketchup from the corner of his mouth with a napkin. "You late for school?"

"Exams today. Start at nine. And by the way, just for the record, I've *never* been late for school in my life."

"You? You're late for everything. Unless Wendi's with you to keep you on time."

"Well, that *might* be true. But I've never been late for school."

"You willing to take a polygraph on that?" he said.

Chapter Nine

Giving exams is boring. For me, the exciting part of teaching has always been interacting with kids, moving around the room, asking questions, pulling answers from them, building their confidence and competence.

But exams, especially in mathematics, are a necessary evil. They show just how much the students have learned and retained. From the student's side, they're a stress-filled exercise. Sometimes stress leads people to make bad decisions. Especially kids. To do things they know, deep down, are wrong. Like trying to cheat. It's the teacher's responsibility to do their best to keep students honest. That's why, no matter whether it's an exam, a test, or just a quiz, I always watch them as they work. I stay on my feet. Moving around. When teachers are distracted, busy doing other things, like grading papers, punching around on a computer keyboard, or reading a book, they fail to eliminate the opportunity for students to be dishonest. Sometimes the best way to keep people honest is by removing temptation. People in general are more likely to break the rules when they know no one is watching.

And so the morning Pre-Calculus exam passed. An excruciatingly slow two hours, but without incident. One down. Four to go. I ate lunch at my desk and started grading. Over the years, I've learned the most efficient, methodical way to get through the stack of papers is by working a page at a time. Do everybody's first page, then second page, and so on. As you go, record the number of points taken off at the bottom right corner of each page. In the end, tally up the points by fanning out and folding over the pages so all the numbers are visible. If only everything in life could be reduced to such an orderly process.

In mid-afternoon, I took a break for a while and made about half a dozen phone calls. Over the years, I'd made a lot of contacts in the community. I'd learned to differentiate between the petty gossips and those with reliable information. The ones who made note of the comings and goings around them. But no one I talked with had ever heard of Tammy Tydiss or Melissa Adamson.

I went back to working through my exams until dismissal time. Before the last of the big yellow buses pulled out of the parking lot, I caught up with a few of my colleagues and the front office secretary. No one was familiar with the name of either of the two women in question.

That evening, Wendi came over for dinner with take-out from the Chinese restaurant in Weston. We ate beef and broccoli, chicken and snow peas, and egg rolls. I had my usual bowl of wonton soup.

After having our fill, we were sitting together on the sofa, watching the news on a Washington D.C. station. The first ten minutes of the broadcast were devoted to murders, shootings, and carjackings. One of the stolen cars was the unmarked vehicle of an on-duty police officer. As the crow flies, D.C. is not all that far away, but an entirely different world.

We cracked open our fortune cookies. They were a little on the stale side. Wendi's fortune said, *Love is within your grasp.*

She reached out and squeezed my arm. "It's true, it's true!" she squealed.

Up on the TV, there was a story on about a rich guy who'd been accused of making unwanted sexual advances toward a blonde actress who had a minor role on a popular streaming show I'd never heard of. The male reporter mentioned an out-of-court settlement for an undisclosed amount. The accompanying video clip showed the man trying to avoid being interviewed outside a lawyer's office in Fredericksburg.

"*Beware of darkness,*" I said, reading my fortune out loud. "Looks like they're running out of ideas. They've resorted to quoting George Harrison."

"Not a bad source," she said. "But maybe George got his idea from a fortune cookie."

"Inspiration comes from all places," I said. "But knowing George's interests leads me to believe the idea had a deeper origin."

"Maybe we should turn off this depressing city news and listen to *All Things Must Pass*."

"Good suggestion," I said. "And a good tag line for a future fortune cookie."

Within a minute or two, I'd found the album on my music app on the Roku. Listening to George never got old. We ate our tasteless fortune cookies and talked quietly with the music turned low.

After a while, Wendi decided it was time to get back to her apartment in Weston. She had some end-of-year paperwork to take care of and laundry to do. At my insistence, she took most of the leftovers with her. When she went out the door, George was singing *I Dig Love*.

I spent the hour after she left sending out emails and text messages and making calls, still trying to find anyone who'd ever heard of the elusive Tammy Tydiss. Receiving no positive responses, I went back to work on grading my exams. I was a lot slower at grading than I used to be. It seemed the older I got, the longer it took to finish a set of papers. These days, I was having a hard time staying up late and working. It seemed like the later the hour, the slower I got.

Around ten o'clock, I got a call back.

The call was from a guy named Buck Widrig. He ran a ten-acre truck farm out where he lived on Slipstone Road, a mile or so off the main highway. To make ends meet, Buck also hired out to work on other people's farms. He and his wife, Rosie, were in their early thirties now, with two kids in elementary school. He knew I'd pay for good information.

"I know her name's Tammy. Least ways that's what she called herself. She said her last name kinda fast. But it sounded like Tydiss, or something like that anyway."

"So, you talked with her?" I said. "Face to face?"

"Yessir, I did. Our daughter, Clemma. She was out for a bike ride Saturday, a couple of weeks ago. Chain broke. She couldn't fix it, of course. She went over to the Kroft house to call us to come fetch her. But there weren't no one home. So she went across the road to this Tammy gal's place where the woman was out working in her garden. Now we told Clemma never to do that. Talk to strangers, and all. But you know how kids are. Clemma figured it'd be all right. Her being a woman, and all. And she had her little boy working with her there in the garden. She let Clemma use her phone to call us. When I went on down the road to fetch her, the woman seemed to be right nice. I'd seen her before, though. Out working her garden when I drove by. The sight of her was right hard to miss."

"Oh," I said. "Why is that?"

"She's kinda one of them hippie types. Got real, real long brown hair. Wears them tie-dyed shirts and skirts sometimes. But most of the time, when it's warm and sunny, she's just out there in her little old tiny red bikini."

"I would guess that might stop traffic."

"It sure does! She wears it well. And let me tell you, there's been more than one old boy who damn near ran off the road there. Now don't tell my wife I said that, Mr. Barrow."

"No, sir. Not a word from me," I laughed. "And where exactly is her house?"

"Right across the road from the Kroft's. You know where that is. But where she's living ain't exactly a house, Mr. Barrow. I mean, there *is* a dwelling there, but it ain't fit for nobody to live in. An old green place with the roof caved in, and the front porch collapsed. Trees growing up through the middle of it."

"So, she's in a trailer, or something?"

"More like something," he said. "She's got an old, blue-painted school bus parked there. Looks like it used to belong to the Baptist church. Got a stove pipe sticking out the side where a window used to be. Blue curtains all around the inside. Reckon she's got it all set up to live in. That's why some of the folks around here call her the Bus Lady."

Chapter Ten

The next day seemed more like three. No matter how often I glanced at the clock on my classroom wall, the hands refused to move any faster. A Calculus exam in the morning. Algebra II in the afternoon. Kids working hard. Relieved when it was over. Most of them left with some degree of a smile on their face. As they headed out the door, we would wish each other a good summer.

When one kid started to leave without saying anything at all, I said, "Have a great summer."

To which he replied sharply, "I intend to."

Oh well. Can't win over all of them.

Working through lunch, I managed to finish the exams from the previous day. But the stack of papers continued to grow. Piling up like snow on a car. Needing to be dealt with before starting on your way to wherever you needed to go.

At the end of the day, I should have gone straight home and dug into the day's accumulation. But I didn't. I headed out of Weston toward home but turned off onto Slipstone Road.

When I arrived at Tammy's place, there was a big yellow school bus coming from the opposite direction, stopped at the end of the driveway. Red lights flashing. Stop sign swiveled out from the driver's side. I stopped ahead of it, at more than the legally required distance. She had been standing there, waiting, her tall, thin form dressed in a tie-dyed skirt and a plain, faded-pink t-shirt. A little tyke was making his way carefully down the steps of the bus, one at a time, hanging on to the chrome railing with one hand.

There was no grand, welcome-home hug. She didn't take his hand in hers. They just turned and walked up the driveway, the boy a step behind, kicking at loose stones as he went, past the garden, toward the big blue bus parked in the yard near the collapsed structure Buck Widrig had described.

The flashing red warning lights on the bus went off as it surged on down the road. When it passed, I pulled ahead into the dirt and stone driveway and parked.

There was no mailbox at the end of the driveway. Just a white-painted post with the required 911 address hand-painted on in black numbers. The garden was well-maintained, few weeds, with straight rows of young growth, and a long line of staked-out tomato plants. Off to one side of the blue bus was a set of four solar panels, mounted to a metal frame on the ground, slanted up at a fixed angle. Sitting next to the array of panels was an old machine that looked like a generator. Behind that was a shed made of concrete blocks with a rusted tin roof and a splintered wooden door. There was a round concrete cap over an old well next to the shed. A double clothesline ran from the shed to a pole at the side of the bus. Except around the wheels, the bottom of the bus was shielded with a dented green-metal skirt, haybales pushed up against it here and there.

A rusted white Chevy pickup sat parked at the end of the driveway near the collapsed house. There was a faded logo on the driver's side door. A silhouette of a green lawn tractor in the center flanked on either side by images of a weed-trimmer and a chainsaw. Block lettering above and below spelled out the name, POTOMAC PERFECTION LANDSCAPING. Listed at the bottom were two phone numbers and a dot-com website.

Even though the woman had turned her head at the sound of my car pulling onto the driveway, she and the boy had retreated inside by the time I'd walked half the distance to the blue bus. When I got there, the door was folded open. I knocked hard on the glass and stepped back. After a minute, she came into view and descended the steps. Her light brown hair was pulled back and tied up high, into the longest ponytail I'd ever seen. In the interim, she'd removed her t-shirt to reveal the red bikini top Buck had been so delighted to describe. Perhaps I'd interrupted her change of clothes.

Sometimes I walk too fast.

"Yes?" she said, looking a little wary, cautious.

I was still dressed in my school clothes. Khakis with a blue oxford shirt, complemented with a brown and blue slant-striped tie. Official-looking, but non-threatening attire. I introduced myself, handed her my card, and flashed my P.I. license. I decided not to tell her I was also a math teacher. No need to frighten her.

"Tammy Tydiss?" I asked.

"Yes," she said, folding her arms. "What do you want?"

"I'm trying to find a woman named Melissa Adamson. I was told she might be staying here with you."

"Who are you working for?"

"My client is a close friend of hers. A woman named Kasey Dylan. She's concerned about Melissa. She'd like to talk with her. Make sure she's okay."

"She's not here."

"Do you expect her?"

"No," she said, turning her head away, looking at nothing.

"But she *was* here?"

"How do I know you're not trying to help her husband find her?"

"I'm not. I understand the situation with her husband. I don't work for people like that."

"She's not here," she said, making eye contact again. "She was here for a while, but she left with a friend a couple of weeks ago."

"Do you know where she went? Who she's with?"

"No. She called someone. They came and picked her up."

"This friend male or female?"

"I don't know. Came after dark. Didn't get out of the car. Melissa just got in, and they left."

"You know what kind of car it was? Color? Virginia plates or not?"

"I told you it was dark."

"Melissa's not answering her phone. You happen to know if she broke hers? Maybe got a new one for some reason?"

"I wouldn't know anything about that. Maybe she just doesn't want to talk to anyone. I've told you all I know."

"Have you known Melissa a long time?"

"No. Just since she's been here. I help other women sometimes. When they need to get away from a situation. I don't like a lot of people knowing about it."

While we were talking the boy came outside, repeating the cautious way he'd stepped off the other bus.

"This young man must be your son," I said. "How you doing, buddy?"

He didn't look at me or say anything.

"My nephew," Tammy said. "He's staying with me for a while."

The boy stepped away from Tammy and looked up at me in a disconnected way.

"I'm Pete," I said to him. "What's your name?"

"It's Kyle," Tammy said, for him. "If there's nothing else, it's time for me to make our supper."

She turned and coaxed the boy back inside.

"If you hear from Melissa, I'd appreciate a call," I said. "Or if you think of anything else that might help."

She nodded and went back inside the bus, unfolding and closing the glass and metal door behind her.

On my way out, I maneuvered my phone into a discreet position and snapped a photo of the pickup truck.

Chapter Eleven

Wendi stayed away that night, leaving me alone to concentrate on attacking my papers. I finished the first set, Algebra II, at a little after nine o'clock. Feeling sleepy, I took a break and grabbed a Coke from the fridge. One of the little glass bottles. As advertised, it was cold and refreshing. It's funny how the same Coke, in cans or plastic bottles, never seems to taste quite as good.

I grabbed another one and went back up to my desk in the loft. I might not drink coffee, but I'm not morally opposed to the occasional, moderate consumption of caffeinated drinks. Caffeine has its purpose. And its purpose that night was to keep me awake long enough to at least make a dent in the Calculus papers that required my attention.

With my red pen back in hand, I continued to scratch at the papers until midnight. By then, I was physically exhausted, but not necessarily sleepy. I didn't finish, but only had two pages to go.

Once in bed for the night, trying to drift off to sleep seemed futile. Every time I closed my eyes, the image of my hand holding a red pen appeared. I thought for a while about the place in which Tammy Tydiss and her nephew dwelled. An old school bus converted into a home. Maybe it was the best she could do. All she could afford. Everyone has to live somewhere. I'd seen worse places.

Thinking about her garden drew my thoughts, once again, to my grandfather. Out near the back of his property, there were two fruit trees. A Bartlett pear and a Macintosh apple. But most of the space between the cabin and the fruit trees was devoted to his garden. It had easily been three times the size of Tammy's. He grew just about everything. Carrots, squash, cucumbers, broccoli, two kinds of beans, peas, and more. The only thing he never seemed to bother with was corn. As a kid, I did what I could to help with the garden while I was there. Probably motivated to get the work out of the way so we could get to the fun stuff we had planned.

All the food he grew was way too much for him to eat or preserve for later, even with my temporary contribution to its consumption. So he gave a lot of it away. Once a week, we'd load up his pickup and head out for some isolated place down the back roads of Potomac County.

Sometimes the folks we visited were White. Sometimes they were Black. No matter which, I could see they were poor. They lived in rusted trailers, or dilapidated houses with peeling paint, boarded-up windows, and sagging porches. If the people had kids, we'd usually play at kicking a ball around or something, while my grandfather sat and visited with the adults, often of more than one generation. Sometimes they would give him some small item in return. Some goat's milk, a dozen eggs, or even a chicken. Other times, they would fix something broken that he'd brought along or give him something useful that they'd made. The people were always grateful and humbled by my grandfather's gesture of kindness and friendship. I don't think they looked on it as pure charity.

I think, in some way, my grandfather's giving humbled him as well. Whenever we left one of those places, he was quiet for a while. Once, when we were pulling away, I wondered out loud about how people could live in a place like that. I remember him leaning his head in my direction, easing his grip on the steering wheel, and speaking in a kindly, low, teaching way, saying, "Everyone has to live somewhere, Pete. Folks do the best they can with what they have."

* * *

With less than adequate sleep, I felt like a walking zombie the next morning. It was a struggle to remain on my feet for the last two exams, Precalculus and Algebra II again. But I managed to stay focused and at least projected the appearance of being alert.

Off and on all day, I thought about Tammy Tydiss and her little nephew, Kyle. Wondering how the kid had come to live with her. Thinking it likely she hadn't told me all she knew of the whereabouts of her former guest, Melissa Adamson.

At lunchtime, instead of trying to finish up the last two pages of yesterday's Calculus exam, I went online to the website for Potomac Perfection Landscaping. The information on the site was barebones. Not much more than what was on the truck door. Phone numbers. A few action photos of people of various races, hard at work, mowing and trimming. Most of the workers shown were women. The banner at the bottom of the page read, *Serving Potomac and Dominion Counties on Virginia's Northern Neck. An Old Dominion Services Company.*

There wasn't any information about who owned or managed the landscaping business. A search for Old Dominion Services Company identified it as a Fredericksburg company, but otherwise came up empty.

At the end of the day, when the kids were, at long last, gone for the summer, one of my younger colleagues down the hall let out a long, loud, "Yeeeee Haaaa!"

I laughed and closed my door, wondering who was happier, the students or the teachers.

Sitting at my desk, I looked up the phone number for a mowing service that served Potomac and Dominion Counties. It was run by a former student of mine named Tater Knox and his father-in-law. Word was that Tater did most of the work while his wife's daddy played cards and drank moonshine in between taking phone calls at a rented garage they called *the office.* I skipped the office listing and called the second number that looked like it might be Tater's cell.

I got lucky when he answered on the third ring. We took a minute or two to catch up and exchange pleasantries before I got to the reason for my call.

"You ever heard of a landscaping company called Potomac Perfection, Tater?"

"Yeah, Mr. Barrow. I heard of them. Seen one of their trucks a time or two. Why you ask?"

"I'm checking into the background of one of their employees," I said. "You know anything about the business?"

"I know I ain't worried about any competition from them. All of us in the business, we keep track of each other. Looking out for who might be out there trying to steal away our customers. No one I've talked to has ever seen them working anywhere. They ain't took nobody's regular clients away from them, as far as anyone knows."

After that, I put in a call to Simon Wadsworth's office. His secretary took a message.

Wadsworth's law firm was responsible for somewhere around eighty percent of my investigative work. Sometimes when I was overwhelmed with schoolwork, I had to decline a job. He didn't like that and always threatened to get someone else to do his snooping around. He never did. I was willing to put up with his condescension and whining as long as he didn't go too far. He wasn't the most pleasant employer, but he paid well, knowing he'd have to pay even more to hire some big-city investigator out of Richmond or Fredericksburg.

While I was packing up my bag to leave, Wadsworth called back, sounding like he was already in a bad mood.

"I need you to check on something for me," I said.

"Isn't that what I pay *you* to do?" he said.

"Usually. But I'm up to my ass in exams, and I've hit a dead end on an internet search. I thought with your legal connections, you might be able to find some info on a Fredericksburg company, named Old Dominion Services, that supposedly owns a local landscaper called Potomac Perfection."

"Well, all right," he whined. "What is it you need to know?"

"I'm not exactly sure," I said.

"That doesn't help."

"How about who owns the company. Names of employees, maybe."

"What are you into, Pete? You're not working for another law firm, are you?"

"If I was working for another law firm, then why would I bother to call you?" For a smart lawyer, sometimes common sense eludes him.

He made no promises, but begrudgingly agreed to let me know if he found anything. No timetable was given. I hoped he'd get back to me before Labor Day.

Chapter Twelve

At four o'clock, I met up with Wendi in the Weston Elementary School parking lot, where we swapped vehicles. Her white Toyota for my gray Mazda SUV. I was headed out to see the Kroft family, where they lived on Slipstone Road, directly across from Tammy's place. Just in case she was outside, I didn't want to take the chance that she might recognize my vehicle and suspect I was checking up on her with the neighbors. Which, of course, is exactly what I *was* doing.

When I got there, as far as I could tell, Tammy wasn't outside. I turned into the Kroft's driveway. The first fifty feet or so was covered in loose limestone that looked like it was a recent addition. The rest of it had a scattering of crushed oyster shells, but mostly just dirt with a green trail of grass and weeds up the middle. The driveway made a loop encircling the house, so I pulled around behind the one-and-a-half-story structure and parked out of view from the place across the road.

The front of the house and half of one side were covered in what looked like new white vinyl siding. The rest was sheathed in old, gray-weathered asbestos shingles. Out back, a battered metal storage shed leaned toward a rusted, thirty-foot windmill tower, the multi-bladed rotor on top removed long ago and replaced with a TV antenna.

I was greeted by a long-eared beagle and basset mix named Dusty, pointing his nose to the sky, howling out his tepid warning in a hoarse, gravely, non-melodic sort of way. When I bent down and scratched him behind the ears, he settled down and leaned into me.

Nealy Kroft came out the back screen door to welcome me. He was dressed in brown paint-splashed jeans with black cowboy boots and a green t-shirt with faded-out lettering on the front. The John Deere cap on his head looked new.

Nealy was in his mid-forties, a native of Potomac County, but friendly to Yankee come-heres like me. Not everyone was. He was a jack-of-all-trades sort of guy who'd been everything from a waterman to a farmer to a general handyman. An honest man with a good work ethic; he had a reputation, with some, as a man who at times left jobs half-done while he started something else. I'd taught his wife, Dora, years ago. They had a fourteen-year-old son named Arlo.

Inside, Dora was busy in the kitchen, putting baking potatoes and a pot of something in the oven. Arlo had been watching TV. When I came in with his father, he turned it off, gave me a quick *hello*, and bounded, two at a time, up the stairs, out of sight.

We made small talk for a few minutes about the weather and sports and where Nealy and Dora were working these days. Then we got around to talking about the reason I'd come for a visit.

"I'm looking for a young woman who was staying with your neighbor, Tammy, across the road," I said. "Her name is Melissa Adamson."

"Don't know the name," Dora said. "But then, we don't get much of a chance to visit with them folks much."

I showed them the photo of a younger Melissa sitting on the porch swing.

"Kinda looks like a girl that was there for a while. A ways back, maybe a month or more," Nealy said. "But there's a lot of women that comes and goes."

"You know much about your neighbor, Tammy?" I asked.

"The Bus Lady?" Dora said. "She keeps to herself, mostly. Don't want to talk to anyone much. But she'll sure parade around out in her yard, half-naked in that bikini all the time."

"Now, Dora," Nealy said.

"Well, she does," Dora said. "Acts like she wants to be left alone, then struts around like that. Drawing attention to herself."

"I doubt that's her intention," Nealy said.

"Well, whatever her *intention*," Dora said. "It is what it is."

"About how long has she lived there?" I said.

"More than a year, I'd say. Moved in there with her bus last year in the spring," he said.

"And her nephew was with her then?"

"Aw, no," he said, looking at his wife for confirmation. "We didn't see the boy around until the school bus started stopping there for him a couple months ago."

"And she lived there in the bus all winter long?"

"Oh, no," Dora said. "She went somewheres else during the colder months. I'd say from the beginning of December until early March. March was right warm this year."

"She go in the bus?" I said.

"No," Nealy said. "The blue bus stayed parked there all winter. I wonder if it'll still run."

"Would you happen to know who owns the property?"

"Indeed, I don't," Nealy said. "We been here a long time, and I never did hear anyone say."

"Have you ever been over there? "

"I did some work for her," Nealy said. "A couple of weeks ago. Tree came down across her driveway in that big storm we had. She came across the road and asked me if I knew anyone who could take care of it for her. Told her I had a chainsaw. Did that kind of work from time to time. Took me the better part of a day to cut it up and haul it out of there. She paid me in cash. Four hundred dollars. Didn't seem to fret much over the amount."

"You know where she works?" I said.

"I believe she works for a landscaper. Drives one of their trucks. Don't seem to have a car of her own. I thought it right odd that she works for a landscaper, but didn't know anyone who could take care of that tree for her."

"That is peculiar," I said.

"She don't work long hours, though. Especially since that boy come to stay with her. She leaves after he gets on the school bus in the morning. But then she's always home well before the bus comes back to drop him off in the afternoon."

"Never seems to work on the weekends," Dora added.

"Mmm," I said. "And you say you've seen a lot of women coming and going there?"

"Well, we don't like to gossip," Dora said. "I mean, we're good Baptists and all. But yes. There's been quite a few that comes to stay with her for a week or two. Not so much recently. Mostly one girl at a time, but sometimes two. They come, and then we don't see them anymore. And then after a while, there's somebody else there."

"Can you describe any of the women?" I said.

"Well, we seldom see them up close," she said. "But I'd say they were all fairly young. Maybe still in their twenties. Mostly White girls. Though a couple weren't. Other than that, I can't say."

"And you didn't recognize any of the women? No one from around here?"

"Not that I could see from over here," Dora said. "We didn't see anybody we knew. And there's been a bunch of them."

"But none of them was wearing bikinis," Nealy said with a grin. Dora reacted with a nasty scowl aimed in his direction.

I decided it was time to change the subject. "Listen, I hear Arlo's done a great job on the robotics team this year."

"Yes. Yes, he has," Nealy said. "We don't pretend to understand a lot of what he does, but we're right proud of him."

"You mind if I go up and congratulate him before I leave?"

"That would be fine. He'd appreciate that, I'm sure," he said.

Arlo was a little surprised when I knocked on his open door and walked in. The room was small with a low ceiling. A tall person would have a problem standing up straight. He'd have a problem himself as he continued to grow.

He was sitting on the bed, fiddling with something on an iPad. Over on the wall in front of a tiny dormer window was a narrow table with a lamp and a pair of binoculars on top.

"Hey, Mr. Barrow," he said. "What's up?"

"Just wanted to congratulate you on your work with the robotics team this year. Heard you took second place in the regionals last month."

"Yeah. We did all right."

"Hear you're a leader on the team. That's quite an amazing accomplishment for a freshman."

"Yeah. I guess so. I really like it. It's a lot of fun. I've learned a bunch of stuff."

"How'd your math class go this year?"

"I aced it."

"Really? Well, that's great! Hope I get the chance to work with you next year."

I glanced at the binoculars on the table again but decided it would be too awkward to ask him about what he'd seen of the bikini-clad Bus Lady across the road.

"Well, you enjoy your summer, Arlo. And you know it's never too early to start thinking about college. You've got the brains for it."

I just hoped he could find the money for it when the time came.

Chapter Thirteen

When I got home from my visit with the Krofts, I made another call to Tater Knox. I got his voicemail and left a message. Five minutes later, he called me back.

"Would a company like Potomac Perfection be able to handle tree removal?" I asked.

"You mean a standing tree?" he said. "There's specialty companies for that."

"No. I mean a fallen tree."

"For one that's already down, it's just a matter of using a chainsaw to cut it up to haul it away. Most of us in the business can handle that."

"So, you'd say it would be unusual for someone who works for a company like Potomac Perfection to not have any idea about who to call to take care of removing a downed tree?"

"I'd say so, yeah," he laughed. "Especially since they got a damn picture of a chainsaw in the company logo on their truck."

* * *

Just after six o'clock that evening, Wendi arrived with a bag of burgers and fries from Tiny's Takeout in Weston. The town wasn't big enough to attract any of the big fast-food franchises, so Tiny had cornered the local market. His burgers were bigger and better than anything McDonald's or Burger King could offer. I'd worry about getting back to eating healthy in a few days, when all my schoolwork was done.

After devouring every greasy ounce of artery-clogging food, we planted ourselves out on the deck in a pair of Adirondack chairs. We sat quietly for a while, watching the evening sun glistening off the moving water. After a few minutes, I broke the silence with an update on what little I'd learned about Tammy Tydiss and the comings and goings around the blue bus.

"Her nephew's not a student at Weston Elementary," Wendi said. "If they live on Slipstone Road, then he goes to Maple Grove Elementary."

"So she would've registered the kid. Had to show the proper paperwork to get him enrolled."

"Yes," she said. "Birth certificate. Proof of residency. Proof of guardianship or custody. Immunization record. Why the interest in the kid?"

"I don't know. All these women are coming and going. And then a kid suddenly shows up? Something just doesn't seem right. Maybe it's just another thread to pull on until a more prominent snag comes along. I guess the other thing that bothered me was how he didn't seem to be all that connected to Tammy. He just seemed disconnected in general."

"Well, she is only his aunt, not his mother. He might not have spent much time, or any at all, with Tammy before moving in with her. Maybe the kid's just shy. Or on the spectrum somewhere."

"I just wonder how bad things must have been with the mother, that coming to live with his aunt on a school bus would be a step up."

"We've both seen worse living conditions," she said.

"You know the teachers over there?"

"And the principal."

"You think you could talk to them? Find out if they know anything about the kid and his aunt."

"I have to go there tomorrow morning. To talk to the principal about some students transferring over from Weston next year. A couple of them have some serious learning problems and socialization issues that the staff members need to be made aware of. I can ask around for you. What's the kid's name?"

"She called him Kyle. I don't know about the last name."

"I'll figure it out."

I wondered out loud about Ben Skoville, how he was recovering after his surgery, how he was enduring the chemo. That led to my telling her about his physical characteristic that had reminded me of my grandfather.

"You seem to be dwelling on memories of your grandfather a lot these days," Wendi said. "I hadn't heard you speak of him in a long time, until the past few weeks."

"Yeah. It's about that time of year again. It's occurred to me lately that I'm nearly the age he was when he died. And now I'm a grandfather myself. His death seems to linger close by. It still feels recent. Like it was yesterday."

"You were close. The pain of losing someone you love never really goes away completely."

"I suppose not. Especially when the method of his demise can't be reconciled with the man he was."

"There are always doubts with suicide," she said, reaching over to place her hand on mine.

"My doubt has always been whether it really *was* suicide. As far as I'm concerned, there was never anything to say for sure, one way or the other."

"A problem without a solution. Difficult for a man of mathematics like you, where there is always a definitive resolution. One answer. Backed up by logic and the strict rules of the discipline."

"Not so with life," I said. "Or death."

"Maybe that's why you occupy yourself with two very different pursuits. As a math teacher, there's a solution to every reasonable problem."

"And as an investigator, not so much. The solution to a problem may be less clear, or nonexistent."

"You're a problem solver," she said. "You want everything in life to have a solution. A clear line of reasoning to reach a logical conclusion. But with your grandfather's death, that never happened. You've looked into his death a few times over the years and found nothing conclusive to contradict the official ruling. No leads. No next step. Maybe that's why you do what you do for others. Help them find a solution to their problems. You couldn't resolve the problem of how *he* died, so you help other people with *their* problems. Maybe, in a way, that's your grandfather's legacy."

"Maybe so," I said. "I've never thought about it in quite that way before. You sure you're just a school psychologist?"

"That's what the degree says. You ever consider talking to a real professional therapist about dealing with what happened to your grandfather? And how closely it followed the loss of your father?"

"I thought about it when I was younger. Maybe twenty or thirty years ago. Always felt like I was too busy. Seems a little late to bother with it now. At my age. And hey, who needs a real shrink when I've got you? You're much cheaper, and you make house calls."

We sat in silence again for a while, her hand a perfect fit in mine. Until we had to break apart to swat at the mosquitoes that had decided to join us.

"Well, I hate to always be the one to end the party," I said. "But I've got more exams to grade."

"You should have been a gym teacher," she said. "They never have homework."

Chapter Fourteen

I was at the desk in my classroom by seven o'clock Thursday morning. After Wendi left the night before, I'd found my second wind and managed to put a pretty good dent in my stack of papers. It was starting to feel like I was on schedule to finish in a reasonable amount of time. There was no great pressure to finish grades for seniors. We'd been required to report seniors in danger of failing two weeks ago. I'd had none in that last-minute predicament, and seniors with A's were excused from taking exams. Final grades for all students were due to be entered by Monday morning. Report cards were mailed out a week later.

After grading more exams for a while, at midmorning, I took a break and used an old metal AV cart to shuttle my student textbooks down the hall to the bookroom. Other teachers were coming and going as I stacked the books neatly on the shelves reserved for the math department. Some of my colleagues were eager to share their travel plans for the summer. I was embarrassed to admit I didn't have any travel plans. In an odd sort of unplanned, unofficial exchange program, the French teacher was headed to England, and an English teacher was traveling to France.

After shelving the last of the books, I went back to my classroom and pulled out the file on Melissa Adamson that Skoville had given me. He'd told me he had no luck in reaching any of the people listed as possible contacts, all names and numbers he'd gotten from Kasey Dylan. I thought it might be worth another try.

Of the four contacts listed, only three of them came with phone numbers. I tried calling all three. From the three-digit exchange code, I could tell two of the numbers were for land lines. The third looked like a cell number. The call to the first landline number ended in a message reporting it was no longer in service. The second resulted in twenty unanswered rings with no opportunity to leave a message. The call to the cell number got no answer, and my attempt to leave a voicemail failed with a generic, no-name recording that said the mailbox was full. I studied the four names for a few minutes, storing them away in my memory, just in case I came across them again.

Wendi and I had planned to meet for lunch at 12:15. By the time I got to Paco's Pizza, a block up the street from the Sheriff's Office in downtown Weston, it was just after half past twelve. When I slid into the booth, Wendi looked dramatically at the time on her phone, set it down on the table, and gave me her best *late-again* look. She didn't bother to say anything other than, "I've already ordered. Cobb Salad for me. Crab cake sandwich for you. With chips. Not hush puppies."

For a pizza place, they make a better-than-fair crab cake. Not mushy. Not too much filler. Lightly seasoned with good-sized chunks of meat. Not jumbo lump, but big enough. And reasonably priced.

The place was packed. Deputies Carter and Pugh were seated two booths over. Simon Wadsworth was seated at a table with a couple other lawyers and workers from his office. He nodded when he saw me, but didn't come over to talk. Other teachers and administrators were scattered about the room. A group of six teenagers, most of whom I'd taught this year, were at a table across the room, sharing a couple of pizzas. They were laughing and clowning around, already enjoying their summer freedom. I resisted the habitual urge to ask them to keep it down.

While we waited for our food, we talked about Wendi's morning and what she'd learned about Tammy's nephew, Kyle.

"The aunt told them the boy was homeschooled," she said. "So there's no record from a previous school. He's very quiet. Rarely smiles or gets excited. Never chatters on about his home life, the way a lot of first graders do."

"Do they think he's somewhere on the autism spectrum?" I said.

"No. But he seems troubled. They've tried to get him to talk about his life outside of school, his aunt. He won't open up. It's almost like he's afraid to talk about anything."

"How's his academic progress? If that's what you'd call it in first grade."

"His teacher says he does okay. Better than some of the other kids in the class. He's below grade level in some respects, but they say he's made progress in the two months since his enrollment. He knows his numbers. He's beginning to read. Sadly, some kids can't."

Myra, the waitress, brought our food. She gave me the salad and Wendi the crab cake sandwich, then stood there for a second, waiting for my reaction. When she got it, she laughed and switched the plates.

"You know, Mr. Barrow," she said. "You always order the *same* thing. A little salad once in a while wouldn't kill you."

She and Wendi looked at each other and laughed. I took a defiant bite of my sandwich.

Myra walked back to the kitchen, and Wendi picked up her fork and shuffled around the contents of her bowl.

"He's learning to add and subtract," she continued. "On grade level with his math. His teacher did say she had trouble getting him to print his name. He knows how to make all the letters. He has the motor skills. But he resists. They said when he first got there, he was very slow to respond when they said his name. At first, they thought he was just sort of zoned out."

"He socialize much with the other kids?"

"He does okay in class, working in a group with other kids. But otherwise tends to keep to himself. He'll kick a ball around with some of the other kids out on the playground sometimes. But mostly, out at recess, he likes to sit by himself under a tree."

"You get his last name?" I said.

"It's not Tydiss. It's Ballinderry." She spelled it for me.

"No wonder he didn't want to print that. It would take him half the day."

Chapter Fifteen

Graduation rehearsal started promptly at 2:00 P.M. I was not late. The music teacher and choir director, Reverend Lucious Thornaby, was in charge of the potential chaos taking place out on the football field. The faculty was employed to set up the white-plastic folding chairs, evenly spaced in straight rows in the bright green grass that probably should have been cut much shorter. Out in front of the goalpost, the stage had been constructed the previous day by the maintenance staff, with help from members of the Parents' Association.

The weather for Friday evening was expected to be nearly perfect, with a light breeze and temperatures in the mid-seventies. Some years we hadn't been so lucky. In the case of storms or excessive heat, the ceremony had to be moved into the crowded gym, where the air-conditioning had a hard time living up to its name.

When the rehearsal began, the faculty filed in behind the administrators. The graduates followed us. Some were marching with serious expressions, preparing for the real thing. Others were laughing, looking all around in a nervous, self-conscious sort of way. A few of the girls were crying. Maybe they'd be able to get it out of their system before the next evening. But experience told me it would probably be worse.

Once in their seats, Thornaby told them about the order of events and speeches. He issued a stern, sermon-like reminder that the ceremony was to be a joyous but serious celebration meant just as much for their parents and families as it was for them. He cautioned them to avoid the temptation to do anything stupid or hurtful that might embarrass their family.

I always had mixed emotions about graduation time. Too many personal memories interfered with the joy I should be feeling for the students and their achievements. My own high school graduation had been relatively ordinary, with my parents and grandfather in attendance. But over the next four years, circumstances would change suddenly and forever. I'd lived at home after high school. Got a steady part-time job at a local supermarket and furthered my education right there in town at Riverport State College. Midway through my sophomore year, my mother was diagnosed with a rare, aggressive form of cancer. She passed away that summer. Two years later, three weeks before graduating with my teaching degree, my father died of a sudden massive heart attack while out mowing the lawn on a Friday evening.

Of course, my grandfather was there for me. He stayed after the funeral to help me get through my last weeks of classes, exams, and graduation. We celebrated that commencement day at the home of a friend and classmate. His large family, gathered together for the event, welcomed the two of us, the last of the Barrows. We put on our happy faces and ate hot dogs, hamburgers, potato salad, and decorated cake. But that night, when we went home to that dark, empty house, as I unlocked and opened the door, I could feel the hard rush of loss hit me in the face, like a blast of heat from an oven, escaping, dissipating in the cool darkness of the mountain evening. I didn't know what was yet to come.

* * *

Wendi went out with some of her co-workers that evening, to celebrate the end of the school year at a bar and restaurant out along the Rappahannock River, over in neighboring Dominion County. After a quick dinner at home, I drove the forty miles up Route 3 to Fredericksburg alone, contemplating all the way on my lack of progress in finding the whereabouts of Melissa Adamson. Every thread I'd pulled on so far had unraveled and revealed next to nothing.

When I got to the hospital, a woman named Mrs. Sorrel, citing HIPAA regulations, was reluctant to tell me anything specific about Ben Skoville's condition. I wasn't a relative or listed as one of his approved contacts. She did tell me that, as far as they were aware, he had no relatives and no one at home to care for him. In her guarded words, she said the surgery *had not gone well*. He'd been transferred across town to a nursing home facility.

A few minutes later, when I arrived at the nursing home, his condition was described as *less than optimal*. He was in and out of consciousness, unable to speak or communicate much at all. I left without seeing him.

From there, I went back downtown to the Crisis Center. I followed two women in through the front door. They checked in at the front desk, where the big, hairy guy was on duty, this time without his chatty female companion. When the two women went on through a doorway into the back, the hairy guy stood and looked at me like he was trying to figure out where he'd seen me before. I could almost see the wheels turning. I reintroduced myself and placed another business card on the counter in front of him. He didn't make a move to pick it up. When I asked, he told me his name was Harry. I was tempted to ask him if he spelled it with an *ai*, but decided he probably wouldn't get it.

"Have you been in touch with Flo?" I said. "I really need to speak with her. I could make it worth your while."

"How much?" he said.

"Maybe a hundred, or so. Depends on whether you can put me in touch with her *soon*. The sooner the better."

"I might know somebody."

I tapped my finger at the card on the counter in front of him. He picked it up and looked hard at it. I couldn't tell if his lips were moving.

"Call me," I said.

* * *

Before leaving town, I decided to drop by to see my client again, on the off chance that she'd remembered anything else of importance. By the time I wrangled my way through traffic over to her place on Hawke Street, the daylight was beginning to fade, and the air was beginning to cool. All of the nearby parking spots out on the street were taken. The lights inside her house were on, and there were people standing and sitting out on the porch. The men were dressed in sports jackets with no ties. Most of the women wore summery dresses with bright colors and flowery patterns. They were all sipping on drinks and munching on hors d'oeuvres. Perhaps my invitation had been lost in the mail.

I could see Kasey Dylan, standing next to the railing at one end of the porch. She was smiling and nodding at a man in a pink shirt who was talking and waving his arms around. Standing with his arm around her waist was a tall, thin guy dressed in a navy-blue jacket. He had dark hair and a bushy-looking mustache. Most likely Rutherford "Fordy" Dylan. I looked for a Ford parked in the driveway, but didn't see one. Sometimes my theories don't pan out. I decided to go home.

Chapter Sixteen

By midafternoon on Friday, I finished grading my exams. Hallelujah. Calculating final grades these days was a breeze. Just enter them into the computer. The program did the rest. Back in the day, it took hours of punching numbers into a hand-held calculator to come up with the end results. I don't miss those days.

The Potomac County High School's letter-grade system was on a ten-point scale. Ninety to a hundred was an A, and so on down the line, with intervals for plus and minus grades. Below sixty percent was failing. I didn't like it when a grade average ending in a nine came up. If a kid was a hard worker, the kind that always had their homework done, I'd bump the grade up to the next level. I never lowered a grade from a calculated average. Whether or not I liked a student had no bearing on what grade they got. I didn't give a kid a grade. They earned it.

The graduation ceremony went relatively well that evening. Although the graduates behaved better than some of their parents. Maybe Reverend Thornaby should have lectured the adults instead. There was a lot of over-the-top hooting and hollering when some of the kids walked across the stage to receive their diplomas from the Potomac County Superintendent of Schools, Dr. Freddie P. Tower. At times, an airhorn blasted from somewhere up in the bleachers. So much for decorum.

The graduates were clad in traditional caps and gowns in the school colors. The boys in navy blue. The girls in gold. The faculty wore black caps and gowns, like we were in mourning. I always felt a little silly in that attire. We weren't the ones graduating. For some reason, seeing some of my younger colleagues goofing around in their dark commencement garb reminded me of the hilarious Three Stooges episode in which they perform the novelty song "Swingin' the Alphabet." I always thought it would be great fun for the school choir to perform the song at graduation. But then I've sometimes been told I have a slightly warped sense of humor.

Some might call me a hypocrite for instigating a further decline in decorum.

The graduation speaker was reportedly an old friend of Dr. Tower's. Picked by the current principal for his supposed success in the business world. Like many of the dozens I'd witnessed before him, he had nothing innovative or memorable to say to the young adults about to head out to work or college. At least he was brief in speaking.

After the ceremony, I engaged in a lot of handshaking, hugging, and posing for photos. With some of the students I'd grown close to, there were always promises made on both sides to stay in touch. But I knew from experience, for many different reasons, however unintended, I would never see some of these people again. And many of them would never see each other again. Just another example of life's joy and celebration tempered with a measure of loss.

I was invited by the parents of several graduates to join them for a celebration at their homes the next day. I politely declined each invitation. I just wasn't in the mood. Besides, I had work to do.

After my own college graduation, my grandfather had hung around for a few more days before heading back to Virginia. He knew I had things that needed to be done. Unlike many of my classmates, I hadn't secured a teaching position yet. It seems hard to believe these days, but back then, there were more teachers ready to enter the workforce than there were jobs available. Especially in Pennsylvania, with an abundance of schools that were still often referred to as State Teachers Colleges.

My grades from the first two years after high school were not the best. I spent too many hours working at the grocery store each week, and hung around at off-campus weekend parties in an inebriated condition way more than I should have. After my mother passed, I got more serious about what

I was doing and earned nothing less than a B in my last two years. But as a result of my earlier indiscretions, when it came time to compete for a teaching position, I often lost out to a candidate with a better GPA.

For three weeks after earning my degree, I continued to complete and mail out applications to school systems in most of the surrounding states. I went on a couple of interviews. Nothing panned out.

And then the unthinkable happened. A call came from the Potomac County, Virginia, Sheriff's office. My grandfather, Paxton Isaac Barrow, was dead. He'd been found on a dirt road, off in the woods, not far from the Rappahannock River. The driver's side door of his old pickup was open, the window half-lowered. His body was on the ground where he'd fallen from the truck. The gun found beside him turned out to be his old service weapon, a Colt .38 Special double-action revolver, from when he'd been a cop in North Carolina. The town government lacked adequate funds, so he'd been required to purchase his own gun. When he left for Virginia, he took it with him.

I'd only seen it once. That first summer, I'd come to stay with him when I was nine. He'd caught me picking it up from the desk drawer where I'd found it while looking for a deck of cards. He'd been harsh about it at first. In a panic, I suppose, seeing me holding it, the barrel pointed toward my face. Then he calmed down as quickly as he had angered, warning me to never touch it again. Telling me it was not a toy. He took it and put it away someplace where I wouldn't find it. I never saw the gun again, until a deputy returned it to me, the month after my grandfather's funeral. When his death was officially ruled a suicide.

Chapter Seventeen

After dark that Friday evening, I was sitting alone, out on the steps to the deck, sipping from a long-neck bottle of Bud, watching the slow rhythmic pulse of the moonlit water lapping against the shore. When my phone rang, I got up, retrieved it from the picnic table, and went inside. It was Nealy Kroft. He immediately apologized for calling so late.

"Not a problem, Nealy," I said. "I'm usually up late on weekends."

"I wanted you to know something as soon as I found out. Tried to catch you at graduation but couldn't find you in the crowd of all of them folks. We was there for Dora's nephew."

"Oh, yeah. I thought I saw you all, up there in the bleachers once. What's up?"

"Well, first of all, I want you to know that Arlo is a good boy at heart. He ain't never give us a lick of trouble. Like a lot of kids his age can do."

"I know that, Nealy."

"And he ain't no pervert neither. But he did confess to us today that he's been watching, with his binoculars, all the comings and goings across the road there at the Bus Lady's place. And well, he told us he seen something a while back that might be of interest to you. He saw a local girl that stayed over there for a time. An older sister of a friend of his. Says her name is Darlene. Darlene Morvine."

"Thanks, Nealy. That might turn out to be helpful. I know who she is. And I know her family. Tell Arlo he may have helped."

"Now, we told him, Mr. Barrow, we don't approve of him looking over there all the time. We don't want him becoming no sort of what-a-you-call-it…peeping Tom."

"Don't be too hard on him, Nealy. It's hard to resist looking at a pretty woman in a bikini. Especially when you're his age. You and I were both fourteen once."

"That we were," he said. "That we were."

* * *

When I got off the phone, Wendi was coming in the door. She dropped the leather bag she was carrying on the floor by the sofa and headed for the fridge. She grabbed a bottle of water, and we met on the sofa.

"You spending the night?" I said.

"I brought my special pajamas," she said.

"Not the ones with the dozens of little sheep on them?"

"The very same."

"You do realize, that as a man of numbers, I'm always tempted to count them?"

"Mmm. Well. We wouldn't want to run the risk of you falling off to sleep. I actually had some other, *more* tempting activities in mind."

She smiled her most encouraging smile.

"You shameless seductress," I said.

"You really know the words to flatter a girl. Remind me why I ever left you, back in the day."

"Temporary insanity?" I said. "And maybe the fact that Devin made a lot more money than I did."

"Yes, but he never let me *spend* any of it."

"That's because it was *his* money. He never really bothered to invest in your marriage."

"I think part of going back to him at the time was guilt. He'd been so devastated when I dumped him for you. My college friends convinced me I'd made a mistake. But I suppose money was important to me then. I'd never had much growing up. I wanted more than a two-teacher salary could give me. And then of course, after the divorce, I ended up living on a one-teacher salary with two kids."

"And now?"

"Age does make us wiser."

"Not everyone."

"Do you ever wonder about what it would have been like if we'd stayed together? Got married. Had our own kids."

"Mmm. If that had happened, then we wouldn't both have the amazing adult kids we have now. Neither of us would wish that. The older I get, the more I believe things happen for a reason. The way they're supposed to. Not always good. Not always bad. Sometimes impossible to understand."

"But I did love you back then," she said. "Maybe more than I was capable of knowing at the time. At the innocent age of twenty-three."

"Maybe it was my fault for putting too much pressure on you. I was too eager to start a family of my own. That wasn't fair to you."

"But now, looking back, I understand why. You'd lost your entire family in such a short period of time. I couldn't see that clearly back then."

"It doesn't matter anymore. We're together now. We both have families we love. Life is good for a while."

"Should we continue this conversation elsewhere?" she said.

"Mmm. Let's start a new one," I said. "While you attempt to dissuade me from counting sheep."

Chapter Eighteen

Darlene Morvine had graduated from Potomac High around seven years ago. I hadn't taught her, but knew her parents, Bud and Cornelia, who owned and operated the Weston Market. I'd heard she'd floundered after high school, given her parents a lot of headaches and heartbreaks. She'd refused to work with them at the store, had a few scrapes with the law. An assault accusation and a trespassing charge, underage drinking, and a DUI. She'd gotten tangled up with a dude named Trip Fallston, who was rumored to be peddling pills around the county and beyond. Fallston spent some time in jail for beating the crap out of Darlene after finding her in bed with another woman. I guess his fragile manhood had been insulted.

When I caught up with Darlene's father at the Weston Market on Saturday morning, he was hoisting five-pound bags of sugar onto a shelf in aisle three. He seemed less than thrilled to discuss the whereabouts of his daughter.

"Last I heard, she's living over in Glover. Shacked up with some hard-looking woman she brought by the house once. Her mother tells me she works at some kind of women's center. Doing what, I couldn't tell you."

"You have an address or phone number?" I said.

"I don't talk with her," he said. "I suppose her mother does."

I walked across the store to the office where I found Cornelia sitting at a desk, focused on the computer screen in front of her. She seemed annoyed at the interruption. I explained that I was trying to locate another woman her daughter may have known. Without saying much, she wrote down Darlene's cell number, handed it to me, and went back to work on her computer.

On my way out, I passed by Bud again. He was rearranging a display of cakes near the checkout counters. He avoided looking at me. I picked up a candy bar from the rack near the express lane and paid with cash. It never hurts to support a local business.

* * *

Glover was a small town on the other side of the Rappahannock River, a few miles south from the town of Tappahannock. Calling Glover a town these days was a stretch. But then the state of Virginia is populated with road signs marking places with just a house or two still standing.

What remained of Glover wasn't much. There were boarded-up houses and clusters of mobile homes with junk cars up on cement blocks in yards that hadn't been mowed in a while. Here and there, a well-maintained home or two broke the pattern, with a fresh coat of paint, a paved driveway, and an uncluttered yard. The tiny post office looked like an old gas station where the pumps had been removed. A once-grand, three-story home stood across the street from the post office. It was painted white and had a covered entranceway with a roof that extended out across the circular driveway from a wide veranda that wrapped around three sides of the house.

The Women's Center was housed in an old schoolhouse that likely dated back to the nineteen thirties or forties. It was a brick structure with tall, individual-paned windows. There was a covered sign by the entrance listing some of the services provided. Underneath was a bin of folded brochures. I opened one and scanned through terms like legal representation advice, referral services, family law, domestic violence protection services, employment law, intimate partner violence shelters, and battered women support groups. I pushed a call button and talked into a video camera and speaker at the front door, and was allowed to enter.

The inside of the building looked surprisingly fresh and new, like it had been recently remodeled. I was greeted guardedly by a muscular woman with long dark hair and shown to a conference room at the end of a short hallway. Darlene Morvine was waiting there for me. Her appearance had changed since high school. Her hair was shorter, and she was heavier. There were scars on her face and arms.

"I'm sorry you had to come all this way," she said. "But I didn't want to talk on the phone about all this. When someone calls, you don't know if they're who they say they are. I was a little surprised my mother gave you my number."

"I understand completely," I said.

"I remember you from Potomac High. Are you still there, or is this what you do now?"

"I'm still there. Though I'm not sure for how much longer. The investigative work has always been sort of a sideline for me."

"Is Mrs. Brinwell still there? She was my favorite teacher. I just loved her. She was tough, but you could tell she really cared about you. As a person."

"Yeah. She's still hanging in there. I'll tell her *hello* for you when I see her."

"So, you said on the phone you wanted to talk to me about Tammy."

"That's right. I heard you stayed with her for a while?"

"I did. After all my trouble with Trip Fallston. Tammy's a wonderful person. She helps women like me who've been battered. Offers them a temporary safe place to stay. I don't have anything bad to say about her."

"I'm not asking for that," I said. "I've been hired by a woman who's concerned about the safety and whereabouts of a friend who also stayed with Tammy for a while. A woman named Melissa Adamson."

"I don't know who that is. There was another woman staying with Tammy when I was there. But her name was Lettie Midland. She left before I did. Tammy hooked her up with a job and a really nice place to live for a time."

"You've stayed in touch with Lettie?"

"Well, no. Not really. I ran into her last month. At a women's rights conference in Richmond. We exchanged numbers then."

"I'd like to talk to her," I said.

"Well, I wouldn't want to give her number without permission, Mr. Barrow. But I could talk to her. Have her call you. I'd vouch for you and all. I know you're a nice man."

Before I left, she snapped a photo of me with her phone. She said Lettie Midland would insist on knowing who she was talking to.

Chapter Nineteen

Back at home, later that afternoon, I took the time to enter my grades through the faculty portal linked to the secure school website. By the time I'd double-checked my entries and finished, it was time to head into Weston for dinner at Wendi's. She was currently residing in one of the two apartments above the Weston Quality Furniture store, directly across the town square from the sheriff's office. Throughout the years, both apartments had almost always been occupied by teachers, usually female, the tenants often directly referred by the personnel department at the school board office. The woman who owned the furniture store enjoyed the stability of professional renters with a steady income and quiet habits. Over the years, only a few teachers had failed to live up to those expectations. Parties were discouraged, but sometimes, especially with younger teachers, they happened spontaneously. Always when the store beneath was closed. And with the sheriff's office in close proximity, things rarely got out of hand.

I was not the only guest that evening. Wendi had invited a few friends from her school, including the young first-grade teacher named Niki from across the hall. It was a diverse group in age, race, and place of origin. A compatible mix of locals, Yankee come-heres, and a couple originally from North Carolina. Beer, wine, and cocktails were flowing freely. The mood was decidedly festive, but relaxed, with everyone more than ready to decompress after another long school year.

Dinner was satisfying and filling, with a wide assortment of flavorful dishes supplied by Wendi and all the guests. There was a green salad and macaroni salad. Casseroles and breads and deviled eggs. Fresh strawberries and blueberries. Beef and chicken dishes. I'd brought my famous crab and seafood dip, made from my grandfather's carefully guarded recipe.

I was deep into a conversation about the music of The Beatles in their final years, talking with a young guy named Bruce, the husband of a third-grade teacher, when my phone rang. The incoming FaceTime call was from a number not in my contacts. I excused myself, walked to the bedroom at the back of the apartment, and stepped out the door onto the porch with a commanding view of the front of the sheriff's office across the courthouse lawn.

The face that popped into view when I touched *accept* was that of a beautiful young woman with long, wavy, blonde hair and a flawless complexion. She had a round face and wore eyeliner and shadow, but little more in the way of makeup. Her voice was low at first, cautious and apprehensive.

"Mr. Barrow?" she said.

"Yes, it is," I said, trying my best to sound pleasant and reassuring.

"My name is Lettie Midland. A friend of Darlene's. She asked me to call you. Said you wanted to talk to me about my connection with Tammy. Are you alone?"

"At the moment. Outside on a porch. There's no one around to hear us."

"Okay then. Let's talk. What would you like to know?"

"Do you know a woman named Melissa Adamson?"

"I wouldn't say I really know her. I know who she is. But not from her being at Tammy's. We weren't there at the same time. We met at the place we were moved to, after Tammy's."

"Moved to?"

"Yes. By friends of Tammy. Joan and Phil. The place was really nice. Such a relief after hiding out at Tammy's for weeks. No offense to Tammy, but her bus was kind of a dump."

"I've seen it," I said. "From the outside. I'm guessing it's a little crowded in there. With two or three women and a kid."

"Kid?"

"Yeah. Tammy's nephew, Kyle."

"He wasn't there when I was."

"When were you there?"

"Middle of March. Right after they let my boyfriend, Clint, out on bail. Son of a bitch said he'd kill me. Said a restraining order didn't mean nothing to him. I watch the news. I've seen it happen to other women. The cops say they'll protect you, but they can't. Not all the time. Told them he had a gun. Cops said they didn't find one. Clint was mean as hell, but not stupid. He stashed it someplace."

"How'd you get hooked up with Tammy? Someone refer you?"

"Yeah. A woman named Flo. At the Crisis Center in Fredericksburg. Got some other woman to drive me down the country to Tammy's."

"And the place this Joan and Phil had you staying. You met Melissa there, you said. Were there other women there as well?"

"About five or six while I was there. Women came and went. Sometimes we'd get up the next morning, and someone would just be gone. Like this one girl named Roma. Not much of an explanation. Joan just made some remark about her *moving on to the next level.* We all had our own rooms there. It was a really nice place. You couldn't see any other houses around. Kind of an estate, I guess you'd call it. Good, healthy food. They had us exercise. Me a lot. You probably can't tell just by looking at my face on your phone, but I'm a little on the heavy side. Curvy, I like to say. Folks tell me I'm pretty and all, though."

"So, they were trying to get you to lose weight?"

"Yeah. I guess so. Didn't have much luck with that. Some of the other girls, they tried to get them to gain a few pounds. You know, the ones that was way too thin. Anorexic looking almost."

"And you were okay with that?"

"I reckon it was for our own good. And they was doing a lot for us. Life coaching and such. But most of all, they was hiding us from our abusers. Husbands, boyfriends, stalkers, whatever. We all felt safe there. Protected."

"They ever ask you to do anything in return?"

"Nothing nasty. If that's what you're getting at. We did some work around the place. Cleaning the house. Taught us how to clean and maintain the indoor pool. Mow and trim. Sometimes they put us in uniform-like t-shirts that said *Potomac Perfection* on the front. They said it was job training. Nobody complained much."

"But you left?" I said.

"One day, Joan just up and showed me a newspaper. There was an article about Clint. Said he'd been shot dead by a man seen driving from the alley where it happened. Said the cops were looking for his ex-girlfriend, meaning me. They were concerned for my safety, since I hadn't been seen in a while. Joan and Phil said since Clint was dead, there was no threat to me anymore, I was free to go. They told me to pack a bag, gave me five hundred in cash, and said they'd give me a ride to wherever I wanted to go."

"Melissa was still there when you left?"

"Yes. She was. She just got there a week or so before I was let go. Sent away. Whatever."

"You think she's still there?"

"I have no idea. Like I said, people came and went a lot."

"Can you tell me where this place is?"

"No. But not because I don't want to. I don't know where it is. They took me there in a van. I rode in the back. There were no windows. I left the same way. They said it was to protect the other women. That no one could tell where the place was if they didn't know."

"You have any idea how long it took you to get there from when you left Tammy's place?"

"It's hard to say. Maybe an hour or so. But we was making a lot of turns. Left and right. So, I reckon they could've been just driving around for a spell. Going in circles for all I know."

"Were you ever in contact with anyone while you were there? Friends? Relatives?"

"No. They kept our phones. They said it was necessary for everyone's security. We all bitched about it to each other, but with everything Joan and Phil were doing to help us, nobody complained to them. When I left, they gave me a new phone. Just a cheap one. They said mine got broken. I didn't believe that, but there wasn't anything I could do about it. So I lost all my contacts. Like an idiot, I didn't have them written down anywhere."

"So, you had no way to get in touch with anyone when you left?"

"Just my sister in Richmond. Hers was the only number I could remember. Same one she had for years. I remembered it because she had a phone before I did. I'd have to borrow one from a friend to call her to come give me a ride home from wherever. You punch a number a bunch of times, you remember it. You just bring up a contact and punch the call thingy all the time, you don't."

"So, I'm guessing you don't know how to get in touch with any of the other women who might've been there when you were, but also left?"

"Nah. I know some of their names. If they gave them to me straight. Don't know all the last names for sure. I can give you what I know, if you want. We weren't really supposed to talk to each other about our past. It was against the rules. The gospel according to Joan, you might say. But it's hard for girls to keep quiet about all the shit that's been dumped on us all our lives. From what I could tell, none of us had many close friends. We pretty much all hated our parents. Not much in the way of close family. But there was one girl I got to be right close with. She was from a town somewhere south of D.C. Alexandria, I think. Her name was Noranne Dubart. Husband broke her arm. Twice. He'd cut her hair real short, all uneven. Made her look kind of crazy like. Kept threatening to cut up her face."

"Any idea why Darlene Morvine never made the move to the estate?"

"Oh, I don't know. She told me Tammy sent her off to meet some folks over in a town called Glover, I think."

"Why there instead of the estate?"

"Maybe she didn't make the cut. Fit the what-a-you-call-it…profile."

"What's that mean?"

"Well, not that we was all conceited or anything. But all us ladies at the estate, we were all right pretty. You know what I'm saying?"

"I believe I do," I said.

"I'm really not supposed to be telling about any of this. Before I left, they had me sign some papers. One of them… non-somethings."

"Non-disclosure agreement?"

"Yeah, that's it. But I got to thinking about why they made me do that. It was like, if they wasn't doing anything wrong, then what the hell? I don't like people telling me what I can say and what I can't. Had enough of that with Clint and too many before him."

"You're not afraid of a lawsuit?"

"I don't give a shit about that," she said. "What they gonna get from me? I got nothing."

* * *

By the time I rejoined the party, people were beginning to leave. Once everyone was gone, we started to clean up the place and put away what was left of the food. When everything was cleared out and tucked away, we collapsed together onto the sofa.

"You spending the night?" Wendi said.

"I don't have any pajamas," I said. "There'd be nothing for you to count."

"Hmm. Perhaps we could find another activity to lull us off to sleep."

"We could always count each other's freckles," I said. "The search might lead us to some interesting places."

Chapter Twenty

In the morning, we breakfasted on leftover deviled eggs and whole-wheat toast topped with strawberry jam. Before I left, we made a plan to meet at my place in the afternoon. In the meantime, Wendi would be checking on the price and availability of steamed crabs, and we'd both take some time to catch up on necessary chores at our respective homes.

At my place, I set about doing my laundry, vacuuming, and emptying the dishwasher. When I came back inside after taking care of some yard work, Wendi called.

"Oscar and Elnora are joining us for crabs at your place," she said. "Two o'clock. I'll pick up the crabs. I decided on a half-bushel of number twos. The price is reasonable. Gus at Weston Seafood claims they're running heavy this week."

"If you can believe him," I said. "He's exaggerated that before."

"I'll pick up some hot dogs and rolls. You have gas in the grill?"

"Got a fresh tank last week. Oscar's taking the day off, huh?"

"Elnora insisted. Said he's working too hard. Their afternoon was free. She said it would be good for them to get out. She even dragged him to church this morning."

"I'll bet he was praying for bacon."

"What?"

"Never mind," I said. "I'll tell you the story later. But I wouldn't count on him eating many hot dogs. He may have been involuntarily placed on a diet."

While waiting for everyone to arrive, I contemplated what to do with the list of five names Lettie Midland had texted me after our lengthy conversation. There was Noranne Dubart. Maybe from Alexandria. Abused by her husband. Roma Coltrell, who abruptly disappeared. A woman named Lexi, whose last name might have been Fincler. Not sure of the spelling. A Latina girl named Rita. Last name unknown. And a tall black woman named Alta with short-cropped hair, whose last name started with an S. Or maybe a C.

And of course, there was Joan and Phil. The benevolent couple who watched over the group. Again, no last names. No idea if they were married, just friends, kissing cousins, or simply platonic co-workers and gatekeepers.

I kept getting more names, but not much else. Little to help me get any closer to locating Melissa Adamson. If I thought about it too much longer, my head might explode. Or worse, it might spoil my appetite. I had to stop thinking about it. There were crabs on the way at that very moment.

After icing down the glass-bottled beer in a cooler, I rolled out some brown craft paper onto the picnic table and placed a roll of paper towels at the center. I secured the paper to the table with clips in the middle and at the corners, then laid out a few pewter mallets and a couple of crab knives. People often have differing opinions on the best way to pick a crab. Some are meticulous about getting every shred of the tasty white meat out of each tiny crevice. Even picking out the scrawny little legs. Others are sloppy and wasteful. Just going after the big chunks. Thankfully, no one who would be sitting at the table today had a history of being wasteful.

When it came to getting the meat out of the claws, Oscar and Elnora always used a knife. I preferred the mallet. Wendi just punted and pushed her claws over to me to deal with. I'm not complaining. I like claw meat. It adds a variety of flavor to the experience.

Everyone arrived by two o'clock, and the feast began. There was mild conversation about this and that, nothing heavy or serious. No talk of school or law enforcement. Elnora was a retired accountant who did tax returns in season, including a lot of pro bono work for low-income families and the elderly. She asked about my daughter, who'd entered the same profession a while back.

More than an hour later, after everyone had their fill, I fired up the grill and attempted not to burn a few hot dogs. The ladies declined the delicacy. I ate one. Despite Elnora's dirty looks, Oscar had two. As usual, smothered in ketchup to begin with, but dipped again, for extra measure, in the red glob on his plate before each subsequent bite.

Despite a fair amount of cloud cover and a mild breeze, it was starting to get hot out on the deck. Wendi and Elnora retreated inside to pick out what was left of the crabs and divide up the meat.

"Aren't hot dogs and bacon in the same nasty food group?" I said.

"Shhh," he said. "Don't bring that shit up. You'll get her all fired up on *that* again."

We finished eating, then rolled up the crab mess from the table and slipped it into a trash bag. When I returned from a visit to the trash and recycling bins, Oscar had settled into an Adirondack chair with a fresh bottle of beer. I followed his lead, grabbed a cold one for myself, and plopped down in the chair next to him.

"You had any luck finding that woman yet?" he said. "What's her name? Melissa—"

"Adamson," I said. "Not much. I did locate the woman she was staying with for a while. Tammy Tydiss. She lives in a blue school bus, out on Slipstone Road."

"The Bus Lady? I heard about her. Never caught her name, though."

"You're the sheriff. Shouldn't you know everyone?"

"I'm too busy to know everyone. She doing anything illegal out there?"

"Not as far as I can tell. She seems to be providing abused women with a place to stay for a while. Less than stellar accommodations, but a place to hide out from their husbands, boyfriends, whatever. She has a little boy staying with her now. A first grader. Her nephew, she says."

"She *says?*"

"Yeah. I know. You think I'm suspicious about everyone."

"Guess that's your nature. You're always watching for the cheaters in life. People hiding the truth. You do what we've both been doing for as long as we have, you tend to get that way."

"Ain't it the truth," I said.

"You turn up anything I should know about, you tell me."

I told him about the rest of what I'd learned. About Darlene Morvine leading me to talk with Lettie Midland about the group of women staying somewhere on what she'd described as an estate.

"Sounds like a dead end," he said. "You can't find the place, you can't find her. Just don't go asking me for any help. I'm way too busy. On top of all the usual troubles, we've had a rash of thefts of catalytic converters being stolen from cars all over the county. I got a deputy out sick and another one on vacation."

"Well, there is just this one thing I was wondering about. Lettie Midland gave me a list of names. Only a few are complete. You think you could find the time to run them? See if anything unusual pops up."

"*All right*. Send me the damn list. But I'm not making any promises. Damn. Why you always have to be asking me to do your homework for you?"

"Well, you are the smartest kid in the class," I said.

"Suck-up," he said.

Chapter Twenty-One

On Monday, I decided to play hooky. Though I'm probably the only one left on the planet who calls it that anymore. I had two unused personal days left, so I emailed the Vice Principal, Mrs. Friday, and told her I wouldn't be in. Carmella Friday was a pleasant lady from a nice family. I liked to say I'd never met a Friday I didn't like. Both the people and the day of the week.

Most of the day would've been consumed with meetings, finishing up discussions on this year, planning changes for the next. Administrators like change. Even when something isn't broken, they want to fix it. Over the years, it had also been my experience that a lot of administrators didn't really listen much to teacher input. Some might politely pretend to be open to suggestions made by faculty members, then end up doing whatever the hell they wanted anyway. In school, we teach about democracy, but in its operation, we often don't practice what we teach. I'll leave it to the history teachers to grapple with that hypocrisy.

A few years back, some Bozo came up with the idea for each member of the faculty to share, out loud, their goals for the next year, at one of our closing meetings. I'm not against goals in general. Everyone should have them. I have them. I'm certainly not against sharing them. But this ritual took a lot of time away from finishing up our paperwork, packing away books, and neatening up our rooms. In recent years, I found myself wanting to present my three goals as (1) Retire, (2) Go fishing, and (3) Go crabbing. Since I'd be skipping out on the day's festivities, the temptation to make a spectacle of myself this year would be removed. I suppose there's always next year. Until there isn't.

Nealy Kroft and his family had left early that morning, gone away for a few days to visit with his sister's family down in the mountains near Blacksburg. He'd given me permission to park my vehicle at his house, so I could watch Tammy's place across the road. He told me where a spare key was hidden, in case I needed to keep an eye on things from the vantage point of Arlo's room. But being in the house would require too much time to get back out to my vehicle in order to follow Tammy when she left for work. So, not wanting to take the risk of losing her, I sat and waited in the gray Subaru sedan I'd borrowed from the car rental place in Weston. It's not always easy to follow someone out on country roads. It helps if the car you're driving doesn't attract attention, and your quarry isn't expecting to be followed. I was hoping that would be the case here.

Since school was out for the summer now, I was wondering what Tammy would do about the kid when she was working. That question was at least partially answered when the pair emerged from the blue bus, and she strapped the boy into a child safety restraint in the back seat of the truck. At least she was attending to the boy's safety. I'd seen a few too many others around the county who neglected to use the proper seating restraints required by law.

The truck rolled out of the driveway, and I followed. Not too far back at first, until we turned off Slipstone Road, headed toward Weston. Out on the main highway, I kept a fair distance between us, trying my best not to be noticed. About a mile before we got to Weston, she turned left on Durn Road. By the time I turned to follow, another car had pulled out of a driveway and gotten between us. For the next couple of miles, the car rolled along at a rate a little slower than Tammy's. Somewhere in the back of my mind, there was a *distance, rate, and time* word problem taking form. I shook off the distraction and concentrated on my current occupation. Despite the separation, I managed to keep Tammy's white truck in sight.

Not long after the car between us turned off, Tammy made a left onto a paved driveway, flanked on both sides with stone pillars. From my view behind her, I could see part of an iron gate that had been swung open.

I couldn't follow her in there, so I drove past the entrance, looking for somewhere to park or turn around.

The next driveway was about fifty yards further up the road. Near a brick-encased mailbox, a big wooden real estate sign had been posted, advertising the place for sale. At the bottom of the sign, it said *Shown By Appointment Only*. Taking a chance that no one was home, I drove up a slight incline to the end of the driveway where it looped around in front of a sprawling, modern-looking, one-story place with a lot of sharp angles, dark windows, and a roof full of solar panels. When I stopped in front, I had an unobstructed view of the house where Tammy had gone.

She was out in front of a big white Colonial-style house, standing at the open door of the pickup, unhooking the kid from his car seat and helping him to climb out.

Lettie had told me there were no other houses visible from the estate where she and the other women had stayed. So I knew this wasn't the place I'd been hoping to find. I powered down my windows and turned off the car. Without knocking, Tammy and the kid went inside the house. I'd just wriggled into a reasonably comfortable position when a man with thick, white hair, dressed in white shorts and a red polo shirt, came charging out of the house in front of me.

He circled around to my side of the car and said, "May I help you?" Not sounding at all like he meant it.

"I saw the *For Sale* sign," I said. "Just thought I'd take a look around."

He looked up and down at the car I was driving, as if assessing my worth from the condition of the little gray sedan. I wanted to tell him that my own vehicle was much nicer, but decided it was better to stay in character than to defend my social standing.

"I'm afraid, *sir*, that *if* you wish to see the house, you must *first* contact the realtor," he said. "She can arrange an appointment for you. *If* she deems it appropriate. You can't expect to just *stop by* and *look around*. This isn't that type of listing."

"Of course," I said. "My apologies. But I do want to compliment you on your lawn, sir. Do you use the same landscaper as your neighbor?" I pointed to Tammy's white truck, parked next door. "That Potomac Perfection outfit?"

"Certainly not!" he barked. "I have no idea what quality of work they might do. From the looks of that truck alone, I wouldn't hire them."

I apologized again, started up the car, and drove off down the hill. In the rearview mirror, I saw the indignant man retreat back inside. I parked out behind a hedgerow along the road, between the two driveways, and waited for something to happen.

About forty minutes later, another truck arrived, pulling a long trailer behind it, loaded with mowers and trimming tools. It was a big, silver, late-model Dodge with the same *Potomac Perfection* logo on the side. I wrote down the license number of the truck and the address of the place. Then I left.

* * *

Back at home, after lunch, I sat on a barstool at the kitchen counter with my laptop open in front of me. From the address of the place Tammy had driven to that morning, I was able to get the names of the owners. John Philip Trunvid Jr. and Joan Pomeroy Flaith. A lot of *Juniors* go by their middle name. It wasn't much of a stretch to deduce that this was more than likely the Phil and Joan that Lettie Midland had told me about.

After a few more deep searches into marriage and divorce records, an interesting profile of Joan emerged. At the ripe old age of forty, she'd already been married four times. Never to Phil. The last marriage had been to a guy named Norman Flaith. Her second husband was a man named Destry Dylan.

In mathematics, there are no coincidences. In life, there are few. Some, more skeptical than I, don't believe in them at all.

Chapter Twenty-Two

It didn't take much more poking around to find out that Destry Dylan had a younger brother. Joan Flaith had previously been married to the brother of Rutherford "Fordy" Dylan. That made it more than likely that Joan and Fordy knew each other. Of course, it didn't necessarily mean that Fordy was somehow involved in hiding out a bunch of women from their abusers. But if he were involved, then why conceal such a thing from his wife, who was attempting to do the very same thing for her friend Melissa? Then again, Joan *was* just his brother's ex. It could be entirely possible that Fordy had no idea what his former sister-in-law was up to. But that theory threw the whole mess back into the uncomfortable realm of coincidence. Perhaps it was time to fall back on an old investigative maxim I'd been taught years ago. *When all else fails, investigate your client.*

But before I got started on that, there were other threads that needed to be followed. I spent some time looking into the Potomac County public records and found out the property where Tammy parked her bus was owned by a man named Driscoll Ballinderry. Same last name as the kid staying with Tammy. The taxes on the property hadn't been paid in a while. The address I found for Ballinderry was near the town of Polts Corner, just west of Fredericksburg. If I left right away, I might get through the city before the afternoon traffic rush.

* * *

Driscoll Ballinderry's place was a two-story shack with not a speck of paint remaining on the weathered-wood clapboard siding. The glass in one of the second-story windows was missing. From the inside, a piece of plywood leaned against the opening. There was a pesky swarm of carpenter bees buzzing around the front of the place. When I stepped onto the porch, most of them scattered. Two of them remained, circling around my head in a weaving pattern.

I knocked hard, three times, on the dirty-white aluminum door. The lone screen panel on top was full of dime-sized holes. A mangy-looking gray cat slinked up to the door, ready to dash inside at the earliest opportunity. I knocked again, longer and harder this time. Finally, a hefty, sagging man, leaning on a wooden cane, shuffled into view, half-hidden by the inner door. The smell of whiskey wafted through the screen, and my escort of carpenter bees seemed to retreat.

"What you want?" the man growled.

"Mr. Ballinderry?" I said, holding up my license. "My name is Barrow, sir. I'm doing a background check on an individual who's applying for a job with Potomac County Public Schools. I wonder if I might ask you a few questions?"

"You ain't the cops?"

"No, sir. I'm a private investigator. I have nothing to do with law enforcement."

"Well, come on in, then. Make sure you don't let that goddamn cat in. Fuckin' cat'll piss on everything."

I blocked the cat with my leg and opened the door just enough to slip in sideways.

Inside, Ballinderry plopped down into a wooden rocker with a cane-bottom seat. I sat across the room, on the edge of an old brown sofa that did, in fact, smell like cat piss. I started to wish for the odor of whiskey to return, but he wasn't offering to share the half-empty bottle of *Old Crow* perched on the table beside him. His cheek was puffed out with a wad of chewing tobacco. An old Maxwell House coffee can sat on the floor on the other side of his chair.

"Who you wanna ask about?" he said.

"A woman named Tammy Tydiss," I said, watching his face for any sign of recognition.

"Who?"

"Tammy Tydiss," I repeated, spelling out the last name. "She's living on a piece of land you own, down in Potomac County."

"I got a daughter named Tammy," he said. "But as far as I know, her name ain't Tydiss. Shit…Tydiss was her grandmother's name, on her mother's side." He grimaced and took a spit at the can but missed. By the looks of the floor, it wasn't the first time.

"Have you seen or talked with your daughter lately?"

"I ain't seen her in years. That bitch ain't been around since I tried to knock some fuckin' sense into her. She comes back, I'll try again. She's as stupid as her damn mother was. Man crazy, the both of them. They'd both fuck a wooden dick and enjoy the splinters."

I gave him a general description of Tammy that included her extra-long hair. I decided it was best not to mention her bikini.

"Sounds like her," he said. "What kinda job you say she's trying to get?"

"I didn't say. She has a nephew? About six years old? Name's Kyle Ballinderry?"

"Whaaaat you talkin' about, mister? She *had* a nephew. Her brother's boy. Died a couple of years ago. Down in Virginia Beach. Drowned in one of them kiddie pools. His *father* was supposed to be watching him. But he's a fuckin' worthless drunk! I might be an alcoholic, but I ain't no fuckin' drunk. There's a difference, you know. A fuckin' drunk just don't give a shit about nothing!"

For a fleeting moment, I considered explaining the concept of a double negative to him. One of the few grammar lessons a math teacher is qualified to deliver. But then, there is no point in attempting to reason with *Old Crow* logic.

* * *

On my way back through Fredericksburg, I decided to try another run at

Harry from the Crisis Center. He'd hinted that he might be able to come up with some information on where the woman named Flo had wandered off to. He was supposed to call me when he had something. Maybe punching up a ten-digit phone number was too much for his brain to handle.

If he had anything for me, he'd be expecting cash. I wasn't in the habit of carrying much money with me these days, so I stopped in at a gas station with an ATM, pulled out two hundred bucks, and charged the fill-up on my credit card.

When I got to the Crisis Center, Harry was alone, inside at the front desk. He seemed jittery, looking at the door behind him and out the front window.

"I was gonna call you tonight," he said. "We can't talk here. There's a cafe around the corner. *Treasures.* They got tables out on the sidewalk. I'll be out there in about ten minutes."

Halfway down the block, I passed Harry's tall, redheaded female co-worker, heading in the opposite direction, toward the Center. She walked past without looking at me. Maybe short people were invisible to her.

I parked myself at a table for two on the brick sidewalk. A waitress came over, and I ordered a glass of iced tea. She looked less than thrilled. She should've been more optimistic. I might be a big tipper.

The sun had dropped behind the three-story buildings, casting the street in shadow. The temperature was starting to drop. The waitress brought my tea. I smiled and thanked her. She walked off without returning the gesture. I was halfway through my tea when Harry showed up, still antsy, looking all around. He sat down, and the waitress came back. He waved her off, and she walked away.

"You got the money?" he said. "You said a *hunred.*"

I wanted to tell him the word *hundred* had another *d* in it. "Depends on what you can give me," I said.

"I got an address. Where she's staying."

"Here in town?"

"Nah. She's down closer to where you're from. A place called Province Beach." He reached into his pants pocket, pulled out a slip of paper, and handed it to me. "That good enough?"

"As long as she's really there," I said. "I could give you fifty now. The rest when I find her."

"That's not fair. You said a *hunred*."

"Okay, Harry. But if you're scamming me, I'll be back. And maybe I'll tell your red-headed co-worker, what's-her-name, what you've been up to."

"It's Margaret," he said. "But you can't tell her."

"Let's hope I don't have to," I said, motioning for the waitress to bring the check.

The tea was only two-fifty. She explained it was senior-discount day. I gave her a five and told her to keep the change. A one-hundred-percent tip. She almost smiled and walked away.

Harry started licking his lips at the sight of cash. I handed him his hundred, and he got up and walked off. Does anyone say *thank you* anymore?

I stayed for a few minutes, finishing my tea, watching the slow traffic, enjoying the early evening air. Back in my car, across the street from the Crisis Center, I saw Harry walking away with the red-headed Margaret and another guy, big looking, wearing a dark ballcap and sunglasses. I couldn't see his face. They climbed into a green panel van and drove away. My car was aimed in the wrong direction to follow, and there was too much traffic to risk a U-turn.

Chapter Twenty-Three

On the way home from Fredericksburg, I called Wendi. She was at my place, watching television, waiting to hear from me. I told her about what I'd been up to all day and invited her to join me on an unannounced visit to the reputed residence of the woman named Flo.

Back at my place, I took the time to grab a quick sandwich. Then the two of us headed out, backtracking about sixteen miles north, on a road that ran mostly parallel to the main highway, following another winding road along the river to the address hairy Harry had given me.

Way back before the Potomac River Bridge opened in 1940, Province Beach had been a popular tourist destination, with many of its visitors arriving by the ferry that connected the Northern Neck with Maryland. Over the years, I'd seen numerous nostalgic photos of the place and heard many of the stories that went with them. In addition to the swimming area at its well-maintained beach, the place had boasted a short boardwalk, populated with quaint shops, simple amusements, lower-end eateries, and a twenty-room hotel with a long, wide veranda overlooking the river. After the opening of the bridge, the tiny community eventually fell out of favor with the tourist trade, being eclipsed by its larger, more popular rival, the town of Colonial Beach, over in Westmoreland County.

The old hotel and virtually everything else from the heyday of Province Beach was gone.

In its place was a sorry-looking trailer park. By the time we got there, it was dark. Our headlights illuminated crowded lanes populated with rusted rectangular structures, just sitting there waiting for a tornado to blow by and wipe the place off the map.

When we found the address, I parked out in front by what was left of a mangled, white- painted metal picket fence with no gate. A yellow porch light was on by the front door. A bright light atop a short pole in front of a neighbor's metal carport cast long shadows across the yard. I caught the scent of something like burnt motor oil. From somewhere across the street came the intermittent bark of a large dog, accompanied by the rattle of a metal chain. Parked behind the fence was a faded-green John Deere lawn tractor with its hood up. The grass hadn't been mowed in a while.

"Nice trailer," I said.

"Yuck," Wendi said. "But aren't we supposed to call them mobile homes?"

"It's parked on a concrete block foundation. I think it has officially lost most of its mobility."

Parked in what amounted to a driveway was an old ninety-something Chevy sedan with a cracked windshield and a flat tire. Behind the fractured windshield, propped up on the dashboard, was a hand-painted *For Sale* sign.

"In the market for a used car?" Wendi said.

"I believe they're now called pre-owned automobiles," I said. "Implying they may have been previously owned, but not necessarily used."

"I'm pretty sure that one's been used."

"I hope that's not her only means of transportation," I said.

Through the translucent curtains, we could see the flickering light of a television.

"Let's go ask her," she said. "Looks like someone's home."

I knocked on the door, but no one came. I tried again with the same result. It was late, and I didn't feel like exercising my patience. I told Wendi to wait by the door and keep knocking. She ignored my directions and followed me around to a high, curtainless kitchen window at the end of the trailer.

"Boost me up, so I can see inside," she said.

I ignored her suggestion and moved a rigid, plastic chair from the yard over to the window. When I climbed up and stood on the seat, I could see inside. Stretched out on the floor, in front of the TV, was the motionless body of a woman.

* * *

Nearly two hours later, we were still there, leaning against the front of my car, waiting for Sheriff Oscar Murphy, his deputies, and Potomac County Coroner, Dr. Ted Rodrigo and his crew, to finish attending to their assigned duties. The dog across the street was still barking, and most of the neighbors had come out to watch. It would have been difficult to sleep through all the initial sirens and the continuously flashing red and blue lights.

When we saw Murphy duck and exit through the front door, we stepped over and stood by the hole in the fence where a gate had once been.

"Looks like a drug overdose," he said. "Probably dead before you got here. Too far gone for the Rescue Squad to bring her back."

"So, it's not a homicide?" I said.

"Hard to say, this early. Some bruises on her wrists. Like she might have been restrained at some point. Don't know what she took for sure yet, or whether she took it on her own. Found a few pills scattered around the table and on the floor. Could be opioids. Maybe something laced with fentanyl. We're being careful."

"Any of the neighbors see or hear anything?" Wendi said.

"Didn't hear anything unusual," Murphy said. "Claim that damn dog barks all night, all the time, anyway. Didn't see anything suspicious. Just you two. If y'all would confess, we could lock you up and go home early."

"Very funny, Oscar," she said, not meaning it. "I wish we could have done something to help her. Given her Narcan or whatever. Not that we carry any with us."

"Don't beat yourself up over it. You did the best you could. You called 911. Sometimes that's all we can do."

"I suppose so," she said. "I'm just not used to dealing with this sort of thing."

"Hanging out with a math teacher is a dirty business," he said. "Hard to avoid the seamy side of life."

"I've tried to warn her," I said.

"You saw the body through the window?" Murphy said, getting serious again. "Then went inside?"

"The door wasn't locked," I said. "We checked her, then came back out and made the call."

"You didn't touch anything else? Look around inside?"

"Nope."

"What's your connection with the deceased woman?"

I filled him in on what I'd learned since we'd talked the day before. I told him about Flo's previous employment at the Crisis Center, and Harry's telling me where to find her. About her connecting both Melissa Adamson and Lettie Midland with Tammy, the Bus Lady. I decided not to tell him yet about what Driscoll Ballinderry had told me about Tammy's nephew. As far as I knew, that had nothing to do with the situation at hand, or my search for Melissa Adamson.

"You get anything yet about the women on Lettie's list?" I said.

"Not yet," he said. "Be patient, schoolteacher. I'll let you know when, and if, I find something useful. In the meantime, just in case this wasn't an accident… I'm serious now, Pete. You watch your ass."

I put my hand on Wendi's shoulder. "That's her job, " I said.

Chapter Twenty-Four

Despite having little sleep the night before, I arrived at school extra early the next morning and got right to work on packing up my room, neatening things up, and polishing off what was left of my required paperwork. As department chair, I was responsible for checking the rooms of the other math teachers, making sure that their space had been left neat and clean, and all their paperwork had been completed. As soon as each of them arrived, I checked things off and signed their clearance sheets. By noon, everything was finished.

After a special parting lunch that included fried chicken and chocolate cake, put on by the PTSA in the cafeteria, we got together for one last department meeting in my classroom. Everyone filled me in on what I'd missed at the previous day's gatherings. It wasn't much. Some of them wished they'd thought of taking a personal day like I had.

At two o'clock, Mrs. Friday got on the intercom and announced that anyone who had handed in their clearance sheet was free to leave. It didn't take long for the parking lot to clear out.

It was always a great feeling to be finished, though the thrill of it seemed to become less and less with each passing year. Teaching is one of the few occupations in the world with such a well-defined end to a year's labor. Followed by a hard-earned break from the routine, with a chance to unwind and reflect, before a new beginning each fall. A fresh chance to start over. Another opportunity not afforded by many other careers.

Now I was a free man. Sort of. I still had another job that required my attention. After taking a nap, I'd get right on it.

I woke just past five-thirty, feeling groggy and out of sorts. After throwing together a sloppy sandwich of ham and cheese with lettuce, tomato, and mayo, I stumbled out to the table on the deck to eat. It was still hot, and the breeze off the river was minimal. Eating slowly, I watched the water and thought about Melissa Adamson. One of the people who might have led me to her was dead. Flo had died by her own hand, or someone else's. But that was Murphy's problem to solve. Not mine. My only job was to find Melissa Adamson. I needed to keep reminding myself of that. The possibility that the boy living with Tammy was not really her nephew may have nothing at all to do with helping me to find Melissa. The drunken… correction, *alcoholic* ramblings of Driscoll Ballinderry might be true, but I had no clear sense of how that might help me.

Knowing now that Tammy's real last name was most likely Ballinderry helped little in finding more information on her. She had an old social media account with few pictures and not much else that revealed anything useful. Tammy's father had more or less admitted to physically abusing her. Which explained, at least in part, her motivation to help other women. If, in fact, that was what she was doing.

Online, I found the sad obituary and a newspaper article detailing the life and death of a kid named Kyle Ballinderry. If the real boy with that name was deceased, then it stood to reason that his Aunt Tammy might've had access to his documentation. And that she might have used some of those real documents, along with other false ones, to register another boy for school here in Potomac County. Schools don't have the resources to verify the documentation supplied in registering a new student. Unless it was poorly done, few administrators would recognize a fake document if they saw one. The birth certificate used by Tammy probably would have been real. But the custody papers might not be. I'd need to try to get a look at those, if I could.

But if the kid wasn't really her nephew, then who was he? I found no record of her having any children of her own. I wanted to believe that all of this was none of my business, if it didn't help me to find Melissa. But if the kid wasn't who she said he was, then I was obligated to report what I knew or suspected.

There were more threads I hadn't pulled on yet. Kasey Dylan had told me that Melissa's mother was dead. Killed while driving impaired, in a single-car collision with a utility pole. Her father was living somewhere in California. Melissa had told Kasey she didn't know where, and that she didn't care if she ever laid eyes on him again. I thought it seemed unlikely that she'd seek him out. Even to get away from an abusive husband.

But Melissa's husband, Greg Adamson, needed to be checked out. I thought it unlikely that he'd been able to track her down when I hadn't. But then, I didn't know what he knew about his wife. It was a rock that needed looking under. Even if it was hiding something slimy and unpleasant.

Wendi stayed at her apartment that night. Her plans included reading and an early bedtime to make up for the sleep lost the night before over the unsettling incident at Province Beach. She doesn't believe in naps. I'm pretty sure she views taking naps as a sign of weakness. When we talked on the phone to say goodnight, I didn't bother to tell her about the long one I'd taken that afternoon.

I spent the rest of the solitary evening on my laptop, poking around here and there, taking notes. It didn't take long to find out where Greg Adamson lived and worked. His social media accounts revealed more than I wanted or needed to know. From the suggestive pictures he'd posted, it looked like he had a new girl in his life. Emphasis on the word *girl*. She looked younger than most of the high-school girls I taught. Maybe he'd decided to expand his criminal repertoire beyond wife-beating, into the territory of child abuse. But of course, it wasn't always easy to judge a person's age by their looks. Wendi and I had both looked quite young, right out of college. I remember us being at a mom-and-pop store out on Route 3, one evening during our first week as teachers. The middle-aged woman behind the counter was teasing us about being back to school already, asking us what grade we were in that year. I remember the stunned look on her face when we told her we were teachers, not students.

* * *

By midmorning on Wednesday, I was back in Fredericksburg, parked across from the cycle shop where Greg Adamson earned a living. It was a deep and narrow cinderblock building, in a mostly residential neighborhood of older homes dating back to the 1940s. The high garage door that took up most of the front of the place was pulled up. Inside, people were scrambling about, shouting orders at each other, the clink of metal-on-metal echoing around them.

At half past ten, a tattooed guy in a black t-shirt with the sleeves cut off slipped on a pair of aviator sunglasses as he swaggered out to the sidewalk in front. His long dark hair was pulled back in a braided ponytail. Leaning against the building, between the garage opening and the office door, he pulled a chrome lighter from the pocket of his sagging jeans and lit up a cigarette. From the pictures I'd seen on social media, I knew he was Greg Adamson. I got out and walked across the street to him.

"You Greg?" I said.

He took a long drag on his cigarette while he looked me up and down. I was wearing faded jeans and a black polo shirt with matching black Nikes. If I needed to run, I was ready. Like him, I was wearing a pair of aviators. Same shirt color. Same sunglasses. Perhaps we could bond over our similar choices in life.

He exhaled a puff of smoke and studied the curled brim of my Nationals ballcap.

"The Nationals suck," he smirked. "Yeah. I'm Greg. Why?"

No doubt a Yankees fan. I flashed my license and identified myself as a private investigator. He seemed unimpressed.

"I'm looking for a woman named Melissa Adamson," I said. "I'm told she's your wife. That you might know where she is."

"Legally, we're still married. But we're not together anymore. She split, man. I don't know where the fuck she went. And I don't care anymore. What the fuck you want her for?"

"I represent her father," I lied. "He's inherited some money. He wants to share it with his daughter, but can't find her."

"That sounds like bullshit, man. Nobody in that family ever had a pot to piss in. Like I told you, I don't know where she is. I don't know if you're hooked up with those other guys that paid me a visit or not. And I don't really care. But I ain't looking for her anymore."

"What other guys?" I said.

He took off his sunglasses, revealing bruising around his right eye.

"Ones that gave me this. Along with the message to stop looking for Melissa. If they're your friends, tell them I got the message. It still hurts."

There was a slight quiver to his voice. He looked like he was about to cry. Apparently, he could dish it out but couldn't take it.

He put his aviators back on, dropped his cigarette, and stomped on it.

"Now get the fuck out of here," he said. "And leave me alone."

Chapter Twenty-Five

I considered trying to call and meet up with my client before leaving Fredericksburg. After all, she was the one paying the bill. She deserved to be kept informed of my progress. If it could be called that. But I had to be careful about what I told her. Letting her know that her brother-in-law, Destry Dylan, had an ex-wife who'd turned up in the investigation could present a problem. You never knew how a client might react to unexpected information. If the facts led her into a confrontation with her husband, that could end up hindering my search for Melissa. And if the tangential connection between Joan Flaith and Fordy Dylan turned out to have no bearing on the case, the bond of trust between Kasey and her husband could become strained. Not to mention the trust between me and my client.

I also saw no reason to alarm her over the death of Flo. Kasey said she didn't know her. And there was no solid reason to suspect the woman's demise had anything to do with Melissa's alleged disappearance.

So I decided to drive on back to Potomac County. Maybe later I'd send Kasey an email or a text message to update her on some of the things I'd been checking into. But not all. Not yet.

I didn't go directly home. Deciding instead at the last minute, to drive on past my turn, toward Weston, and off onto Slipstone Road. As expected, Tammy's truck wasn't in the yard. So I turned around and headed back to the place on Durn Road she'd visited on Monday. The place owned by the enterprising couple, Joan and Phil. From the road, I could see there were no vehicles out front and the three garage doors were closed. I went on past the for-sale house, around a bend, and did a U-turn at the next driveway.

When I drove back past the place for sale, the indignant white-haired guy was out at the road retrieving his mail from the box. He stopped and glared as I drove by, looking like he recognized me. I considered stopping to give him a tour of my much nicer vehicle, but decided against it. He didn't seem like the kind of guy who could change his opinion of someone.

* * *

On the drive back from Fredericksburg, I'd called Murphy and set up an appointment to chat with him. He said he could squeeze me in at 12:15, right before lunch. It was 12:37 when I slipped into the chair in front of his desk.

"Where's Wendi?" he said, without looking up from his laptop.

"Shopping in Richmond for the day," I said. "Why?"

"I knew she couldn't be with you."

"And why is that?"

"Because you're late," he said, closing his laptop and grinning at me. "Proving my theory that you're *always* late when she's not with you."

"You're using inductive reasoning," I said. "Drawing a conclusion based on past observations. That makes your conclusion *probably* true, but not *necessarily* true. I could be on time without her."

"Hmm. Maybe someday. But I'm not holding my breath. So what is it you wanted to talk about?"

"What about your lunch?"

"I already ate. I knew you'd be late."

I ignored that and got to the point of my visit. Telling him about Tammy's real last name, her dead nephew, and my resulting suspicions about the boy living with her. Murphy listened and took notes.

"We'll check with the school on the kid's documents," he said. "If the boy's not who she's presented him to be, then she could be in some deep shit."

"If that's the case, any chance you could hold off on coming down on her right away? I'd like to be closer to finding Melissa before the shit hits the fan with Tammy."

"I'll do what I can. But the safety of the child has to come first. You know that. I can't be worried about tipping your hand in looking for someone who might not even want to be found."

I conceded that point and moved on. "Any news about Flo's death?" I asked.

"Not much. Her full name was Florence Peeke. It'll be a while before we know exactly what killed her. You know how that goes."

"Toxicologists are slow and deliberate, but precise. Four to six weeks?"

"Yep. That *palace* in Province Beach where you found her belongs to a relative. An uncle who rarely comes there anymore. She stayed there off and on. Neighbors said they didn't know much about her. Said she kept to herself mostly. Sometimes they saw other people with her. Mostly women. Never saw the same person twice. People came and went. Often at night. Neighbors said they'd see things when they were outside for a smoke, or out with the dog taking a piss."

"Hope the dog was the one pissing," I said. "Not the neighbor."

"Who knows," he said. "Maybe both. It *is* Province Beach."

"A true paradise lost," I said. "Pissed on by many."

"I connected with the authorities in Fredericksburg. Told them where you got the info on Flo's whereabouts. Said they'd question this guy Harry and his friend Margaret at the Crisis Center. See if they can squeeze anything useful out of them."

"Any security cameras in the neighborhood?"

"Not many in working order. Not even the doorbell kind. The crime rate is surprisingly low in that corner of our little county. We don't get that many calls out there."

"Hmm. Maybe it's populated with very honest and trusting people. Or they just feel like they've got nothing worth stealing that would justify the expense of the equipment. What about the bruises on her wrists?"

"Autopsy report says they were recent. That's troubling. Might mean someone forced something into her."

"Any progress with the names on Lettie Midland's list?" I asked.

"Not yet. Like I said, I'll call you when I have something."

Before I left, I told him about my encounter with the recently threatened and bruised Greg Adamson.

"I should let the Fredericksburg cops know about that," Murphy said. "In the meantime, don't do anything stupid and get yourself in a bad situation. You keep snooping around, someone might decide to play rough with you, too."

Chapter Twenty-Six

When I got back home, I worked for a while on typing up an email to my client, Kasey Dylan. I used a lot of vague language, like *promising leads* and *persons of interest*. I told her I'd located Tammy and confirmed that Melissa had been staying with her for a while but had since moved on. I urged her to continue her attempts to contact Melissa on the phone she had given her to hide away in the false-bottomed purse. And to let me know if Melissa answered her calls or responded in any way.

I read the email over a couple of times before sending it. For bullshit, it wasn't bad. It sounded encouraging and full of promise. Maybe when I finally retired, I could carve out a new, more sedentary career as a professional bullshitter. It's so easy to fall in love with your own words.

What I didn't tell her was that Tammy had lied to me. She'd claimed Melissa had left with someone she didn't know. But Lettie Midland had placed Melissa at the estate with Joan and Phil, whom she'd described as *friends of Tammy*. With my own eyes, I'd seen Tammy at a house owned by them. It was also looking more likely that Tammy had lied about the identity of the kid living with her. The real Kyle Ballinderry was dead. Who the kid with her might be, and who he belonged to were questions that needed to be addressed. I understood that Murphy was legally obligated to pursue the answers to those questions in a timely manner, for the welfare of the child. But if he blew the lid off the Tammy situation too soon, doors leading to Melissa Adamson's whereabouts were sure to close.

I was deep in thought about my next move when Murphy called.

"Got a hit," he said. "One of the names on the list. Noranne Dubart."

"The one Lettie Midland said she was close to," I said. "From Alexandria, she thought."

"That's where she is now."

"You have an address?" I said, grabbing a pen and pad from the kitchen counter. "I need to move on this before she decides to take off for parts unknown."

"I don't reckon you need to worry about that. She's not likely to be changing her place of residence anytime soon."

"She's not dead?"

"It's not that permanent," he said. "She's in jail."

* * *

By ten o'clock the next morning, we were on our way to Alexandria for an appointment to talk with the incarcerated Noranne Dubart. Murphy had made the necessary arrangements. He was driving an unmarked, official county vehicle. A big black SUV that looked more like it belonged to the FBI than the county cops. Slow, dark clouds were creeping in from the west as we headed north.

We'd decided to make a day of it. Murphy knew a guy and had secured tickets to a Nationals game in D.C. The Brewers were in town for the second day of a three-game series. Starting time was 1:35. Wendi was off to Annapolis for a quick visit with her daughter and granddaughter. She said she'd be back late on Friday.

By the time we got to the city lockup in Alexandria, a light rain had started to fall. Murphy got us through the normal progression of security procedures. We met up with Noranne Dubart in a stark room with cinderblock walls, painted in the same depressing, institutional green as a classroom I'd once inhabited. It took years of complaining to get my room repainted in a more mentally stimulating color. This room would never be repainted. It wasn't a place for intellectual stimulation.

Noranne had initially been arrested on Monday at a shady downtown hotel on a charge of prostitution. But the more serious charge she faced was for an incident from the previous day. She'd allegedly attacked her husband with a knife while he was sleeping, then fled the scene. The cops claimed she'd come back to town for the sole purpose of inflicting harm on her allegedly abusive spouse. He'd never spent a day in jail for the things he'd done to her.

Murphy had convinced her lawyer that our line of questioning had nothing to do with her current situation. That she was not a suspect in any other crime, and we were only there to seek information about some women she had known.

Despite her orange jumpsuit attire and lack of makeup, it was obvious that Noranne Dubart was a beautiful woman. Showing an inch of dark roots at the top, her long blonde hair hung past her shoulders. Her eyes were a mesmerizing shade of green. Lips perfectly proportioned and shaped. A beauty-mark mole, just above and to the left of the corner of a mouth that was twisted into a barely perceivable smirk. I didn't get the impression of an attitude. It was simply the way she carried herself.

Her lawyer was a public defender, a skinny young guy in a wrinkled suit. He stayed silent for most of the interview, offering an occasional nod of assurance when she paused for his approval.

Murphy introduced us and reminded them both of our intentions.

"We'd like to talk to you," Murphy began, "about your time staying at a place with Lettie Midland and some other women. A place Lettie called an *estate*. Reportedly run by a woman named Joan Flaith."

"Yeah. Joan," she said. "I didn't know her last name, but she was in charge."

"And her partner?" I said. "A guy named Phil Trunvid?"

"Phil was there. He came and went. He really didn't have anything to do with us. Joan liked to let him know she was the boss. Treated him like an assistant. Sending him off to get stuff. Joan kept him away from us. He was kind of a creepy guy. None of us really wanted him around. We didn't trust him. Or any man, for that matter. Given our histories with men, we had a reason."

"Do you know a woman named Tammy Tydiss?" I said. "Or maybe Tammy

Ballinderry?"

"I know *a* Tammy. Didn't ever get her last name. Woman with really long hair?"

"Sounds like her," I said.

"She came around once in a while. Another woman named Roma staying there knew her better than I did. They'd walk off alone together and talk sometimes."

"So you didn't stay with Tammy at her place before going to the estate?" I said.

"No. But I think Roma did. I figured that's how they got close. Before I got there, I stayed a couple of nights in some really shitty places. In a messy trailer, in a park out by the river with a woman named Flo. Then out at some cabin in the woods. When I got to the place Joan was running, it was like I'd gone to heaven. A nice, clean place. Good food. New clothes. A room of my own. An indoor pool. In our private counseling sessions, Joan made a point of comparing some of the shitholes I'd lived in all my life to that place. She wanted me to understand that I might never have to live like that again. Wallowing in some hovel, while some man does whatever he wants to do to my mind and body. I guess she was trying to show me how good life could be. Build up my expectations, Joan would say. My self-confidence. You know?"

"Sounds like the care you were getting would cost a good bit," I said. "Any idea if Joan was the one paying for all this?"

"I don't know. Didn't think about it much. But sometimes I got the feeling that she answered to someone else. I'd hear her talking on the phone. Not much of *what* she was saying. More of *how* she was speaking to the person on the other end. Kind of how you'd talk to a boss."

"Do you know who owns the estate where you were staying?" I said.

"No. But I don't think it was Joan. Or Phil," she said. "Their attitude toward everything was more like they were taking care of the place for someone else."

"Did you ever feel you were being kept there against your will?" Murphy said.

"No…not really. I mean, they didn't lock us up or anything. But it *was* against the rules to leave. And none of us wanted to get booted out. We had it made there."

"But they kept your phones," I said. "You weren't allowed to call anyone. Stay in contact with friends or family?"

"That's true," she said. "But Joan explained it was for our own good. So our abusers couldn't find us."

"You never got to use your phone?" Murphy asked. "Never to even call someone to tell them you were okay and safe?"

"Sometimes Joan would help me to make a call. Or send a text. After we'd talked and decided it was time to remove someone from my life. Cut out a contact. None of us had many. But Joan was good at explaining why our lives needed a fresh start. That to get away from our tormentors for good, we had to cut off any chance of a connection."

"Lettie Midland said that this Roma you spoke of *disappeared* from the estate," Murphy said. "That Joan's explanation was something vague about having *moved on to the next level.* You know anything about that?"

"I know that Roma broke the rules. More than once. The first time had to do with phones. She was snooping around one day, in a room where she wasn't supposed to be. Looking for where they were hiding all our phones. She didn't find any of ours, but she did find a stash of phones in a locked desk drawer that she got open somehow. A shit-ton of burner phones. Some were still wrapped up. Still in the store package. Joan came in and caught her red-handed, trying to turn one on. Made her put it back. Joan was pissed as hell. Thing is, Roma already had another one in her pocket. I guess Joan didn't think to count them, to make sure they were all there. Maybe she didn't know how many were there to begin with. So Roma got away with snatching one."

"Did she use the phone?" I asked.

"Couple of times, that I know of. She remembered some numbers. Not many. Then one Saturday night around 11:30, she came to my room and said she'd talked to someone. She didn't say who. Just that there was an emergency she had to take care of that couldn't wait. She told me she'd taken the keys to one of the cars parked outside the garage, down by the gate. She said she'd be back as soon as she could. She knew it wouldn't be easy. She'd have to sort of figure out which way to go when she got off the grounds. Then find out how to get where she needed to go. And hope she could find her way back."

"When did Joan and Phil discover she'd left?" Murphy said.

"Almost right away. There was a remote to open the gate in the car. Joan must have got an automatic text message, or some kind of alert when the gate opened. She and Phil were running around through the house and outside, screaming their heads off at each other in a panic. Phil got in his SUV and went looking for her. He came back at two in the morning without Roma. He and Joan spent the rest of the night down in the library room, bitching at each other. Calling people on their phones."

"But Roma did come back?" I said.

"Yeah. About ten o'clock the next morning. Looking all sheepish, like a guilty dog. Joan and her spent a lot of time in the library with the doors closed. Later that day, Roma told me she'd apologized to Joan but wouldn't tell her where she'd been or who she'd seen. She didn't tell me either. Not because she couldn't trust me. More like…I couldn't be made to tell what I didn't know. The next day, when we got up, Roma was gone."

"Getting back to Tammy," Murphy said. "You know anything about a six-year-old boy in her care? You ever see the child with her? Hear anything about him?'

"No. When she came there, she was always alone."

"Roma never mentioned a kid in relation to Tammy?"

"No."

"How about a woman named Melissa Adamson?" I said. "Was she staying there at the estate while you were there?"

"Yeah. She came there in early May. Didn't get to know her that well. Kept to herself a lot."

"She was still there when you left?" I said.

"Yeah."

"And when did you leave?"

"This past Saturday."

"Can you tell us where this estate was? How to get there?" Murphy said.

"I don't know exactly. When I left, it was dark. I was on a lot of backroads, trying to find my way out of the place. Turned around a bunch of times. Finally came to a town called Parkville. Then I remember seeing a sign that said *Thanks for visiting Dominion County.* From there, I followed Route 3 north."

"What were the circumstances of your departure?" Murphy asked.

She paused for her attorney's approval, then continued. "The night before Roma disappeared, or whatever, she told me she'd hidden the phone under a rock down by the garage.

I found it there and kept it hidden. I used it to call my sister once in a while. When I called her last week, she told me my husband had been at her place looking for me. He beat the hell out of her, and she was in the hospital. He said he'd kill her if she squealed to the cops. When I heard that, I went ballistic. I just had to get the hell out of there. That son of a bitch might've got away with what he did to me, but he wasn't getting off messing with my little sister. I took Joan's car and left. After the thing with Roma happened, I thought they would've been more careful with where they left the keys, but they weren't. Phil's an idiot. It was easy. After I had my little…um…*chat* with my husband, when I went out to where I'd parked Joan's car, it was gone. I figure they must've had a GPS in it or something. Tracked it down. Took it back."

"What kind of car was it?" I said.

"A gray Mercedes sedan," she said. "Not very old."

"Do you remember the license plate number on the car?"

"No. I'm not sure I ever looked at it."

Murphy backed his chair out from the table, signaling it was time to go.

"Noranne," I said. "Thank you for talking with us. I just have one more question for you. In the time you were there, can you recall any link with someone or something outside of the estate? Like any kind of delivery? Any service to the plumbing, or the pool, or the HVAC system?"

"There were times when we were all gathered together at the center of the house and had to stay there for a while. A room with no windows. Sometimes we could hear sounds. Like maybe something being fixed. But we never saw any kind of truck or anything. Never a person."

"Anything else?" I said. "Anything at all. Any unusual sounds or smells outside?"

"I think we might've been somewhere near the water. The air smelled that way. You know what I mean? And sometimes there was a buzzing sound in the distance. Like boat motors. There were trees at the back of the property. Behind the house. There was a locked gate and a path through the trees, but you couldn't see where it led to. We weren't allowed to go back there."

"Anything else you remember?" I said.

"There was one more thing," she said. "A drone that would fly over the place all the time. Kind of low-like. Buzzing really loud. Not that big. It was red. Always on weekends. I heard Joan threaten to blast the damn thing out of the air if it kept coming back. Phil had a shotgun he'd use to kill groundhogs sometimes. We'd hear him shoot it off. Most of the time in the evening. When it was starting to get dark. I wondered if maybe he didn't get the drone, too. Because I don't remember seeing or hearing it anymore after the Memorial Day weekend."

Before we left, her skinny lawyer made a desperate plea to Murphy for anything he could do, as a member of law enforcement, to help his client in exchange for the information she'd given us. Murphy thanked them both, and said he'd put in a good word for Noranne. We all knew that wouldn't do much.

"I know I've put myself in here," Noranne said, before being led off by the guard. "If I'd had better control of my emotions, I would have stayed with Joan. I threw it all away because I couldn't break the connection with my sister. I'll never live somewhere as nice as that again."

On the way out, through the long hallways and clanging locked doors, Murphy commented on Noranne's predicament. "Attempted murder charge. That's some serious shit."

"Hard to help with that," I said.

"And prostitution charges."

CHAPTER TWENTY-SIX

"Probably had no money," I said. "Tough situation. A girl's gotta eat."

Outside, the rain had stopped, and the sky was beginning to clear.

"Looks like the game is still on," Murphy said, looking up at the breaking clouds. "About a thirty-minute drive from here up to the ballpark. We might be a little late."

"Not my fault," I said. "You're the one driving. Maybe we should've brought Wendi along to keep you on time."

Chapter Twenty-Seven

Nationals Park is located up in the District, south of the Capitol Building, along the Anacostia River, slightly north of where it flows into the Potomac. Along with the tickets, Murphy's connection had provided a VIP parking pass that put us close enough to keep our walk into the ballpark relatively short, getting us inside just at the beginning of the bottom of the first.

Before heading to our seats, we made a stop at the chili concession. I went for a single jumbo beef chili dog. Murphy exercised restraint, ordering a jumbo beef and a jumbo turkey dog. The dogs were loaded with mustard, onions, and a special, spicy, homemade chili sauce. I was pretty sure he'd just be telling Elnora about the turkey dog. No matter how much his wife would have approved, he decided to skip the vegetarian option. With her concerns in mind, we limited our alcohol consumption to one Leinenkugel's each.

Our seats were out behind first base, three rows back, where we'd have to remain alert for foul balls. The Nats were off to a rough start that season, with a few more losses than wins at the moment. But that day, they were looking to extend a four-game winning streak, on their way to a possible homestand sweep against the Brewers. There was still plenty of time left in the season to turn things around. True fans remain ever hopeful.

Soto got on base twice in the early innings, knocking in three runs and scoring once. His two-run homer in the eighth sealed the deal for the Nats. The Brewers had nothing to show in their last time up at the plate. They would head for the locker room with a final score of eight to two. Maybe they could live up to their name and brew some beer to cry into.

At the ballpark, we'd kept the topic of conversation on baseball in general, and the game in front of us in particular. But on the way home, amid the rush-hour traffic, our talk turned back to our business from earlier in the day.

"What do you make of that talk about Joan Flaith persuading Noranne to cut people out of her life?" I said.

"Sounds like some kind of brainwashing," Murphy said. "Kind of thing they'd do in one of those damn cults."

"Cut everyone out of your life, lose contact with people, then who's left to alert anyone that something may have happened to you?"

"Good point. Hard to solve a crime if no one knows it's happened."

"If a tree falls in the woods…?"

"Exactly."

"Sounds like Joan Flaith knows what she's doing," I said.

"Be nice to know why she's doing it," Murphy said. "Especially if it's for nefarious purposes."

"But from what some of these women have told me, she doesn't seem to be taking the same track with all of them. Cults don't generally turn people loose. Or refer them to other services. Be good to know more about Joan's background."

"Gives you something to do with all your free time. Keep you out of trouble."

"I have plenty to do. I *am* a licensed fisherman."

"Considering how few you catch, I don't think the fish are worried."

"Hmm. Probably how the Potomac County criminals feel about you."

"Besides her being his former sister-in-law, you find any more of a connection between her and your client's husband? What's his name… Chevy?"

"It's Fordy," I laughed. "Not Chevy."

"I knew it was one of those car names."

"No. Nothing more than that passing family connection, yet," I said.

"Noranne's description get you any closer to figuring out where this estate might be?"

"Sounds like it's over in Dominion County. Somewhere outside of Parkville. That narrows it down some. Being near the water helps. The drone she talked about is something to look into. I might know a guy who could help with that."

"That's good. As long as it's not me," he said.

"Yeah, yeah. I know. You're busy chasing down confirmed criminals. Not potential ones."

"Speaking of criminals. Be interesting to know if Joan Flaith reported her car being stolen when Noranne ran off with it."

"It would," I said. "The report would include where the car was taken from."

"I might have the time to look into *that* for you."

Chapter Twenty-Eight

Noranne Dubart's parting comments from the previous day's interview had stuck with me. As I went about my usual household chores that Friday morning, my thoughts kept returning to the predicament she was in, and how the biggest regret she'd expressed in the whole affair had been that she would never live anywhere as nice as the estate again. She was probably right.

At least as long as she stayed locked up. Which held the potential to be for an extended period of time. Looks could be deceiving, but her young, skinny public defender didn't appear to be the kind of savvy lawyer she would need to mount a vigorous defense on her behalf. She didn't have the money to hire someone better.

I started to think about the importance we attach to the places in which we dwell. In a way, many of us allow ourselves to be defined by our environment. It's often difficult for people to rise above their circumstances. Usually, rising up takes hard work. Less often, it requires good luck. Sometimes it takes both. Often, *where* you're placed in the world determines the opportunities available. An education helps. Sometimes, a run of really bad luck can beat a person down to the point of no return.

I'd grown up in an aging house in a small town. My mother always kept the inside of our home clean and tidy. But the structure itself was old and often in need of repair. The facade was brick veneer. But even that was of dubious quality. There was one place where the bricks had bowed out from the wall, on the verge of collapse. The view across the street was the office building and drive-on scale for a metal scrapyard. Around the corner was a dry-cleaning business.

As a small kid, I suppose I never thought much about the place in which I lived. But as I got older, I had school friends with much nicer homes, and parents with professional jobs. One of my friends, in the later years of elementary school, was the son of a surgeon at the Riverport hospital. His home was on a wooded hillside in an upscale neighborhood populated with people of means. For a while, especially one particular summer, I was invited there often, to play and swim in their inground pool, and sometimes to spend the night. I suppose, in some way, it was then that I began to really notice the difference in what people possessed. At the time, the experience made me feel like I was less. It left me wanting more than an old house in an old part of town. Over the years, I've shaken off that notion. I've learned that the things we have and the places we live need not define us.

When my father died suddenly and unexpectedly, just before my college graduation, I was thrust forward into instant adulthood, faced with responsibilities I had never considered. I became a homeowner with an inherited mortgage. And nothing more to support myself than a part-time job at the local supermarket. It would have been easy to give up on my aspirations. To forget about continuing to search for a teaching position. To remain in the safety and familiarity of the deteriorating house in which I'd grown up. Continue to chip away at the mortgage that my father had left unfinished. It would have taken less effort to stay. I knew others who had made that choice.

But when my grandfather died just weeks later, I inherited yet another dwelling. Hours away from where I'd grown up. Far from the steady job with a paycheck. This place had no mortgage. It was paid for, free and clear. In solid shape, with a magnificent view of a miles-wide river. It beat the hell out of looking at the scrapyard.

It was a place where some of the happiest times of my life had played out. The most important people in my life were gone, but the dwellings with their memories remained. And so I made the choice to leave Riverport behind. To dwell in the house that Pax Barrow had built.

I quit my job at the store and put my childhood home up for sale. It sold quickly for less than it was worth, but for a few thousand more than the cost of paying off the mortgage. I had enough to live on for a while.

I spent a lot of time that summer alone at the cabin, watching the pulse and sway of the river. Feeling the need to become more familiar with my new home, I explored every nook and cranny of Potomac County, driving down backroads, sometimes past the places my grandfather had taken me, wondering if the same people still lived there. I got to know some of the folks who weren't dismissive of young Yankee come-heres. Watermen and farmers. Store clerks and auto repairmen. Tour guides at the nearby historical sites. In early August, I heard about an unexpected opening for a math teacher at the local high school. A week later, I had the job.

I realized later how much I needed the time I'd taken for myself that summer. Time to think. Time to heal. Time to put things in perspective. At some point, I began to realize that there were people everywhere in the world, in all walks of life, who'd faced much more loss and adversity than I had. Some had lost entire families in an instant. At some time during that interim of summer, I made the conscious choice not to dwell on my own losses. None of those I had lost would have wanted a life of sorrow for me. For a time, death had been chasing close behind me, snatching away the people I loved. But now, I was pulling ahead. I was at the beginning of a new career. A fresh start in a familiar place with the promise of new possibilities. There were new people to meet. Young, old, and in between. People I wanted to help. Professionally. Personally. Privately, when needed.

And so I chose joy over sorrow. Moving forward, over looking back. The possibilities of gain over the certainty of loss. Flowing on with the current of life, like the wide-open river before me.

Chapter Twenty-Nine

I spent a good part of Friday afternoon poking around into Joan Flaith's background. I already knew about her multiple marriages, including the one to Destry Dylan, brother of my client's husband. Her education included a bachelor's degree in psychology from a small college in Kentucky I'd never heard of. From what I could tell, she seemed to move frequently, and her employment history was long and sporadic. Her ex, Destry, seemed to be out of her life now, living in California. Lowering the chances that he had anything to do with her current situation.

Among the more interesting things I learned was the revelation that Joan P. Flaith was an author, of sorts. Five years ago, she'd co-authored a self-help book with the wordy title, *Stepping Back and Cutting Out: Reassessing Negative Relationships*. The book was put out by a company with the provocative name of *Bottomless Pitt Publications*. It was presented for sale as a three-hundred-page e-book on Amazon for the reasonable price of $2.49. The book was described as a how-to guide for deciding when it was time to terminate physically and mentally harmful relationships that contributed to stagnation in one's life. The publisher was an outfit from Pittsburgh, Pennsylvania. As far as I could tell, it was the only book they'd ever published. The owner of the company was listed as Damon Radburke.

A search into Phil Trunvid's life turned up little of interest. He'd worked for several landscapers before starting a company of his own for a while. That business failed shortly before he and Joan Flaith bought the house together out on Durn Road.

When I'd had enough of burning my eyes on a computer screen, I switched gears and called a guy I knew, who might be able to help with locating the estate through the drone angle suggested by our conversation with Noranne Dubart.

Clark Early was a guy in his late twenties who'd taught Physics for a couple of years at Potomac County High before defecting to Dominion County for a significant pay raise and the opportunity to coach their robotics club into becoming a competitive team. In his spare time, Clark was also the president and founder of a drone club that served enthusiasts in Potomac and Dominion Counties. I told him all of what Noranne had remembered about the low-flying, red drone that had pestered the estate on weekends until Memorial Day. About its likely location in Dominion County, somewhere outside of the town of Parkville. And the threat that might have made the drone a target. He said the group had a meeting coming up the next week. He'd ask around, but didn't make any promises about when he'd get back to me. Where have I heard that before?

That evening, after dinner, I was relaxing in my recliner in front of the TV, somewhere in that dreamy state between wakefulness and true sleep, when Wendi slid the door open and stepped inside. She was carrying her overnight bag. I was instantly revived from my drowsiness by the prospect of counting sheep in the very near future.

She showed me new photos on her phone of her five-year-old granddaughter and talked about the visit to Annapolis. When she finished, I caught her up to date on the details of the interview Murphy and I had with Noranne Dubart, and our manly outing at the ballpark. When I told her about the book that Joan Flaith had co-written, she seemed interested.

"You *are* planning to read it?" she said.

"I don't know," I grumbled. "Only if I have to. It is over three hundred pages. I'm not sure it's worth my time. Or that there's anything in there relevant to finding Melissa."

"I could read it. Let you know what it's all about."

"Like a book report?"

"Yeah."

"That might be helpful. I'll reimburse you the $2.49."

"And pay me for my time?" she said, flashing me her most inviting smile.

"Hmm. Maybe. What sort of compensation might your services require?"

"Something beyond the value of two forty-nine. But not necessarily monetary. I'm flexible."

"You certainly are," I said.

Sometime later, we were back in the bedroom with the lights out, just beginning our negotiations when I heard my phone ringing, out in the living room. By the time I flipped on the lamp, pulled on a pair of boxers, and stumbled out to the end table where I'd left it, the ringing had stopped. When I saw it was Murphy, I called him back.

"You asleep?" he said, sounding amused.

"Not even close," I said. "What's up?"

"Thought you might want to know about what I found. For starters, far as I can tell, neither Joan Flaith nor her partner, what's-his-name…Phil Trunvid, have reported a stolen late-model, gray Mercedes sedan. In fact, neither of them seems to own a gray, or any other color, Mercedes. I got the Fredericksburg cops to pull up video from a street camera that shows Noranne leaving the parked car. And then, a few minutes later, a guy who looks a lot like the photo on Trunvid's driver's license getting in and driving off. From the car tags, we got the owner's name. It's registered to a guy in Fredericksburg named Karl Bassle. Cops drove by his place. Said the car's parked in his driveway. Google machine says he's a lawyer. Ever heard of him?"

"No," I said. "I wonder if he knows Fordy Dylan. Same city. Same occupation."

"That's for you to figure out. But lawyers are a dime a dozen in the city."

"True," I said. "Might not even count as a coincidence."

"You want to hear the rest, or are you feeling sleepy?"

"There's more?"

"When I do someone's homework for them, I do it thoroughly."

"Okay, I'll owe you my lunch money. Please carry on."

"I sent Deputy Carter down to Maple Grove Elementary School today. She examined the paperwork for the kid, Kyle Ballinderry. In her opinion, the copy of the birth certificate looks genuine. But she thinks the letter from the lawyer, signed by the kid's parents, granting temporary custody, looks fake. She brought copies of everything back to the office with her. I tend to agree."

"So what's next?" I asked, not wanting to hear the answer.

"We're going to need to talk with the Bus Lady, Tammy Tydiss… Ballinderry, whatever the hell her name is. Sooner than later."

I spent a few minutes making my case again for why I needed more time before he confronted her with what we suspected. Murphy listened, but didn't budge much.

"The welfare of the child has to come first. You know that. I'll need to put a call into the lawyer's office to check on the document, but that's as long as I can wait. It's the right thing to do. It's the law. You know that."

I did know that. "At least give me a few hours' notice before you talk to her."

"I can do that. And I suppose you can come along, if you want."

"Might help to convince her to tell the truth. With someone less official there."

"Might hurt," he said. "Sometimes, too many people plus too many questions equals too much pressure."

"Sounds like a physics equation," I said

When I got back to the bedroom, the light was still on. Wendi was sitting up, her back braced with multiple pillows, reading from her iPad. She looked at me, raised her eyebrows, and shrugged. "Sorry. I didn't know how long you'd be. I downloaded the book. I'm reading now. You officially owe me $2.49."

Some deals come back to bite you in the ass.

Chapter Thirty

In the morning, we resumed negotiations on Wendi's compensation for reading Joan Flaith's book. After reaching a satisfying conclusion on both sides, we showered, then retreated to the kitchen for a hearty breakfast.

I proceeded to whip up my Saturday morning special, a pair of crabmeat and cheese omelets, while Wendi sat on a stool at the counter reading the book on her iPad. I burned and buttered some toast and poured some orange juice into a pair of long-stemmed wine glasses. Pete Barrow, Master Chef. If only I'd thought of cloth napkins.

While we ate, Wendi continued to read, ignoring my questions about her initial opinion. After breakfast, she left for her apartment in Weston, citing numerous pending chores, errands, and, of course, reading more of the book.

I was in one of those phases of investigative work that I most despised. Waiting for people to get back to me. It was my nature to keep moving. I wanted to be in control of where I was headed. But a lot of what I wanted or needed to know was in the hands of others at the moment. Simon Wadsworth was supposed to be using his legal connections to check on the ownership and employees of Old Dominion Services, the company that owned Potomac Perfection Landscaping, the outfit that Tammy supposedly worked for. It had been ten days already since my request. Murphy was trying to verify the validity of the documents used to register the kid called Kyle Ballinderry for school. Clark Early had promised to ask around about a drone that might help in locating the estate where Melissa Adamson had last been seen by the now-incarcerated Noranne Dubart. Even Wendi was in the process of plowing through Joan Flaith's book, withholding her summary until she'd finished.

I decided to spend some time digging around through some of the usual databases and websites, looking into the background of Roma Coltrell, Noranne's friend at the estate, who had, against the rules, fled the place one night for unknown reasons. Only to return the next day, then vanish altogether by the following morning. Like a lot of the women in the orbit around Melissa Adamson's disappearance, Roma's social media presence was nearly non-existent. She had few relatives, but I managed to find a record of her mother and a stepfather. Both had taken up separate lives in different parts of the country. The only somewhat local relative was a half-brother named Riley Zerco. His address was in a little town called Hofflinsburg, just north of Richmond, only a mile off Route 360.

I had no other pressing matters to attend to that day. If there was even an outside chance that Zerco had recently been in touch with his sister, it might be worth the ninety-minute drive, each way. At least I'd be in motion. Not just waiting.

Along the way, I stopped at a Tappahannock drive-thru for a quick lunch. By the time I got to the address I'd found for Riley Zerco, it was past one o'clock. The sun was high and bright, but the air was thick with humidity in a way that made walking a struggle that felt more like swimming.

Hofflinsburg was a nice little town, with well-manicured lawns and paved driveways that led up to mostly moderate-sized ranch-style homes. Zerco's place was a little smaller than those around him, but just as neat and uncluttered. I found him out in front, busy spreading mulch in the flower beds by the front porch.

When I introduced myself and flashed my license, he stood up, removed his brown gardening gloves and stuffed them into the back pocket of his baggy cargo shorts. He was only slightly taller than me and looked to be in his mid-thirties. His dark hair was cut short, as neatly trimmed as his lawn.

"I'm trying to locate a woman," I said. "She may have recently been staying at a place where your sister, Roma, also resided. I was hoping you might be able to put me in contact with Roma. That maybe she could tell me where this place is located."

He didn't say anything. He tugged at the sleeve of his shirt and bent his head down to wipe the sweat from his brow.

"Have you been in contact with your sister?" I continued. "Or happen to know where I could find her?"

"I haven't seen or spoken with Roma in a couple of months," he said. "The last time we met, she was really pissed at me."

"I'm sorry to hear that," I said. "Would you mind telling me why?"

"Could I see that license of yours again, please?"

I got it out and handed it to him. He studied it for a long moment, like he was trying to discern if it was real or fake. He gave it back to me and stood with his hands on his hips, looking past my shoulder to somewhere in the distance behind me.

"I've always tried to help my sister," he said. "But sometimes she's her own worst enemy. She's too trusting. Thinks everyone is her friend. Has a habit of taking up with the wrong kind of men. She's pretty and always on the lookout for some slick, handsome dude that'll look good in a picture with her. Never mind how he treats her. As long as they make a nice-looking couple. Which usually ends up with her getting the crap beat out of her. I was doing her a big, big favor, off and on for a couple of years, then full-time for a few months. When I told her I couldn't do it anymore, she got really angry. We met, and she said outright that she didn't care if she ever saw me again. Not the first time she said that. Maybe she meant it this time."

"What was the favor?"

"I was taking care of her son, Bobby."

"A son?" I said, trying not to sound surprised. "How old is he?"

"Six. Nice kid, but super quiet. No wonder, though. The way she's moved him around so much. From one asshole guy to the next."

"Kid's father in the picture?"

"No. Never has been."

"So, your sister was angry with you when you told her you could no longer take care of Bobby?"

"Yeah. I would have kept him forever, if I could have. I love the kid like he's my own. But I had to change jobs. I'm working nights now. Second shift. Before the switch, I had a neighbor who could watch him after school for a couple of hours, until I got home from work. But I had no one who could watch him until near midnight, five days a week. I couldn't afford to pay for that, even if I could have found someone. I told Roma I could still take care of him on weekends, but she said that wouldn't help."

"Tough situation," I said. "So she took her son back?"

"We made arrangements to meet at an all-night diner. Out on 360, close to Tappahannock."

"When was this?"

"Mid-April. It was a Saturday. The thirteenth, I think."

"Did she explain her circumstances to you? Give you any idea where she was staying?"

"She was so pissed at me. Screaming at me out in the parking lot. After a while, she calmed down some. Said she was living in a really nice place. That she had a promise of a good job. But the people helping her didn't know she had a kid. And if they found out, it would screw everything up for her. Before she drove off, she talked about a friend who might be able to help."

"She give a name?" I said. "Maybe Tammy?"

"Yeah," he said. "I think that *was* her name."

Chapter Thirty-One

Before leaving, I promised Riley Zerco I'd let him know if I found out where his sister, Roma Coltrell, was living. But more importantly, he wanted to know where she'd taken his nephew. I could tell he was sincerely worried about the kid. And rightly so. I didn't tell him I was fairly certain Bobby was now living in an old blue school bus with the woman named Tammy, who may or may not have the boy's best interests at heart.

I made it back to Potomac County by midafternoon and parked in an angled visitor's spot out on the street in front of the sheriff's office. Deputy Pugh was on his way out the door. He nodded at me as we passed, but didn't have anything to say. Inside, there was no one stationed at the front desk, so I went on back to Murphy's office. He was at his desk, eyes fixed on his laptop screen.

"Where is everyone?" I said. "No one out front to screen your visitors?"

"That never seems to stop you from getting back here," Murphy said. "I guess I should move out front. But the chair out there is so damn uncomfortable. Ten minutes in it and my back starts aching."

"Why should the boss have to put up with the daily discomforts faced by his subordinates?"

"Exactly."

"But speaking of subordinates, where are they?"

"All out on calls. A domestic dispute. Car accident. And an incident with some clown shooting a bunch of holes in somebody's big damn expensive boat."

We talked about the Nats completing their series sweep against the Brewers and where the team was headed on their next road trip. Murphy complained about constantly being short-staffed, and the county commissioners' repeated refusals to increase the department's budget so he could hire more deputies. It was a complaint I'd heard often. But I thought it best to let him vent. Maybe someday I'd want him to listen to me bitch about my principal. Who, by the way, was neither a prince nor a pal.

When the small talk played out, I told him about the trip down to Hofflinsburg to talk with Riley Zerco about his sister, Roma Coltrell. About her six-year-old son, Bobby, and her efforts to hide his existence from her keepers, Joan and Phil. And finally, about her mentioning Tammy as a friend who might be able to help her in that regard.

"Looks like the kid with Tammy belongs to Roma Coltrell," Murphy said.

"So Kyle Ballinderry is really Bobby Coltrell," I said, knowing what was coming next.

"I have to notify Social Services," he said. "Let them know what we suspect. I'm sorry to piss on your parade, but we'll have to bring Tammy in for questioning. Even if the mother did ask her to take care of the kid, there's still the fact that she falsified documents to register the kid for school."

"But maybe to keep the kid safe. Roma's brother said the father was never around, but he was abusive. Who knows, maybe he was looking for the kid. It's not so different a situation from what happens in a witness protection program."

"That's totally different," he said. "Witness protection is a legally sanctioned and executed program. Not just a couple of women deciding to change a kid's name to hide him out for whatever reason they deem necessary for their own benefit. You're just throwing shit against the wall to see what sticks."

He was right, of course. That was exactly what I was doing.

"What about the kid's uncle?" I said. "Couldn't we get him to—"

"That's up to social services. I'm sure they'll have to put him in foster care for a while. Until they can get things sorted out, to do what's best for the kid. Besides, you said the guy works nights. Can't take care of the kid on his own."

I conceded the argument to Murphy, knowing what he said was what had to happen. I had to accept it, but I didn't have to like it. Foster care was such a crap shoot. You never knew how the dice would roll. The kid had a chance of ending up with someone who cared about his welfare. But maybe a better chance of being placed with someone who just cared about the money.

I left Murphy's office feeling frustrated and powerless. Things were in motion, but out of my control. I didn't feel like Murphy had enough to charge Tammy with abducting the kid. Everything I'd learned suggested otherwise: that Roma had asked her to take care of her son. If Murphy had thoughts of charging her with anything as serious as abduction, he'd need to talk to Roma. And, so far, no one seemed to know where she'd gone. He had more than enough to confront Tammy with providing a false identity for the kid when registering for school. But even if she was charged, I doubted she'd be locked up for long. Especially if someone got her a good lawyer. And when she got out, there was a pretty good chance that her association with Joan Flaith might lead to cutting off my chances at locating the estate and finding Melissa Adamson. I had begun to feel like I was getting closer to achieving that goal. Noranne Dubart had placed Melissa at the estate as recently as a week ago. Now, obligations to do the right thing for the kid had gotten in the way.

I left my car parked out in front of the sheriff's office and trudged across the courthouse lawn on the town square to Wendi's apartment. When I let myself in, she was curled up on the sofa with her iPad on her lap. She held up a finger to stop me from speaking. I took a seat in a wooden rocker across the room and waited. A minute later, she sat up, closed the cover on her device, and let out a long, exhausted sigh.

"You finished already?" I said.

"It's an e-book," she said. "The font was big, and the pages were small. And, unlike you, I *am* a fast reader."

"And you're ready to tell me about it?"

"Yeah. Unless you were expecting a written book report."

"Oral will be fine."

"Where have I heard that before?"

"Are we opening negotiations again?"

"You wish."

"I do, but there's time for that later. So tell me, what did you learn?"

"Well, to start with, the book is poorly written. It reads like someone's failed master's thesis or doctoral dissertation. It's dry. It's repetitive. They seem to be making the same point over and over again. In some parts, I was able to skim, because I knew what was coming."

"So, style aside, what does it say?"

"Pretty much what the long title suggests. But to the extreme. The authors advocate cutting people out of your life who are mentally or physically abusive. But also, others who don't serve to improve your standing in life. Associations that you don't benefit from. Friends. Family. It doesn't matter. Not just the people who are dragging you down, but the people who aren't helping to lift you up. No friends for the sake of friendship. No family connections, unless you profit from them in some way. Monetarily or otherwise."

"Sounds like a handbook for being a sociopath," I said. "With an added twist of narcissism thrown in."

"I felt dirty, just for downloading it. Let alone reading it."

"So nothing in there that's really going to help me find Melissa?"

"No. But it does provide a blueprint for what Joan might be trying to do with the women she's supposedly trying to help. If you find Melissa, it might be good to know what to expect."

Chapter Thirty-Two

"You *do* know what today is?" Wendi asked.

It was Sunday morning. We were back at my place, bright azure-tinted light filtering in through the thin, blue bedroom curtains. I rolled over and squinted at the clock on the dresser. It was only 6:15.

I groaned and rolled back over to face her. "Well, unless we've been asleep a lot longer than it feels, it must be Sunday."

"Which Sunday?" she said, sitting up with her back against the headboard, rearranging the pillows.

"If this is a mental exercise to get me to wake up, it's working."

"You're avoiding the question."

"It's Sunday. The twenty-first of June. Can I go back to sleep now?"

"No. We're awake. Might as well get up and start the day. Now, how many Sundays so far this month?"

Arithmetic. I subtracted sevens and counted. "Three. This is the third Sunday in June."

"And what is the third Sunday in June known as?"

"Oh," I said, turning onto my back. "It's Father's Day."

"When was the last time you talked to your kids?"

"I don't know, "I said. "I'd have to check my phone. Two weeks ago, maybe."

"It's been four weeks."

"How would you know that?"

"Because I've talked with both of them this week."

"You called them?"

"No. They called me. Breana on Tuesday. Bret on Friday."

"Why?"

"They were thinking about trying to surprise you with a visit today. Just the two of them. For a few hours in the afternoon. When Breana asked if you were busy, I couldn't lie to her. Bret called on Friday to say they wouldn't be coming. They didn't want to intrude when you were working on a case."

"They could've come. But it's a long drive for a short visit. I mean, it's just a holiday that the card companies invented. It's not that big of a deal."

"It's a big deal to them. You've been a good father. They want to honor you for that. They miss spending time with you."

"My working on a case shouldn't stop them from visiting. It's not a 24-7 thing."

"They know how you get when you're involved in a case. Or busy with school work, in season, for that matter."

"And how is that?"

"Hmm. How about driven, distracted? Maybe obsessed. Ready to jump up and leave at a moment's notice. From what they've told me, I gather that was one of their mother's consistent complaints."

"Some things need to be dealt with right away," I said, trying not to sound defensive, just stating a fact.

"That's what they said you'd say."

"I wasn't that way when they were growing up."

"That's not what they're saying. I get the impression it's been a progressive thing. Especially since they went off to college. And you got divorced."

"I'm still their favorite parent."

"Having met your ex, Margo, and having spent time with Breana and Bret, I'm sure that's true. But in the three years I've been back in your life, I've seen you become...overly focused on getting the job done. Sometimes, to the detriment of your relationships with your children. And your grandchild."

"She's only two."

"Not for long. It would be nice if she got used to seeing your face. And grew up knowing what a loving person you are. That's harder for her to understand if you're not around much."

"Okay," I said. "I get it. You're right. All three of you. More family time."

"Good, she said. "I'll hold you to that. Have you brought in yesterday's mail yet?"

"Nope. Forgot."

"They said to expect a card from each of them. And they'll be calling today, of course. Make sure your phone is charged and keep it where you can hear it ringing. And one more thing."

"What's that?"

"Happy Father's Day, sweetheart. Stay here. I'll make breakfast."

* * *

It was bothersome that I'd allowed my relationships with my kids to get to the point where they felt more comfortable talking to Wendi about me than talking to me about me. Wendi had danced around using the term workaholic, but I was beginning to see that was what I was turning into. When this current investigation was over, I'd fix it. But at that moment, I was feeling like the Father's Day version of Ebeneezer Scrooge.

Back when I was growing up, Father's Day hadn't been regarded as such an event. More of a mildly special day, rather than an outright holiday. I always gave my dad a card, usually one my mother had picked out for me. We rarely went out to restaurants, so my mother cooked a special dinner for my father. Not always the same. Whatever he asked for that particular year. For dessert, there was vanilla ice cream with fresh strawberries on top. My father's favorite. A couple of times, we used an old hand-crank machine to make homemade ice cream. But that got old pretty fast. It was too much effort. My arm still hurts when I think about it.

When I got older, some of my Father's Days were spent in Virginia with my grandfather.

On those occasions, there was always a phone call with my parents in Pennsylvania. I would wish my father a happy day, and we'd talk about what my grandfather and I had been up to. At some point in the call, I'd hand the phone over to my grandfather to speak with his son. That part of the call never lasted more than a minute, maybe less. My grandfather was always quiet for a while after we hung up.

I used to joke that I was the product of a mixed marriage. My father was tall, and my mother was short. He was six feet tall. She was barely five foot two, and with, like the song says, *eyes of blue.* Their personalities were as disparate as their statures. My father was an earnest man, with intermittent episodes of observable joy in his life. He was quick to judge and slow to forgive. His smiles and laughter were rare and valued. My mother was full of warmth, fun, and enthusiasm for life. When she got going, she could talk a mile a minute.

I was not as close to my father as I was to my mother. Even my height skewed in her direction. My father and I did things together. Sports activities. Some camping and fishing. But when I needed to talk something out, my mother was the one I went to. She was always open to conversation about nearly anything, serious or otherwise. My father was prone to occasional bouts of stoic silence. Especially when his own father came to visit. And that was the only subject my mother ever avoided with me. The trouble between them.

That rift between my father and grandfather remained a mystery for most of my years growing up. Whenever I asked about it, my mother would either change the subject or refer me to my father, knowing that I wouldn't dare to ask him. But after my mother lost her short battle with cancer, and it was just the two of us left, my father and I drew closer. He softened, became easier to talk with. For the first time, it occurred to me that my mother had also been the one *he'd* confided in all his life. That realization made her memory even more precious.

Those last two years of his life, as my father and I became closer, I wondered even more about his relationship with my grandfather. So one day, not long before he died, I asked him what the trouble between him and his father had been. His answer came as a shock to me. It was difficult to accept, at first. It didn't reconcile with the man I knew Pax Barrow to be.

When my father was around nine years old, my grandfather started working two jobs to try to make ends meet. He was a delivery truck driver by day. But four nights a week, he worked as a security guard at the local headquarters for a jewelry company that had a chain of stores scattered across the state. Most nights, when he got home late, he would sit up alone and drink. Hard liquor. After a while, the drinking became a problem. His personality changed from loving husband and father to someone no one recognized. A mean, selfish prick who blamed everyone else for his failures and self-exaggerated troubles in life. He became verbally abusive to both his wife and son, often humiliating them in public and social situations, in front of family, friends, and strangers alike. Once, in a booth at a diner, he threw a glass of water in my father's face for the crime of laughing at his father's drunken attempt to pronounce the name of a menu item.

This turmoil went on for two years. One Saturday night, at the age of eleven, my father sat unnoticed on the stairs, looking through the prison-like bars of the railing, listening to his parents screaming at each other. He didn't remember what the argument was about, only the way it had made him feel. Powerless and sick in his gut. The fight culminated in his father backhanding his mother across the face and charging out the door into the darkness.

He came home the next morning. Nothing was ever said about the incident again. From that day on, he never drank more than an occasional beer at social gatherings. Pax Barrow went back to being the person who had disappeared into a bottle two years before.

My father told me that his mother forgave her husband. But my father could never get past what his father had said and done throughout those two long years of his childhood. Things were never again quite the same between my father and grandfather.

Over the years that followed, their differences grew. My father did well in school, and my grandfather encouraged him to be the first in the family to attend college. My father dismissed the idea, probably, he admitted to me, because it was something my grandfather wanted him to do. He later came to regret his stubbornness. When the time came for *me* to go to college, there was no debate. We both wanted more.

I have often wondered why my father would have allowed me to go off and stay with my grandfather for weeks at a time, beginning at the very age when their own troubles had started. Even as a child, I had always sensed an undeclared competition between my father and grandfather for my admiration. Maybe my father was waiting for my grandfather to fail. To, in some way, reveal the imperfection that my father had witnessed as a child at my age. But perhaps the act of handing over his own son to his father's care was instead a demonstration of trust. A declaration of forgiveness and faith that could only remain unspoken.

Chapter Thirty-Three

Breana and Bret only lived an hour apart. After deciding not to make the trip to see me, they settled for keeping company with each other that day at Breana's home near Westminster, Maryland. They were four years apart in age but had always been about as close and supportive of one another as a parent might hope for them to be. The alliteration with the B's in their names had been their mother's idea. Choosing names for your own children is always difficult for teachers. Especially when both parents are teachers. Too many possibilities, no matter how great they sound, get eliminated because they were the names of less than likable students.

So, instead of two separate calls that day, I was treated to one joyous, early afternoon FaceTime connection with everyone there. Before the call was over, I made a promise to see them all soon. Wendi chimed in with assurances that she would be backing up that promise with action. Not long after the family call ended, my phone rang again.

"You busy?" Murphy said. "Celebrating the holiday?"

"Just got off the phone with my kids," I said. "How about you?"

"Same here. I don't expect them to come home anymore. They're too busy. Hell, I'm too busy."

"You just calling to wish me a happy Father's Day?"

"Hardly. Got some news concerning the business you're messing with."

"Good news, or bad news?"

"Mostly bad. It concerns a body that was found about two months ago. A floater. Across the river, along the Maryland shoreline. Went down as a Jane Doe."

"I remember hearing about it. Just read a follow-up in the paper recently. Asking for information from the public to help in identifying the woman."

"The body was finally identified from an unusual tattoo on the left shoulder. Picture of a bunny rabbit riding a Harley, being chased by a police car. Cops over there finally traced it back to a tattoo parlor in Fredericksburg. Records showed the customer was Roma Coltrell."

"Shit."

"That's what I said. Family has been notified. If her father's still around, it won't be a Father's Day he'll ever be able to forget. Makes her kid essentially an orphan now. Unless his father steps up."

"You said it was *mostly* bad news. What's the good part?"

"At least the family knows what happened to her. If not the how and why. They've got a body to bury. Some never get that."

According to Lettie Midland, Joan Flaith had said that Roma had *moved on to the next level*, the day after she vanished from the estate. I hadn't liked the sound of that description when I heard it. I liked it even less now. For Roma Coltrell, the *next level* was not of this earth. Her son, Bobby, now being called Kyle, had lost his mother. Despite the fact that she'd bounced him around from place to place for most of his short life, the kid probably still loved her. Kids don't give up on people that easily. She was his mother. He would want to see her again. Sit on her lap and be held by her again. Now that was never going to happen.

Murphy went on to tell me that Roma's body had been found floating off the pier at a waterfront home on the Maryland side of the Potomac by a couple headed out for a morning fishing expedition. She hadn't drowned. The autopsy report showed the cause of death was blunt force trauma to the head, possibly due to a fall. But foul play couldn't be ruled out.

A few piers downstream from where the body was floating, a boat was found adrift. It was returned to the owners, across the water in Dominion County. They hadn't even realized it was missing. There was no physical evidence found to connect Roma Coltrell and the wandering boat. Given the distance traveled and the prevailing currents, it was deemed highly unlikely that the vessel had arrived there on its own.

* * *

"So now there are *two* people dead?" Wendi said, kicking off her sandals, propping her feet on the coffee table in front of my sofa.

"First Flo, and now Roma," I said. "Both involved in different ways with Joan Flaith."

"And Oscar's not concerned about this?"

"Of course, he's concerned. He's the sheriff. But you know him. He doesn't get all *riled* up about things."

"So, what's he doing about it?"

"Not much he can do. In Flo's case, there's little evidence of foul play and no leads. As far as we know, Roma Coltrell died in Maryland. Out of his legal domain. It's not his case to investigate."

"Maybe it shouldn't be yours either," she said. "I mean, two people are dead. If you keep poking around, things could get dangerous for *you*. Have you thought about that?"

"Some."

"And?"

"If things look like they're getting sticky, I'll call Murphy. Let the people with guns and badges handle it. I have no intention of putting myself in the line of fire."

"It's other people's intentions I'm worried about," she said, putting her feet back on the floor, slipping on one of her sandals. "Murphy won't always be available when you need him or his deputies. You have your own gun. The .38 revolver that belonged to your grandfather when he was a cop. You should consider carrying it with you."

"It's an antique."

"Does it work?"

"Yeah."

"You keep it cleaned? In working order?"

"I do. But I've never used it outside of a firing range. You know that."

"So would it hurt to carry it with you? It's licensed. You have a permit to carry. What's the problem?"

CHAPTER THIRTY-THREE

"It's heavy. I might lean to one side when I'm walking. People would talk."

"This isn't a joke, Pete," she said, standing up, slipping on the other sandal. "Can you at least keep the gun in your car?"

"I'll think about it. But you know how I feel about guns in general. Handguns are dangerous. It's too easy for them to fall into the wrong hands. I worry about that. Too often, innocent people suffer unintended consequences."

"And you know how I feel about them," she said.

"You lived in the city for most of your life. You felt like you needed a gun to protect yourself and your kids. I get that. But this isn't the city. I'm not dodging bullets here. Neither of the people who have died were shot."

"No. But someone with a gun might be able to prevent being forced to take a lethal dose of drugs, or stop someone from bashing your head in."

"We don't know that's what happened to these women."

"But it might have."

"It's a possibility," I conceded. "Okay. You win. I'll keep the gun in the car when I'm out. Just in case."

"And when I'm with you, I'm carrying mine," she said, sitting back down, kicking off her sandals again. "It's a lot smaller than yours. I hardly lean at all."

* * *

I hadn't shared with many people the fact that I'd taken my grandfather's gun to the shooting range. Practiced with it the way he would've done. Wendi knew. Murphy knew. Others I'd confided in thought it strange that I would even consider doing such a thing. Fire the weapon that my grandfather had, by all reasonable accounts, used to take his own life. Most thought it odd that I would even want to keep the gun, not have it destroyed.

My refusal to believe that he had killed himself played a part in hanging onto the instrument of his death. Keeping hold of it, taking it a step further and shooting the very gun that had taken his life, in some inexplicable way, allowed me to keep his memory closer. It was the sort of defiant thing he might have done himself. In our time together, he tried to teach me to face my fears head-on. Not to shy away from the things that make us uneasy or frightened. Get a grip on those fears and take control. Don't let fear control your decisions.

But he did also say that sometimes the right kind of fear can be a good thing. A healthy, natural, rational thing that helps us to stay safe. He said that wisdom comes from knowing the difference between good fear and bad fear. Between the rational and the irrational.

Chapter Thirty-Four

By late afternoon, I was out on the road, headed for the address Murphy had supplied for the people whose boat had been taken around the time Roma Coltrell's body had been found afloat across the river. The place was located over in neighboring Dominion County. From what Noranne Dubart had told me, it was the most likely zone for the location of the estate. The place where Joan Flaith was allegedly indoctrinating young women with her questionable theories on human relationships.

Murphy had given me a mobile phone number for the boat owners. I'd called ahead and was expected. The pleasant-sounding man I talked to assured me that I would not be intruding on any sort of holiday gathering. His father was dead, and he and his wife of thirty-nine years had no children.

Out by the main road, there was a white-painted wooden sign with the name *Marsh* spelled out in raised black letters. The area around it was landscaped with flowers and mulch and decorated with a tiny rowboat, a large black-painted anchor, and a three-foot carved-wood statue of a classic mariner, complete with sailor's cap, boots, and peacoat. The long lane leading into the place was flanked on each side by a row of fifty-foot loblolly pines and a golf-course-quality lawn. Beyond the grassy strips were fields of half-grown corn. Closer to the house, the cornfields gave way to a thick stand of trees on both sides. When I parked by the attached garage and got out of the car, I could see the river, but no other houses were visible on either side.

The Marsh's home was surprisingly small by most waterfront standards.

A single-story, white-painted place with a low-pitched roof and a narrow concrete patio on the side facing the river. Out across the lawn, halfway to the water, was a kidney-shaped pool and a twenty-foot-square pavilion. A few feet beyond, out in the sun, a set of five Adirondacks were arranged in a semi-circle around a brick firepit. That's where I found Buzzy and Orna Marsh. Right where he'd said they would be.

The deep-tanned couple welcomed me like the long-lost friend that I wasn't. They might have been starved for company, but I got the impression they were probably that way with everyone they met. Eager to greet. Ready to party hearty. I accepted the bottle of Bud offered from the cooler under the pavilion and settled into a chair at one end of the semicircle. Over by the cooler, there was a ten-gallon bucket, half filled with empty brown bottles. They were both working on emptying another one. It was difficult to tell, but they looked like they might be around my age. Their skin had that leathery look of a lifetime spent in the sun. They seemed like nice people. The threat of confrontation seemed unlikely. I felt no regrets for leaving my heavy antique gun locked up at home.

I offered to show them my identification, but they waved it off, insisting it wasn't necessary, that I looked like an honest guy. We spent some time on small talk. They were come-heres, originally from a town in Ohio, out near Lake Erie. Buzzy was a retired physical therapist. Orna had been a nurse. When Buzzy got up to go to the cooler, he walked with a pronounced limp. Orna was chain-smoking unfiltered Camels. They spent most of the year here on the river but migrated to Florida's west coast for the winter months.

Buzzy finally brought the conversation around to the boats moored in three of the four slips off his forty-foot pier. The most impressive was a twenty-five-foot cabin cruiser. The others were an eighteen-foot, stern-driven bow rider and a small sloop for the days when they felt like sailing. The bow rider was the one that had been found adrift not far from where Roma's body had been floating.

"We didn't even realize the damn thing was gone," Buzzy said. "Until they brought it back."

"We were off visiting friends in Richmond," Orna said. "Got back late that night. Slept in the next morning, then went out running errands for most of the day. He leaves the damn keys in the thing all the time."

"Guilty," he said. "I admit it. She's always on me about it. How it's not safe. Now she can tell me *I told you so.*"

"I told you so!" she said, cackling until it turned into a coughing fit.

"So, you have no idea who might have taken the boat?" I said.

"No," he said. "Don't even know most of the folks around us. Everybody sort of keeps to themselves. We have a lot of friends who come here to play, but none who would take the boat and just let it go. I figure it had to be that girl they found dead in the water. But where she came from, I couldn't guess."

"You ever recall seeing a drone flying around out here?" I said. "Before Memorial Day? Might've been red."

"I saw that thing a couple of times," she said. "It was flying all up and down through here. Just above the trees. Looked like fun. Told him I wanted one."

"Orna, you don't need no *damn* flying thingy," he said. "You got enough trouble as it is maneuvering yourself around on the ground."

"Oh you shut up, *Buzzy*. You got no reason to talk. The way you stagger around here."

"You have any idea where it came from?" I said. "Or where it went off to?"

"I never paid any attention to which direction it went when it left," she said.

"I heard it," he said. "But I never did see it."

After leaving the Marsh's place, I drove up and down Anchor Road, stopping at most of the nearby lanes, snapping photos with my phone of the address numbers on the mailboxes.

* * *

Back at home that evening, I was seated at the kitchen counter with my laptop open in front of me, looking around on Google Maps. I found the Marsh place on Anchor Road and switched over to satellite view. Zooming out from there, I could see the tops of houses, parked cars, and an abundance of trees. I found two places that fit the sparse description I'd accumulated from talking with Lettie Midland and Noranne Dubart. Both properties had big houses, with a garage located near, but out of sight of the main gate. Both had a thick stand of trees separating the grounds from the river, with a path through the woods leading to a waterfront beach and pier. The tree canopy prevented seeing if there was any sort of gate at the beginning of the path. Most people with property on a river wanted a nice view of the water from their home. Evidently, these were people who valued their privacy over a waterfront view.

One of the properties was just two parcels upstream from Buzzy and Orna's place. The other was three lots downstream. I matched the addresses with the photos on my phone and did a search on each. The names of the property owners were unfamiliar. Geoffrey Weddington and Charles Karruth, Sr.

Chapter Thirty-Five

By seven o'clock Monday morning, I was sitting in the passenger seat of Murphy's official vehicle. We were parked in a gravel lot by an abandoned tobacco barn, just off the main highway at the head of Slipstone Road. Deputies Carter and Pugh were sitting in a marked cruiser behind us. My car was out of the way, over close to the barn. When two women from social services arrived in a white sedan, Murphy got out and spoke to them briefly. He got back behind the wheel, and we rolled out of the lot, leading the three-car caravan up Slipstone Road to where Tammy's blue-painted school bus was parked.

The white pickup was sitting in its usual spot in the yard. We all got out, and Murphy pounded on the glass and metal door, shouting, "Sheriff's Department, Miss Tydiss. Please open the door."

After a couple of minutes of repeated knocks and loud proclamations, Murphy pushed on the door, and it folded open. At his signal, Carter and Pugh stepped inside to check for occupants. They were back out in less than a minute, reporting no one was inside. A quick search of the shed and the yard around the collapsed building yielded nothing. Tammy and the boy were gone.

"So now what?" I said, standing next to Murphy's SUV, the others getting back in their cars.

"I'll have Pugh drive my car back into town. Let's me and you head out to that place you followed her to on Durn Road. We'll take your car. It'll draw less attention. I'll call the deputies and Social Services back in if we need them."

On the way there, Murphy tried calling the emergency contact number Tammy had left with the kid's school. It went directly to voicemail, like the phone had been powered off.

When we got to the house owned by Joan Flaith and Phil Trunvid, there were no vehicles parked in the driveway. The garage doors were wide open. Parked inside was a small, red Honda coupe with a rusted and dented right front fender. We went around to the front of the house, and Murphy pounded on the door. After a couple of minutes, the door opened. Standing inside was a sleepy-looking, young, scrawny guy with curly, sandy-colored hair down to his shoulders. He was wearing a pair of red and green plaid boxer shorts and nothing else.

"Dude. I was asleep," he said, apparently unimpressed by Murphy's uniform, badge, and gun.

Murphy introduced himself. He didn't bother to explain who I was.

"We've had some reports of break-ins in the area," Murphy said. "You live here?"

"Yeah. Sometimes. It's my mom's house."

"What's your name, son?" Murphy said.

"Alex."

"Last name?"

"Dylan. I'm Alex Dylan."

"What's your mother's name?" I asked.

"Joan Flaith."

"Oh, so you're Destry Dylan's son?" I said. "I know your dad. From Fredericksburg, right?"

"Yeah."

"Is your dad living around here again?" I said.

Murphy shot me a look, like he wasn't pleased with my line of questioning.

"Nah, man. He's still out in California," the kid said.

"Is your mother home?" Murphy said.

"No. She and her boyfriend, Phil, are away. I'm watching the place for them."

"You alone here, son? he said. "Anyone else inside right now?"

"Yeah. I mean, no. No one else is here."

"You mind showing me some identification, please, Alex?"

"Okay," he said, walking back into the house, leaving us standing at the open door.

He came back a minute later and offered his wallet to Murphy.

"Please take your I.D. out of your wallet, Alex," Murphy said.

The kid's face twisted into one of those whatever-looks, but he said nothing and obeyed the sheriff's instruction. Murphy glanced at the kid's driver's license and handed it back to him.

"Thanks, Alex. Sorry to disturb you. If you see any suspicious activity around here or at your neighbors, please call the sheriff's department."

Back in the car, as we were pulling away, Murphy said, "You really know that kid's father?"

"Just his name. I didn't even know Destry Dylan and Joan Flaith *had* a kid. Somehow I missed that. I wanted to know if the kid's father is a relevant factor in all this."

"If he's really in California, like the kid said, then probably not."

"Good to know," I said. "If the kid's telling the truth."

"Some kids do."

"Yeah. I heard about that."

* * *

On the ride back to his office, I told Murphy about my chat with Buzzy and Orna Marsh, and how I'd found two properties that were strong possibilities for the location of Joan Flaith's enterprise.

"I can't help you with anything over there," he said. "Dominion County's out of my territory. There is no probable cause for any law enforcement to go onto those properties."

"You could ask, couldn't you? If the owner says no, then we know they might be hiding something."

"We have no evidence that Tammy and the boy might be on the premises. We don't even know if this is technically an abduction. She could just be doing what she can to protect her friend's kid."

"And what about the safety of the woman I'm looking for? Melissa Adamson. Isn't there anything we can use to help her?"

"Look, I'm sympathetic to your cause. But we don't have anything that tells us specifically that she's in any kind of danger. That's going to have to continue to be your problem to deal with. Until…"

"Okay. Okay, I get it."

"I can *ask* the sheriff over there to keep a lookout for them. But he and I are not on the best of terms these days. He's as understaffed as I am, and still pissed that I *recruited* a deputy away from him last year."

Chapter Thirty-Six

I dropped Murphy off, back at the sheriff's department in Weston, and headed for home. About halfway there, I was contemplating my options for an early lunch and the possibility of a clandestine late-morning nap, when my phone rang. The secretary from Simon Wadsworth's law office asked if I was available to meet with him at eleven o'clock. I glanced at the clock on the dashboard. It was 10:22. I said I was, turned around at the state park entrance, and headed back toward Weston.

I stopped at the convenience store on the edge of town for gas and picked up a premade turkey sandwich with a bottle of water. Sitting outside at an umbrellaed table, I ate at a leisurely pace and watched the midmorning traffic roll by. There wasn't much to see. A few people stopped by on their way in or out of the store to say hello and chat about the weather.

By the time I got to Simon Wadsworth's office building, it was 11:07. Close enough. Julia, his secretary, ushered me into his office and directed me to a hard wooden chair in front of his massive mahogany desk, where I sat and waited for five more minutes.

Wadsworth entered the office through another door behind his desk and sat down in his well-cushioned leather chair.

"You are late," he said, shuffling papers on his desk, not looking at me.

"It was short notice. You weren't ready for me anyway," I said.

"I was. At *eleven o'clock*. My time is valuable. I don't have the whole summer off like you do. I have things to do that require my timely attention. I don't have time to just sit around and wait."

"You ever go fishing, Simon?"

"Certainly not. Why on earth would I do that? If I desire fish to eat, I order it from the menu at a proper restaurant."

I let his answer speak for itself.

"I take it you've found some of the information I was looking for?"

"Yes," he said, sitting up straight, becoming less agitated, more businesslike. "As it turns out, much more than I anticipated."

"More is sometimes better," I said.

"The owner of the Old Dominion Services company is, quite surprisingly, a group of young lawyers from Fredericksburg. It appears to be some sort of property management service that specializes in maintenance and security for large properties that are infrequently utilized by the affluent owners."

"So, rich people who own big places they don't use much."

"That's what I just said."

"They have many clients?"

"I have no idea. But rumor has it, the company shows a strong profit."

"You get the names of the lawyers who own this lucrative enterprise?"

"Of course."

"Well, could you *tell* me?"

He picked up a yellow legal pad from his desk, slid on his half-glasses, and read their names. "Dwight Laurelworth, Karl Bassle, Rutherford Dylan, and Charles Karruth, Jr."

"Bingo," I said. Finally, the more than familial connection between Fordy Dylan and Joan Flaith I'd been waiting for. And the likely location of the fabled estate. Despite my enthusiasm, I remained seated, knowing Wadsworth wasn't the type to participate in a high-five.

"I take it the names are familiar?" he said.

"Some. I've never heard of Laurelworth. But Bassle's name popped up peripherally. As did a Charles Karruth, *Senior*."

"I know Karruth Senior. Casually," Wadsworth said. "Retired. A fine attorney. I don't know his son. What's your interest in all this, Peter?"

"My client has asked me to locate a friend, a woman she's lost contact with. She's concerned for the woman's safety. It's beginning to look like the friend may be staying on a property owned by the elder Karruth. But the biggest revelation here is the involvement of Rutherford Dylan. He's my client's husband."

"Interesting," he said. "I should tell you that, despite his father's fine reputation and standing in the legal community, my contacts report that the junior Karruth is not very highly regarded among his peers. He has a reputation as a ne'er-do-well. A slacker. Not without ambition but lacking in the desire to do real work in order to earn what he wants. Rumor has it his father spends most of his time in Europe these days. And that he has completely cut off supplementing his son's income."

"Any rumors about the others in the group?"

"Plenty. Though I'd categorize the information more in the column of fact than rumor. None of the four seems to be excelling to any significant degree in their chosen profession. Not a one is on track to earn partner status in the four different firms in which they are employed. In fact, it's said that Bassle and Laurelworth are in danger of being dismissed."

"And what about Rutherford Dylan?"

"Ah yes, Rutherford Anderton Dylan, III. Not exactly a legal legacy, despite his solid-sounding name. His father owned a failed hardware store in West Virginia. He is the supposed leader of the group. The others all met through him. His three friends seem to enjoy bragging about all the money they're pulling in with their property management group. But more than once, Dylan has been observed, in public settings, chastising the others over their excessive drinking and subsequent boasting. One of my sources, who was very forthcoming with information, said he understood the group was playing with the notion of starting their own law firm. Though how an indolent group like that could summon the work ethic needed to build any kind of steady clientele, he couldn't begin to fathom. His best guess was for them to become a pack of some sort of television-promoted ambulance chasers."

"Thanks for the info, Simon," I said. "You've been very helpful. With details I didn't expect."

"Just don't get in the habit of asking *me* for information. Digging in the dirt is your forte. If these men hadn't happened to be lawyers, I wouldn't have uncovered a tenth of what I've told you. Despite being a profession shrouded in confidentiality, gossip within the legal community is more than common."

"Just one more thing, I wanted to ask."

"What now?" he said.

"There's a woman in police custody up in Alexandria."

I went on to describe the circumstances of Noranne Dubart's predicament and how I was less than confident in her public defender's abilities to serve her best interests.

"Well, I can't help her myself. I wouldn't have the time or inclination. But I can make some calls. I know skilled people up there who do that sort of work, pro bono. I'll see what I can do. You're such a bleeding heart sometimes, Peter."

On the ride back home, I pondered what I'd been told about Fordy Dylan and his cohorts. The fact that Fordy hadn't come from a more noble background didn't surprise me all that much. Plenty of attorneys rose up from humble beginnings. What surprised me most was the fact that a group of lawyers would be involved in something as unrelated to their profession as property management. And that such an endeavor could be so lucrative as to spawn ambitions of starting their own law firm. That required money. Lots of it. There had to be more to it.

Joan Flaith was operating whatever it was she was up to on an estate owned by the father of one of the owners of Old Dominion Services, the parent company of Potomac Perfection Landscaping, Tammy's employer. It all had to mean that something out of the ordinary was going on here. Two people operating within the sphere of my investigation were dead. It was becoming increasingly difficult to believe their deaths had nothing to do with whatever was going on at the estate. What had started out as a straightforward case of locating a troubled woman had taken a hard turn down a much more twisted path into uncharted territory.

I saw no clear line of reasoning that would lead to explaining why Kasey Dylan would hire someone to find her friend, if she knew her own husband might hold the key to her location. So far, I'd avoided asking her about her husband, being afraid that she'd confront him before I had the chance to uncover more about this whole situation.

Maybe it was time.

Chapter Thirty-Seven

"A group of lawyers is referred to as an *eloquence of lawyers*," Wendi said.

She was sitting up, cross-legged in my bed, a pillow under the computer in her lap. It was getting close to midnight. We'd been talking about the information Wadsworth had relayed to me that morning about Fordy Dylan and his merry band of barrister brothers.

"An *eloquence*?" I said. "That name reeks of conceit. Sounds like something they'd *want* to call themselves."

"There are other names," she said, reading from the screen. "A *huddle* of lawyers. A *disputation* of lawyers. How about a *greed* of lawyers, or an *escheat* of lawyers." She spelled the last one for me.

"I'd tend to go with one of the last two."

"I like *a greed of lawyers*," she said. "*Greed* is simple. One syllable. Descriptive of intent."

"Not all lawyers are greedy. For example, Wadsworth is a pain in my ass, but he's never shown an avaricious side. But, considering what we know so far about this particular bunch, I'd tend to agree with your selection."

"Then *Greed* it is," she said. "So you're planning to ask Kasey about her husband?"

"I feel like I'm obligated to tell her what I've found. She *is* the one paying the bill. Hiding the truth from her for too long isn't ethical. I'll ask her not to confront her husband about his involvement. At least until we've located Melissa for certain. Had a chance to talk with her. To know that she's safe and not being kept against her will."

"So when are you planning to have this talk with Kasey?"

"Tomorrow. If I can make sure her husband's not around. I'd like to catch her at a time when there's no chance of her mentioning our meeting to him. Even casually."

"Do you need me to come along? I could cancel my dentist appointment and lunch plans."

"No. That's okay. You'd have to wait months for another appointment. We'd be back at school. You'd need to take time off. Neither of us likes to do that. Unless it's just a professional development day. We all like to skip those. But I might need your help later. If we get to the point where Kasey and Melissa can meet and talk."

"And you have no idea what Joan Flaith and this *greed of lawyers* are up to with all this?"

"Or why," I said. "But my instincts tell me there must be money involved. Maybe lots of it. The kind that would be required to start a new law firm."

* * *

By six-thirty Tuesday morning, I was sitting behind the wheel of a rented gray Toyota Corolla, parked across the street and down the block from the Dylan house on Hawke Street in Fredericksburg. I'd brought along a pair of binoculars and a digital camera with a telephoto lens. It was cloudy, and a light rain had begun to dot the sidewalks and windshield. The early hour had me wishing we'd turned in earlier the night before and regretting the lifelong choice not to take up the habit of drinking coffee.

The street was still quiet for the most part, with a few people dressed in professional attire hurrying to their parked cars. Most with a travel mug of coffee in hand. A guy with a long dark beard, wearing a backwards Yankees cap, drove by, creeping along, tossing newspapers wrapped in plastic out his window onto selected lawns.

At 6:53, Fordy Dylan shuffled out his front door and climbed into the Volvo SUV parked in his driveway. I followed at a safe distance, almost losing him twice in the heavy slog of morning traffic.

We were headed west, out of the city, toward the historic Chancellorsville Battlefield, past a high school and a self-proclaimed country store. The rain had stopped, but the thick clouds still shrouded the morning sun. He pulled off into the parking lot of an old motel that had been converted into a Civil War antiques and souvenir store. Rolling on past, I turned into the gas station next door and parked by the air pump. I got out and fumbled around with the hose while I watched him standing by his car, looking around like he was waiting for someone. He was holding something wrapped in a black plastic bag, tucked under his arm.

After a minute or so, another vehicle pulled in and parked beside him. A big, muscular guy with a shaved head and red-framed glasses got out of a white Toyota SUV with D.C. plates. It was a late model, with a black-painted hood and sporty-looking stripes down the side. While they stood there talking, I slipped back inside my car, grabbed the camera from the front seat, and snapped some quick pictures of the two. Including a shot of Fordy handing over the black-wrapped, book-sized package.

The big guy got into his vehicle and pulled back out onto the highway, headed west.

Maybe he was just a tourist, headed out to spend the day visiting all the local battlefields. And maybe Fordy was just a helpful friend, offering to share the insights of a local resident, handing over a cherished Civil War guidebook. Maybe the Pope was a Bible-thumping Southern Baptist.

When Fordy headed east, back into town, I followed. The morning traffic was building to the peak of its slow-moving frenzy. After a lot of repeated stop-and-go, we made it back into the heart of the city. He turned right, just before the college campus. After a left, followed by another right turn, I was beginning to worry that he'd picked up my tail. My concern ended when he pulled into a labeled parking spot in a lot marked with a sign that said *Law Offices of Ruick and Gartland*. I parked out on the street and watched him go inside. After a couple of minutes, I pulled out and headed back over to the Dylan house on Hawke Street.

When I got there, I spotted Kasey's car in the driveway and drove on around the block. After circling around through the neighborhood, I pulled into a spot a block and a half down the street from her house and called the number on her business card.

She was working from home that day and was available to meet. I'd noticed a small park with a walking path and benches, located off the street behind her house. When I suggested we meet there, she hesitated and asked why.

"You have a doorbell camera on your front porch," I said. "Would you mind telling me who gets the alerts when someone comes to the door?"

"My husband and I both do," she said. "Why would you ask?"

It was time to be straightforward. "Because part of what I have to tell you involves your husband. I'd prefer he didn't know we'd met."

There was a long silence. She started to say something, but stopped. At the end of a shorter silence, she spoke again. "All right, then. I'll be there in five minutes."

Chapter Thirty-Eight

Kasey arrived at the park nearly out of breath, wearing wrinkled white shorts and a faded tank top. Her short hair looked like it hadn't been brushed in a while, and her face was unadorned with makeup. She had running shoes on with no socks. Without all the trimmings, she looked even more plain than she had at our first meeting. It had taken her longer than five minutes to get there. More like ten. But who was I to criticize. The paranoid side of me just hoped she hadn't used the extra minutes to call her husband.

We sat apart on opposite ends of the wooden bench. I leaned back. She sat perched on the edge, half turned towards me. Two young mothers, engaged in conversation, walking behind hooded strollers with unseen babies, pushed past us and nodded an obligatory greeting.

"What's this all about?" she said. "Why didn't you want my husband to know we were meeting?"

"His name came up in the course of my investigation to find Melissa," I said.

"Have you found her? What could Fordy possibly have to do with this?"

"I haven't exactly found her, yet," I said, holding back on answering her other question. "But I'm fairly certain I've found the place where she may be living now. Or at least recently. She's not with the woman named Tammy anymore. It's my belief that she's living on an estate down in Dominion County. Outside the town of Parkville."

"But Melissa's okay? Her husband didn't get to her?"

"I don't have any reason to believe she's not. And someone has warned off her husband from looking for her. But the people she's staying with may have less than ethical reasons for harboring her."

"What people?"

"Do you know a woman named Joan Flaith?"

"Joan…what does…she was married to Fordy's brother, Destry, at one time. I heard she'd remarried a man named Flaith and divorced him. What's she got to do with this?"

"She runs a sort of…group home…for abused women. I think that's where Melissa may be staying. From what I've been able to learn from others who lived there, the counseling she's receiving from Joan may entail some unorthodox methods that encourage permanent separation from friends and family."

Kasey turned her head away and looked around the park at nothing. She'd stopped asking about her husband's involvement.

"The estate where the group home is operating is owned by the father of one of your husband's legal associates. A man named Karruth. In the owner's absence, the place is supposedly being managed by a group called Old Dominion Services. A company owned by the younger Karruth, two other guys named Bassle and Laurelworth. And their friend, your husband, Rutherford Dylan."

She took it all in and sat in silence for a long moment. When she turned to look at me again, tears were starting to roll down her face. She took a deep breath and exhaled slowly.

"Fordy is older than me," she began. "By eight years, to be exact. I knew there were other women before me. I was young when we married, but not naïve. His brother Destry is five years older than him. Fordy told me they were estranged. Never attempted to explain why. Destry didn't attend our wedding. I've never met him. Before we got married, a close friend of mine confided that she'd heard Fordy and Joan had had an affair while she was married to Destry. That their marriage had ended because of it. My friend told me she didn't trust Fordy. That he was probably marrying me because of my parents' money. I chose not to believe her. That same friend came to me again, a few months ago, even before Melissa went away, and told me she'd seen Fordy and Joan together, in a restaurant up in Staunton. They were with two other men who got up and left when they'd finished eating. After that, she said Fordy and Joan sat close together and seemed to be engaged in an intimate conversation. Touching each other. Whispering back and forth. Even kissing."

"I'm sorry to hear that," I said. "Did your friend happen to mention if she knew the other men? Did she describe them?"

"She didn't know them, exactly. One man, a little older, mid-forties maybe, dressed in an expensive-looking suit, looked familiar to her. Not like someone she knew, but someone she'd seen somewhere before. Maybe on television. Not someone famous, though."

"And the other guy?"

"Big. Scary looking, she said. Rough, like he was a bodyguard or something for the other man. She said his head was completely shaved and he wore bright-colored, red-framed glasses. The Devil's spectacles, she called them."

"I followed your husband early this morning. He met up with a man fitting that description. Just outside of town. Before he went to his office."

"Oh," she said. "I...I don't..."

"Have you ever seen these men?"

"No. Not that I'm aware of," she said. "Fordy has lots of business associates, though. I certainly haven't met all of them. I decided not to confront him with what I'd heard. Thought I needed to work harder on my marriage. I've tried these past few months to make myself more attractive. More attentive to his needs. I suppose having Melissa move in for a while didn't help."

I found myself at a loss for words, thinking Wendi would've known what to say.

"He wants me to fire you, Mr. Barrow," she said. "Just yesterday, he said I was wasting my money. That you were never going to find Melissa. That she probably didn't even want to be found. That she'd taken what she could get from me and moved on."

"Are you planning to take his advice?"

"I thought about it. But no. I still want you to find Melissa."

"You told me you put your phone number and your husband's number in the contacts on the phone you gave Melissa to hide. Did you tell your husband about the purse with the hidden phone?"

"No," she said. "I don't know why, but I didn't."

"Good. Do you feel like you'll be able to refrain from confronting your husband about all this? At least for a while."

"It will be difficult. But yes, I can. For Melissa's sake."

"Good. I'll try to get to the bottom of this mess as quickly as possible. But there's something else you should know. Two people involved with Joan Flaith's operation have died. Most recently, a woman who worked at the Crisis Center. Florence Peeke. She was the woman Melissa referred to as Flo. The one who gave her the number to call if she wanted to get away somewhere. I believe it was her job to refer women to connect with Joan. Some through Tammy first, then on to the estate under Joan. She died from an apparent drug overdose, hours after I'd talked to a man who told me where to find her."

"My God!" she said. "You think…"

"We don't know that her death is connected to Joan Flaith. But it pays to be suspicious. And cautious."

"You said *two* people had died?"

"The other person was a woman who was found dead in the river about two months ago. The body was recently identified from a tattoo. Her name was Roma Coltrell. I was told she was living at the estate and being counseled by Joan Flaith at the time of her disappearance. But again, there's no clear proof that Joan had anything to do with her death. Or that your husband has any direct involvement with what's going on there. So, I guess what I'm trying to tell you is, we just need to be careful. Until we know more."

"All right," she said.

"Just one other thing, Kasey. You never said how you came to hire Mr. Skoville to find Melissa."

"It was Fordy," she said. "Fordy recommended him."

Chapter Thirty-Nine

Back at home that afternoon, I settled onto the sofa to watch the Nationals game on TV.

It was top of the third. The Nats were down by one. Their pitcher was looking jittery, turning his head to the left multiple times before throwing, obsessed with the runner on first, afraid he was thinking about going for second. Wendi's lunch outing had turned into an all-day affair of lounging in the intermittent sun by the pool at the home of one of her closest school friends. Some of the others in the group liked to let loose in the summer. Have some wild fun. Shake off the stereotypical image of an elementary schoolteacher. Wendi was generally the voice of reason at these gatherings. I was confident that her younger cohorts would not lead her astray.

When my phone rang, I got up and fetched it from the kitchen counter, watching the runner on first as closely as the pitcher. The call was from the drone club president, Clark Early, living up to his name, getting back to me much sooner than I'd expected.

"We haven't had our meeting yet," he said. "But I was talking to my VP, setting up the agenda for tomorrow night. When I told him what you were looking for, he said he knew a guy. Not in the club. Said the guy's a little on the sketchy side. Into using cameras on his drones. Likes to fly them over swimming pools. Get some pictures, if you know what I mean. VP says the guy leans heavy in the direction of creepy, but he's good to talk to, *if* you can keep him on the topic of technology. But anyway, he said this guy lost a drone. Might've been back around Memorial Day. Told VP someone shot it down."

"You get a name and contact info for this guy?" I said.

"Yeah. His name's Moleville. Willis Moleville."

Clark gave me the guy's number and address. It wasn't far from the Karruth estate, the suspected residence of Joan Flaith and company. He told me Moleville worked from home, that he hardly ever left the place.

When I looked back at the television, somehow the runner had made it to third.

** * **

I found Melville's place across and down the road from what I now knew to be the Karruth estate. The lane going in was all weeds and dirt ruts with rocks thrown in here and there to fill in the holes. The extended branches from the thick, random growth of scattered white pines lining the pathway scraped against the roof and sides of my SUV. I cringed, imagining scratches and streaks of sticky pine sap.

The clearing at the end was a brown carpet of pine needles, with an occasional weed or clump of grass breaking through. The structure was small and old, a one-story rancher with a multitude of shingles missing from the roof, and a crop of six-inch weeds sprouting from the rain gutters that failed to connect with their intended downspouts. Parked next to the side entrance was a shiny-new, green, compact Mitsubishi sedan with the dealer's price sticker still pasted to the window. Its color matched nicely with the mildew covering the white vinyl on the side of the house.

I knocked on the door, and he yelled for me to come on in. I'd called ahead and was expected. The kitchen was surprisingly neat and clean. The rest of the place was not.

I found Willis Moleville on the living room sofa, a wireless game controller in his hands. On the sixty-five-inch screen mounted on the wall, he was maneuvering an armored character through hand-to-hand combat with an endless parade of identical creatures that looked like a cross between an alligator and Mr. Spock. Moleville was a roundish guy with thin dark hair and eyes that bulged every time his on-screen alter ego vanquished an attacker.

"Dude," he said, without looking at me. "Have a seat. Almost done here."

I picked up a pile of tech magazines from a wooden rocker and dropped them on the floor. He didn't seem to mind, or even notice. While I sat and waited, I looked around the room at the clutter of electronic equipment. Scattered about the tables, chairs, and floor were jumbles of power cords draped across keyboards and monitors and outdated game consoles, some older than my children. The worn-out carpet was the same color as the layer of pine needles outside. It was littered with tiny white specks of a substance that was most likely Styrofoam. Against the wall, a few feet behind the sofa, was a large shelving unit that housed a collection of drones of various sizes and configurations.

When he finished conquering his assailants, he let out a sigh of satisfaction and turned off the screen.

"What can I do for you, Mr. Barrow?" he said, easing himself back into a semi-inclined position on the sofa, spreading his arms across the back. "You said on the phone you wanted to talk about a drone I lost?"

"I'm interested in any images you might have captured, before the day it went down. At a particular place across the road, on the river."

I described the Karruth estate and its location as best I could.

"I don't know what you're talking about, dude."

"Sure you do. You take pictures and video footage with your drones."

"Who told you that?"

"Word gets around," I said, trying not to smirk.

"My bad," he said. "My mama always told me I talk too much."

"So, you do have photos or video of that particular place?"

"Some. I got a lot more interesting stuff from other places, if that's what you're into. Not too much going on around there. No outdoor pool. When the girls are out and about, they're all wearing lots of clothes. Boring shit. Not worth my time."

"You report losing your drone to the cops?"

"Now why would I do that? You think I'm a fucking idiot? What I'm doing kind of *buzzes* around the edge of legal. You know what I'm saying?"

"I believe I do."

"But that doesn't mean I just let it go. For nothing."

"Meaning what?"

"I had a live-feed video camera on it. I saw the son of a bitch shoot the thing down. One of my best drones. All that shit's expensive. I was super pissed. So, I went over there. Rang the bell at the gate. Dude comes out to see who's there. I bitch at him for a while. Wave my arms around a lot. Maybe threaten to call the cops."

"And what's his response?"

"Asks me how much the loss set me back. I tell him. Maybe exaggerate a little. He tells me to wait there, outside the gate. So I stand there. Sweating my balls off for about twenty minutes. Wondering if he's ever coming back. Then, finally, the dude comes back with a woman. She's got a big wad of cash in her hand and a paper for me to sign. Agreeing to the payment and to keep my mouth shut."

"A non-disclosure agreement?"

"Yeah. One of those. They paid me three times what I said the outfit was worth. So I signed the damn paper. Whatever."

"And you're not concerned they might find out you've violated the agreement?"

"I run my mouth. I can't help myself. But I figure they're bluffing just as much as I was. They don't want the cops around anymore than I do."

"Can you show me what you have?"

"What's it worth to you?" he said.

Chapter Forty

In his little green car, Willis Moleville followed me to the ATM at one of the three banks in Parkville. After I paid him the amount we'd agreed upon after our previous haggling session, he handed over a flash drive loaded with the video footage he'd taken of the Karruth estate and the surrounding area. The price was a little on the steep side, but at least he didn't drop the *d* out of the middle of the word *hundred* when he said it, preceded by the word *two*. I suppose proper numerical pronunciation is worth something extra. Especially to a math teacher.

At home, I watched the footage, then got busy up in the loft, pulling out a two-by-three-foot whiteboard from the storage closet. I'd used it in the past for private tutoring sessions. There was still an algebra problem involving the Quadratic Formula written on the surface in green marker. I wiped it off as best I could, propped it up on top of my desk, then grabbed some dry-erase markers from the desk drawer.

Like a lot of teachers, I like to make lists. Lists of things to buy, or household chores to be done, or school-related tasks to complete, arranged in chronological order. Sometimes when things start to pile up in an investigation, list-making helps me to visualize and reason through an increasingly perplexing situation. This was beginning to be one of those.

By the time Wendi arrived at my place that Tuesday evening, it was close to nine o'clock, the sky growing darker in the last of the fading light. She found me still up in the loft, standing back from the whiteboard, studying the lists I'd written.

"I see you've been busy," she said. "Making lists."

"Sometimes it helps," I said. "Not always."

I'd separated the names into three columns.

Beginning on the left, printed in green, were the names of the women who'd been trying to escape abusive relationships. All of whom were involved, to some degree, with the program linked to Joan Flaith. Melissa Adamson, the object of my search, headed the list.

"Darlene Morvine stayed with Tammy for a while," I said. "But was referred elsewhere. Never made it to Joan and the estate."

"Lettie Midland implied Darlene wasn't pretty enough," Wendi said.

"Culled out like an undersized crab. So appearance may be a factor here."

"They want to help abused women. But only if they're pretty?"

"Stinks of an ulterior motive. Doesn't it?"

"And next is Lettie Midland herself, who makes it to the estate level."

"But gets booted off the estate," I said. "Ostensibly for the reason that she no longer requires the protective aspect of the program, following the death of her abusive boyfriend."

"But you don't think that's why?"

"Could be. But from what she said of the circumstances, it sounds more to me like they got rid of her because they found out the cops were looking for her after her boyfriend's murder. Might have spooked them. Maybe they didn't want to take the chance that somehow the cops would show up there at the estate."

"Then there's Noranne Dubart," she said.

"She leaves the estate and Joan's program behind. Steals a car. And no one reports it."

"To take revenge on her husband for harming her sister."

"Ends up in jail. Regrets leaving the program and especially the estate."

"Nicest place she ever lived."

"Next comes Roma Coltrell," I said. "The rule breaker. The discipline problem. Runs away."

"To see to the safety of her child," Wendi said.

"Returns to the estate. Repentant, with no explanation of where she's been. Apologizes."

"Throws herself at the mercy of Joan and company."

"And ends up floating dead in the river, soon thereafter."

"Apology apparently not accepted," she said.

"Maybe forgiveness is not one of the pillars of the program. Maybe she stole the boat, trying to escape the wrath of her keepers. She had an accident. Or maybe they caught up with her. Either way, a blow to the head ends her life. End of discipline problem."

"What about these other names?" she said. "I don't remember you mentioning them before."

"Lexi Fincler. Rita somebody. Alta S. or Alta C. All names of other women who were said to have resided at the estate."

"You know anything about them?"

"Not a bit. Other than the fact that Rita was Latina, Alta tall and Black with short hair. and Lexi's last name may be spelled differently."

"So what's next?"

"Murphy has the names. Maybe I'll poke the bear again. Remind him to keep looking for anything on those three."

"He won't mind?"

"He might pretend to, but he'll do it."

We stood and pondered the list again in silence.

"So," I said. "What can we say, in general, about this group of women?"

"They've all been abused," she said. "By a spouse or a boyfriend."

"They are all pretty. In the conventional sense. There are no young teenage girls. All grown women in their twenties."

"They don't have many close relationships with family and friends."

"They're being counseled to feel safe and secure," I said. "And encouraged to cut out the few contacts they do have. Essentially, to drop out of their lives. Disappear. Start fresh."

"Promised a better life, if they do so," she said. "A nice place to live. A good job. But where and with whom?"

"When Murphy and I were talking, the word *cult* came up."

"I don't know. We talked about cults in some of my psychology classes. The leaders are overwhelmingly men. With a charismatic personality. Women are often used as recruiters, but who's the male leader?"

"Certainly not Phil Trunvid," I said. "It doesn't sound like he's well-regarded. He stays in the background. Sounds like Joan is the dominant of the two."

"She's certainly convincing them to throw away their relationships. But the goal of a cult leader is to gain power over followers and usually get money from them. Cults are obsessed with recruiting new members. These people are being very selective."

"And these women have no money. They don't appear to be using them to scam money from other people. They live in isolation."

"No one has described Joan Flaith in terms that would suggest she's charismatic?"

"Noranne seemed to value her advice, but at the same time she still retained enough value in her relationship with her sister to leave Joan behind in order to retaliate against the man who hurt her."

"Maybe they want to be a cult," Wendi said. "But they're just really bad at trying to establish one."

"Incompetent cultists. That's a new one."

"What about the *greed of lawyers*?" she said, pointing at the right-hand column printed in black marker on the whiteboard. "Maybe they're behind this whole thing."

I read the list out loud. "Rutherford 'Fordy' Dylan, Karl Bassle, Charles Karruth, Jr., and Dwight Laurelwood. None of them seems to have the resources to fund all of this. It sounds like someone is giving *them* money. Enough to promote the idea of starting their own firm. That would mean there's someone out there paying them for something."

"For what?"

"Maybe their legal services. A lot of NDAs being signed. People being paid off. And if there's someone else involved, they're being provided with a place to conduct this business with the women. A place not directly linked to this unknown person."

"Maybe this is a sideline," she said. "A temporary one, if they intend to stay in the legal business."

"And maybe it's not a cult, something else altogether. Maybe it's human trafficking. Murphy and I talked about how if the women cut off all contacts with friends and family, then go missing, who's to know. But then, as you said, they're being awfully particular about who they select. Never heard of traffickers being that fussy about the women they sell. "

"Oh wait," she said. "There's something else the women have in common. None of them have children. Except…"

"Except Roma Coltrell. And she might have managed to keep that a secret."

"Or maybe she didn't. And revealing her secret got her killed."

Wendy plopped down into the tufted armchair and propped her feet on the matching ottoman. I picked up her feet, moved them over, and sat down next to them, my focus still on the whiteboard.

"And Melissa Adamson is somewhere in the middle of all this," I said. "If she's still at the estate, then I need to get Kasey Dylan in there to see her. To talk to her and make sure she's okay. If she's a willing participant in whatever this is, then there's not much we can do about it."

"Except to explain the possible dangers to her. Let her know that people have died."

"We'll have to be honest with her. Admit we have no real evidence of foul play."

We sat in silence for a moment, then shifted our attention to the middle column of names printed in red. The movers and shakers. At the top of the list was Tammy 'Tydiss' Ballinderry. Followed in order by Joan Flaith, Phil Trunvid, the late Flo Peeke, and the team of Harry and Margaret from the Crisis Center.

"So Flo was the recruiter," I said. "She referred the women in need of refuge to Tammy or kept them herself."

"Providing a less than desirable dwelling in which to hide out from their tormentors," Wendi said. "Tammy acts as a filter. Culling out those who didn't fit the profile. Whatever the particulars of that may be."

"Joan and Phil run the program in the much more luxurious accommodations at the Karruth estate. Phil in the background, doing the grunt work. Joan at the forefront. Counselor to the battered women. Enforcer of the rules."

"Harry and Margaret?" she said. "Really? They deserve a spot?"

"Well, maybe not Margaret. She's just a grouch. But Harry is obviously afraid of her. He tells me where I might find Flo, but doesn't want Margaret to know he's been talking. After our conversation, I see the two of them get into a van with another guy. A few hours later, we find Flo, dead as a chunk."

"Maybe this guy, someone not on the list, saw you talking to Harry?"

"A strong possibility," I said. "I wish I'd seen his face."

Chapter Forty-One

"Mr. Skoville died last night," Kasey Dylan said.

We were on the phone that Wednesday morning. Wendi had already left for an early pickleball game with friends from school. Through the glass doors to the deck, I could see a bank of thick, dark clouds hanging low over the river. The choppy water looked gray and cold.

"I'm sorry to hear that," I said. "He seemed like a good guy. Dedicated to seeing things got finished."

In recommending Ben Skoville to his wife, Rutherford Dylan had sorely misjudged the man. Probably believing that a person as ill as Skoville would likely fail to uncover Melissa's whereabouts.

"Yes," she said. "I believe he was. I've spoken with the director of the funeral home. Mr. Skoville had no family. He made all his own arrangements well in advance. There will be no visitation. No memorial service. Just a short graveside ceremony. In three days. Saturday morning at ten. I've arranged for a minister to be there. Though he hadn't planned for one, I thought it proper."

"I'm sure he'd appreciate your thoughtfulness. I'll try to be there."

"That would be nice," she said. "If you have the time. But your current pursuit of the living is more critical than paying your respects to the dead. Especially someone you only met once. Any more progress since we last met?"

"Not a lot. But I'm working on it."

"I believe Mr. Skoville chose the right person to continue his efforts. To finish the job."

"I'm trying," I said.

There was a moment of silence where I thought I'd lost her.

"I lied to Fordy," she said. "I told him that I terminated your services. I thought it best for him to believe we were no longer looking for Melissa. That I'd followed his advice."

"Good."

"I intend to leave him. I'll move back with my parents. But not until we've found Melissa."

"If you're afraid, you should go now," I said.

"If I leave now, he might suspect that I know more than I'm letting on. That could make Melissa's predicament worse. I don't want that. I need to feel I'm doing something to help. I'll stay. For now."

* * *

By ten o'clock, I was in Murphy's office, waiting for him to get back from a call. This time, I'd stayed on the proper side of his desk. The solemn early morning news from Kasey Dylan had put me in a respectful mood. When he got there, he looked surprised at my choice of seating, but didn't comment. I liked it when people thought I was unpredictable.

"You wanted to see me at ten," I said. "I was here, you weren't."

"You got any witnesses?" Murphy said.

"Carter will vouch for me."

"That you were here by ten? *Really?*"

"It could've been a little later. Maybe five minutes. I think the clock out there might be a little fast."

"Sure. I'll look into that."

"You've got news for me?"

"Not much. And not the helpful kind. Fredericksburg cops can't find Harry and Margaret to question them about Flo Peeke. People at the Crisis Center say they don't work there anymore. Moved out west somewhere, they say, for new jobs. Left no contact number or address for their new location."

"Let's just hope their new location isn't six feet under, like Flo's," I said.

"Cops also talked to Melissa Adamson's husband, Greg. Said he was less than cooperative. Wouldn't say who roughed him up. Or even admit that he *was* roughed up."

"Any more discouraging news?"

"We've had no luck in locating Tammy and the boy. Doesn't look like they've been back to the bus. Sent Pugh to drive out to Joan Flaith's house. Parked next door for a while. Her teenage son's still there. But no sign of Tammy and the kid."

"What about the chances of getting onto the Karruth estate? To see if she's there. Maybe get an opportunity to see Melissa?"

"I asked the sheriff over in Dominion County. He won't go for it. No probable cause. To be frank, if he asked me to do the same thing over here, I would have to decline."

"Mmm. I see your point. I don't like it, but I see it."

"You could try it yourself. Ring the bell at the gate. Tell them who you are, ask to go in. Say you're there to check on Melissa's welfare. But that might be tipping your hand. They could just say she's not there. Refuse to let you in."

"And as a result, Fordy Dylan might find out I'm still on the job. Causing Kasey to explain why I'm still looking for Melissa if she fired me."

"And then he'd be forced to explain to her just how he knew that."

"And the whole thing blows up, and we still haven't helped Melissa."

"Who maybe doesn't even want help," he said.

"You had the chance to run down anything on those other three names Lettie Midland gave us?" I said. "Lexi Fincler, Rita, and Alta?"

"Nothing on that front either."

"You mind trying again?"

"You're a pest," he said. "You *do* know that?"

"Only when it's important," I said. "You and Elnora want to come over for dinner tonight? I could whip up a batch of my famous crab cakes."

"Sounds like a tempting bribe. But I'll have to say no. We've got a

Juneteenth supper over at the church this evening. *If* I can get out of here on time."

"Don't trust the clock out there," I said, getting up, moving to the doorway, and pointing to the outer office. "It's unreliable. You'll be late for sure."

"I thought you claimed that clock was fast?"

"Sometimes things run fast," I said. "Right before they die."

Chapter Forty-Two

I didn't have to look at the date on my phone to know what day it was when I woke up that Thursday morning. As soon as my eyes opened, I knew. I felt it. The pain of loss was not as sharp as it had once been. But it was still there, twisting deep inside, accompanied by persistent uncertainty. Even after all these years. Decades later.

In my mind, I could still hear his voice. Clear, deep, and melodic. Alternating between silly and somber. Probing me with meaningful questions, teaching a lesson in kindness, or spinning tales from his past.

His face was sometimes not as clear in my mind. A faraway image, distorted in dim light, confused with my own features reflected in the mirror. I would look at photographs periodically to refresh the image, to pair it with voice and movement. To remember a disappointed look or an encouraging smile. To recall his shape and the way he strode across the beach. The way he bent to work his garden. The way he cast his line into the water. The way he twisted to mount the seat of his truck that would carry us away on our small adventures.

The other side of him, which I had never witnessed, had always been the most difficult to visualize, and yet impossible not to. The things others had told me. A drunken man openly tormenting his family, slapping his wife. A secretly tortured man, without warning, pulling the trigger of a gun to end his life. Forcing me to begin my own life anew, with only memories behind me.

Wendi stayed away that day. Knowing I preferred to be alone. Most years, I devoted this day to the memory of Pax Barrow. Why I chose this horrible day to honor his memory, instead of the day of his birth, I can't explain. Maybe it's the power of death itself that demands recognition. In some way overwhelms the joy of beginning.

Sometimes I would go off to the places we'd visited together. Like George Washington's Birthplace. To his favorite fishing spot on the river there, at the end of the long road that passed by the Washington family burial ground. Other years, when I lived in a big house in town with my wife and children, I would retreat back here to spend the day at his cabin on the river. Sometimes, if they wanted, I brought Breana and Bret with me. Margo never seemed to like this place much. Too small. Too rustic, she'd say. In more recent years, seemingly busier with life than I'd ever been, I just visited his grave, planted a flower or two. Said a prayer of forgiveness. Spent the rest of the day in solitude.

But this year, it was the living that demanded my attention. I was already on my way into Weston, headed for the cemetery, potted flowers on the back seat floor, when Murphy called.

"Made an arrest last night," he said. "Related to a person of interest in your investigation."

"Who?" I said.

"Alex Dylan. Joan Flaith's kid."

"What the hell did *he* do?"

"Hosted a party out at his mother's place. Not exactly a small one. Lots of underage drinking. Got loud. Next door neighbor called to complain. When we got there, about half the kids scattered into the woods. Got away. The other half and their host were too far gone to care.

Thought our presence was funny. Offered us all a drink."

"Oh, shit," I laughed.

"Anyway, thought we could talk about how we might use this to help with our situations. Me, to locate Tammy and the boy. You, to get to Melissa Adamson."

"I'm driving into town right now. Just passed the gas station. Be there in two minutes."

"Let's make it five minutes," he said. "Wouldn't want you to be late. *Again.*"

By the time I found a parking spot on the street and got inside, I'd stopped counting the minutes. I met Murphy in his office, where we continued our conversation.

"Kid's been here since about 2:00 A.M. when we brought him in," he said. "Keeps telling us his mother's out of town, doesn't know how to get in touch with her."

"You believe that?"

"Hell no."

"How old is he?"

"Seventeen. Next birthday's in three weeks."

"Still a minor."

"We've tried to explain the legalities of that, but he still won't talk."

"Maybe he's still hungover."

"Strong possibility. Doesn't help his predicament."

"Teenagers will be teenagers," I said. "We'd both be hypocrites if we said our own kids didn't drink at parties before they were of age."

"Thank God none of them got caught," Murphy laughed.

"Would have been awkward. Especially for you."

"We were just out there on Monday," he said. "The county sheriff shows up at his door, snooping around, asking questions, and a few days later, he throws a big party. What an idiot!"

"I've always said there's nothing more clueless than a teenage boy. My younger self included. I remember believing that tall girls might actually be into me."

"I thought I'd be playing pro football *and* baseball."

"See. You've always had lower aspirations than me."

Deputy Carter came and stood in the open doorway.

"What y'all laughing about in here?" she said.

"Just guy stuff," I said.

"Hmm. Not sorry I missed it then. Thought you might want to know, Sheriff. Alex Dylan's ready to call his Mama."

Chapter Forty-Three

We were in the conference room. Alex Dylan sat slouching in a hard plastic chair behind a scarred wooden desk. He was wearing a faded-gray Metallica t-shirt that smelled like stale beer, and a pair of strategically ripped jeans that might have been new. On top of the table was a black landline phone with a lot of buttons and a cord that stretched across the room to a jack on the wall. He still looked hungover and didn't appear all that anxious to make the call.

We were standing. Murphy didn't bother to explain who I was. The kid probably assumed I was some kind of cop, and didn't show any sign of recognizing me from our previous visit to his mother's house. Alex said he didn't know his mother's number, so Murphy gave him back his confiscated cell phone to unlock and bring up the contacts list. He handed it back to Murphy, who punched the number into the phone on the table and handed the receiver to the kid.

When he told his mother where he was and why he was there, we could hear Joan Flaith's obscenity-laced tirade as clear as if she were in the room with us. Despite the circumstances, I felt bad for the kid. I wondered how she'd react to a D on his report card. When she finally slowed her verbal assault, then grew silent, Murphy took the phone and talked for a minute before hanging up. He told the kid he could stay there, and we went back out to his office to wait for Joan Flaith's arrival.

While waiting, we had plenty of time to talk strategy. It took her two hours to get there from wherever she'd been. The Karruth estate wasn't that far away. Maybe she'd needed the extra time to put on her makeup.

Or maybe she'd been off on another romantic rendezvous with Rutherford Dylan. But wherever she'd been, whatever she'd been up to, she arrived looking like she was headed out to dinner and a night on the town. Just not this town.

Joan Flaith was an attractive woman whose internet photo didn't do her justice. She looked to be in her early forties, with long, light-brown hair and a shape like a classic movie star. Poured into a tight red dress that stopped well north of her knees, she sported a pair of matching red heels that added four inches to her height, making her nearly as tall as Murphy.

She wasn't in the mood to see her kid yet, so the three of us were in Murphy's office, where he was seated in his position of authority behind the desk. Joan Flaith and I sat on the visitor's side, my chair turned at an angle so I could see both of them without jerking my head back and forth. She crossed her legs, shot me a curious look, and started bobbing her floating foot up and down. Teenage me would've thought she was flirting.

"So, Sheriff," She said, her voice forceful, businesslike. "Tell me where we are with my son's indiscretion?"

"It's more than an indiscretion," he said. "Alex is a minor, and he has broken the law."

"And what is this man doing here?" she demanded, jerking her chin in my direction.

"This is Mr. Pete Barrow. A friend of the Department, and…"

"I know *who* he is, and *what* he does," she snapped. "I want to know *why* he is here!"

"We'll get to that in a minute," Murphy said. "Please don't interrupt me again, Mrs. Flaith. Your son was caught in an inebriated state. Hosting a party and possibly the one supplying alcohol to others. Some also minors. The State's Attorney usually proceeds according to my recommendations in cases like this. I can tell you this is a road we've been down many times before. The range of consequences can run from a simple fine with community service and counseling, all the way up to a tour through the juvenile court system with possible charges for the parent as well, if a full investigation determines that the parent supplied the alcohol."

"Are you threatening me, Sheriff?" she said, uncrossing her legs, grasping the arms of her chair as she leaned forward.

"No Ma'am," he said, raising his hands, palms outward. "We're just talking."

"Do I need a lawyer already?"

"That's certainly your right. And your choice. But I'd rather you heard me out first."

She leaned back in her seat and folded her arms.

"Well then. Go on," she said.

"I'm looking for a woman named Tammy Tydiss or Tammy Ballinderry," he said. "In relation to a child custody inquiry. I'm told by Mr. Barrow here that you may have a sort of business relationship with her. I was hoping you might have information that you'd be willing to share with us concerning her current whereabouts."

"And what does that have to do with my son's predicament?"

"Nothing," he said. "But if you help me, maybe I can help you. And if you can answer a few of Mr. Barrow's questions, even better."

"Oh. So this is a negotiation?"

"Not at all. Just people trying to help each other out."

She sat in silence for a moment, grimacing, twisting her neck, rolling her eyes. Weighing her options. Maybe considering consequences, deciding on a safe response. Maybe she was thinking about how we'd ruined her plans for a night out.

"All right," she said, speaking in a low, guarded voice. "I know Tammy. Not that well. She sometimes refers women to me for counseling. But I haven't heard from her in a while and have no idea where she might be."

"Do you know a woman named Roma Coltrell?" Murphy said.

"No."

"Were you aware that Roma Coltrell had a son?"

"A son…I…how would I? I told you I don't know her."

"Do you know anything about Tammy having a nephew?" I said, finally deciding it was time to join the conversation.

"She told me she had a nephew staying with her. That's all I know."

"How about a woman named Melissa Adamson?" I said, watching for a reaction that didn't come.

"She's a client of mine. She's currently staying at the place where I work. That's all I can tell you. My work with her is confidential."

"I was previously employed by a woman, a friend of Melissa's who'd asked me to find her. Though I'm no longer employed in that capacity, I believe my former client would still be very much interested in meeting and talking with Melissa. You think you could arrange that?"

"So you could get back on the payroll?"

"Well. A guy's gotta make a living," I said. "So?"

"And you condone this, Sheriff?"

"I'm just here to serve and protect," Murphy said.

"I don't know," she said, turning to face me. "Perhaps."

"Mrs. Flaith," Murphy said. "You mentioned the place where you work. But you didn't say who you work for."

She stood up, smoothed out her dress, and tossed back her hair.

"I need to leave now," she said. "Is my son free to go?"

"You'll need to sign some papers out at the front desk with Deputy Carter," Murphy said. "Then you can take him home. We'll be in touch. We have your number. Please consider the things we've discussed."

I reached out to hand her my business card. She took it without hesitation.

"That goes for me too," I said.

When she left, I walked across the room and closed the door behind her.

"You think she bought the bit about you not working for Kasey Dylan anymore?" Murphy said.

"I don't know. But if she tells Fordy Dylan about this, I hope *he'll* believe it."

"She knew who you were and what you do."

"Would be good to know who told her about me."

"You notice she didn't ask who your client was?"

"Probably because she already knew."

"Because Rutherford Dylan told her."

"You notice she didn't answer your question about who her employer was?"

"I'm the sheriff," he said. "I notice everything."

Chapter Forty-Four

It was late that same Thursday evening when Joan Flaith called. I'd entered the number Murphy had shared with me into my contacts list, so I knew who was calling. I have to admit, I was surprised to hear from her. Our meeting in Murphy's office earlier in the day had ended abruptly, without any sign of future movement on her part.

She made her conditions clear. The meeting between Melissa and Kasey would take place at the Karruth estate, though she didn't call it by name, only giving the address. We agreed to meet the next day, Friday, at two o'clock. Joan claimed that Melissa had asked that she remain in the room for the entire meeting, and that Joan's lawyer attend as well. On our side, no law enforcement or legal representatives would be invited. When I asked if I could bring a female friend with a background in psychology, she hesitated, asked for her name, then finally, after a moment of silence, agreed to allow Wendi to attend.

I said I'd contact Kasey Dylan to see if the arrangements were agreeable to her. If so, I'd send a text message to confirm. The whole thing had the air of a one-sided, non-negotiable business meeting, rather than a simple reunion of two friends. In offering such a gathering, Joan Flaith had to be fairly certain of the outcome. I had a pretty good idea of what it was she was trying to achieve.

I called Wendi first, to explain the details of what was happening, and to see if she was onboard.

"Sure," she said. "I'll tag along. As long as it's okay with Kasey. Though I don't know how much help I'll be."

"You're equipped with a pretty good bullshit detector," I said. "I'd like to get your opinion of these people. If nothing else, it'll even up the teams, if they challenge us to a three-on-three basketball game."

"Except that they're all probably a lot taller."

"Could make them over-confident. Might be to our advantage, if they underestimate our abilities."

"Something we've both experienced many times."

"On and off the court."

"She didn't name the lawyer who'd be there?"

"No," I said. "Should be interesting to see who shows up."

"I think we can be fairly certain it won't be Fordy Dylan," she said.

"Wouldn't that be a shock?"

"You want me to bring my gun?"

"No, Wendi. Please leave any and all firearms at home. This is just talk. I don't think we'll be encountering anything physical enough to require self-defense."

"What about *your* gun? You keeping it in your car, like we agreed?"

"Not yet," I said. "But I'll get around to it. Soon."

"You better."

* * *

When I called Kasey, she didn't pick up. I skipped leaving a message on voicemail and sent a text instead, explaining the offer and terms of the meeting. Ten minutes later, she called me back.

"I'll have to cancel my schedule for the afternoon," she said, in a voice barely above a whisper. "But I can do it. I'll drive down to meet you."

"Good. I'll text you the directions to my place."

"I have to admit I'm nervous," she said. "I'm not sure I'll know what to say. What to ask."

"We can talk a little about that on our way there," I said. "But the important thing is for you to just be yourself. Be the friend you've always been. Ignore the others in the room. Try to focus on Melissa and what's best for her well-being. You'll be okay."

But, in fact, I didn't know that Kasey would be okay. It would be tempting for her to bring up her husband's involvement, though that was something I'd advise her not to do. I didn't know that any of us would be okay. Especially Melissa Adamson. Murphy and I had pitched some pretty big hints about what suspicions we might be harboring. Dropping Roma Coltrell's name in our conversation with Joan Flaith might've been a stupid thing to do. Maybe the wrong card to play at the wrong time. But we were going there in broad daylight. Though the Karruth estate wasn't in his county, I'd be telling Murphy the when and where of our meeting. I really didn't believe they'd be bold enough to do anything then and there. If they wanted to discourage further involvement on our part, the meeting alone might achieve that. If it didn't, there were always other moves to be made later. Perhaps more convincing, more permanent ones.

Chapter Forty-Five

We were sitting in a long room with a cathedral ceiling in a house that deserved the title *mansion*. The elegant furniture was arranged in a U-shape around a dormant, wood-burning fireplace. Two sofas were set facing each other, with a wide dark-stained cocktail table between, and a pair of matching wing-back chairs at the end. At the far end of the room was another fireplace with an identical set of furniture in the same arrangement. I admired the choice of symmetry. At the center of the room, which was largely open space, a large crystal chandelier hung halfway to the floor. Perhaps there would be dancing when our business had concluded.

Introductions were awkward. No one smiled or shook hands. No one said *nice to see you*. Melissa Adamson avoided making eye contact with anyone. Kasey Dylan stared long and hard at her husband's suspected paramour, Joan Flaith, but managed to keep her emotions in check. Joan was dressed in a gray pantsuit and black shoes with no heels, a step down from her attire of the previous day. She introduced her lawyer as Karl Bassle. A tall, pale guy, overly thin with the look of a long-distance runner. His hair was wavy and dark with streaks of premature gray here and there. The black suit he wore looked like it cost more than my entire wardrobe. Despite his association with her husband in the *greed of lawyers*, Kasey gave no sign that they knew each other.

Wendi and I sat at opposite ends of the sofa, with Kasey between us. Across from us, Joan and Melissa were situated next to each other. In the chair closest to them, Bassle sat with his arms and legs crossed, looking at the floor. No one offered refreshments.

Melissa was dressed in a pair of blue slacks and a matching top with trendy openings exposing her tanned shoulders. She wore excessive makeup. The earrings and necklace she wore looked expensive, but not gaudy. Joan placed a hand on Melissa's leg for a moment, signaling for her to begin the conversation.

"I understand you've been worried about me, Kasey," Melissa said, speaking with a dull, unemotional voice, finally making eye contact with her friend. "But I want you to know that I'm fine. Better than I've ever been. There's no reason for you to be concerned."

"But I am," Kasey said. "I care about you. You're my friend. You don't really know these people."

"I know they've helped me. I'm living in this beautiful place. I'm taken care of, body and soul. I have a future. I'll have a job soon with someone important, and maybe an even better place to live. Before, I was suffering. And now I'm not. I've been saved from a life of being beaten down. In more than one way. The people in my life have been holding me back."

"Does that include me?"

"I'm sorry to say, but yes, it does. You were my friend, but I was always less than you. You never saw me as an equal. In your eyes, I was someone who needed to be taken care of. When we were kids, and even now. Working for you and your husband as a maid, that was…demeaning. I was still less than you. Well, now I don't have to be."

Her words came out sharp in intent, but flat in tone. Mean things had been said, but something less hateful, less dismissive was behind her words. It was then that I saw it, beyond her head, on the table behind the sofa. It was the purse that Kasey had given her. Identical to the one Kasey had shown us on her front porch at our first meeting.

Tears had begun to roll down Kasey's cheeks. Melissa's words had done their job.

"I wish you could come home with me," Kasey said. "It would be different this time. We can find you a good job. Or maybe get you back in school."

"While I live with you again? You don't get it, Kasey."

"We've always been so close. Like sisters. I need your friendship as much as I ever have. I don't understand why the help these people claim to be giving you is any different from what I'm offering."

"They're offering me a path to independence."

"Please, Melissa. You know you can trust me. You don't know these people's intentions. Or their history. There are things you don't know. I'm concerned about your safety here and..."

Joan and Bassle shot each other a look. He sat up and unfolded his arms, looking for the first time like he was paying attention.

"Melissa, did you know a woman named Flo Peeke?" I said, tired of remaining silent, figuring it was time to stir the pot.

"Yes. She took me to Tammy's when I left Fredericksburg. Before I came here."

"Did you know that she's dead?" I said.

"No...I...Joan?"

"She died of a drug overdose, dear," Joan said, patting her leg. "She was an addict. Mr. Barrow knows that."

"How about Tammy Tydiss?" I continued to push. "Do you know where she and her nephew might be? Are they here?"

Bassle's eyes widened, and he squirmed around in his chair, sitting on the edge, like he was about to stand. "Don't be dragging Tammy's name into this, Barrow. She has nothing to do with any of..."

"No," Melissa said. "They haven't been around here for a while. Why do you ask?"

"Because no one can find them," I said.

"I don't know..."

"How about a woman named Roma Coltrell?"

"I don't know who that is."

"She used to live here. And now she's dead too." I said.

"Mr. Barrow!" Joan shouted. "That's quite enough!"

"If you're implying, Mr. Barrow," Bassle said, "that anyone here had anything to do with either of those tragedies, I must warn you..."

"I'm not implying anything," I said. "I'm simply stating the facts. Facts that none of you seem to have bothered to share with her. So why don't we let Melissa here decide for herself who she can trust to tell her the truth? The whole truth."

"None of the things you've mentioned have any bearing on Melissa's decision," Joan said. "I believe Melissa has made her point to Mrs. Dylan and to you, Mr. Barrow. I feel that any further discussion would be unproductive. Don't you agree, Melissa?"

"Yes, Joan," she said. "I know you're my friend, Kasey. Trust, between us, has never been an issue. But you need to let me go. Our relationship hasn't helped me. I would prefer that you not try to contact me again. If I ever want your help, I'll contact you. I promise."

No one invited us to stay for dinner and dancing.

Chapter Forty-Six

The ride back to Potomac County was uncomfortably quiet. When I tried to talk with Kasey about how the situation had played out, she got teary again and wouldn't respond. Wendi's efforts produced the same result.

Back at the cabin, she refused our repeated offers to come inside for a while and talk things out. When I brought up the idea that the presence of the purse she'd given Melissa might have been a silent message, she perked up a bit.

"Maybe," she said. "As long as she still has it, there's hope that she'll call. But she said what she said. She could have left with us. She chose not to. I'm afraid it's over, Mr. Barrow. We've done all we can. I still don't understand what my husband's involvement with all this is, beyond his affair with Joan. But I won't be living at the house with Fordy much longer, so please email me your bill. And thanks to the both of you for your efforts."

"I wish I could've done more," I said.

"There's no more to be done. At least nothing that would help Melissa. I'll have to find my own way to deal with my marital situation. Will I see you at the graveside service for Mr. Skoville tomorrow morning?"

"Yes," I said. "I'll see you then."

After Kasey's departure, we went inside and settled onto stools at the kitchen counter. I was drinking beer from a bottle. Wendi opted for a glass of orange juice. She declined my offer to spike it with vodka.

"You finished the job," Wendi said. "You did what she hired you to do. To find her friend."

"Then why does it feel like I haven't accomplished anything?" I said.

"Because, from your point of view, you haven't really solved the problem. *Melissa* chose not to leave with Kasey. Not your fault. Not your problem. You're not convinced that Melissa is safe, but there's not much you can do about it if she prefers Joan's help over Kasey's."

"I suppose you're right. There isn't any more to be done. I've been fired."

"No. You haven't been *fired*. Your services have been terminated at the end of the job."

"Sounds better," I said. "Doesn't feel better."

"I'm afraid I wasn't much help at the meeting," she said. "I suppose I could have said *something*. Could have tried to guide the discussion in a more positive direction."

"Not your fault. You weren't really afforded the opportunity. So, what *was* your take on the whole thing?"

"Oh, I don't know. I guess Melissa's whole spiel seemed rehearsed to me. There wasn't any emotion or conviction behind what she said. Though it was still hard for Kasey to hear. Maybe she was afraid of Joan. Or of losing what she seems to have gained."

"Same feeling I had. Reminded me of a conference in the principal's office where the parents make their kid apologize for being an asshole in class. Just to make the situation go away. But you can tell it's the parents' words spitting out of the kid's mouth. Deep down, the kid still wants to be an asshole."

"At times, it seemed like she might have been sedated," Wendi said. "You get that vibe?"

"No," I said. "But you've seen more people in that condition than I have."

"Unfortunately."

"What about Bassle?" I said. "He sure seemed to get his knickers in a bind when I mentioned Tammy."

"He did. You think he knows where she is?"

"Maybe. Not that it matters to the case anymore. But I do worry about what's happened to her and the kid."

"Oscar will still want to know where she is."

"He will. There's still the matter of who the kid is, and where he belongs, legally."

"Maybe you're right about the purse with the hidden phone being there. Melissa might've been trying to send a subtle message."

"If she still has the phone hidden, then maybe she'll send a real message. One we can read."

Chapter Forty-Seven

On Saturday morning at ten o'clock, we were standing by the graveside of Ben Skoville in Brighton Cemetery, across the Rappahannock River just east of Fredericksburg, not far from the historical site called Ferry Farm, the boyhood home of George Washington. I was wearing my gray suit. Kasey Dylan and Wendi were both clad in black dresses in a style that befit the occasion. It was a cloudy and humid day. Off and on, the sky spit drops, but nothing more came of it.

I'd never attended a burial service for someone I'd known so little. But somehow it seemed like the right thing to do. Besides the three of us, the only other mourner present was the Methodist minister who had come to serve at Kasey's request. It felt sad to see that no one else had shown up. I wondered if he'd had no friends nearby, or none at all. No grateful clients were there. No close associates. I wondered if he had always been an investigator. If he'd always lived and worked here in Virginia. Maybe I'd take the time to look into that. Maybe learning about his life would be a better way to honor his departing from this world.

There were others within the sphere of my search, who had also recently died. The circumstances of their passings were not as certain as those of Ben Skoville. Flo Peeke had been a shadowy figure. One who guided young, vulnerable women toward a life that sought to separate them from those who would care to stand by their graves. And Roma Coltrell, rebel in residence at the estate, whose last significant act was to attempt to ensure the safety of her child. I wondered about who would be standing by their graves, and how many would care about the way they lived and how they died. As if the significance of a life could somehow be measured by the number of people standing around a hole in the ground.

The minister's name was Reverend August Congdon. He had a soft, whispery voice and talked in generic spiritual terms about a man he'd never known. He read some verses from the Bible and ended the short ceremony with the popular Twenty-third Psalm. When he finished, Kasey handed him an envelope, and he shook our hands and walked away. Far off, toward the back of the cemetery, the burial crew stood by their equipment and waited for us to leave.

* * *

In the days that followed, I tried to put it all behind me, to settle down, begin to relax, and enjoy the freedom of summer. Wendi had departed for a trip to Cape May with her daughter and granddaughter, so I spent most of my time alone. I watched mindless television and wandered aimlessly around my place, inside and out, finding it difficult to focus on anything worthwhile for any significant length of time. I paid bills and sent emails and did only the yardwork that couldn't be put off. I could summon no patience for fishing and lacked the concentration to read little beyond the newspaper. I napped too often and too long, which made sleep at night elusive. When I checked my crab pots, they were always empty.

After several days of accomplishing next to nothing, I started to unwind, to gradually break free from my malaise. I spent more time fishing and stopped caring about whether or not I caught anything. I took long walks along the shoreline, gathering up trash to haul away. Attacking it in two-hour intervals, I started in on my fourth time at reading James Michener's *Chesapeake*. Damn those Turlocks!

When Kasey Dylan's check arrived in the mail, it came with a short note thanking me for my help. She included her new address and an alternate phone number. I took the check to the bank in Weston the next day and deposited it into my business account. I figured that was the end of it. Sometimes even math teachers figure wrong.

A few days later, I was watching the news on a D.C. channel, catching up on all the current events I'd missed in the busy weeks since the end of school. In the big city, bad people were still shooting each other, wrecking hijacked cars into buildings, robbing convenience stores at gunpoint, and setting fires. The good guys were making arrests, saving trapped people from wreckage, canvassing neighborhoods seeking information on blurry images caught on tape, putting out fires, and finding missing kids. It was hard to tell which side was winning.

The sports news was more definitive, though nearly as depressing, with the reporter lamenting the Nationals' current three-game losing streak. The perky, blonde weather girl remained upbeat, despite her forecast including the possible threat of coming storms.

When I'd heard enough, I got up from the sofa and retrieved the remote from where I'd left it on the kitchen counter. I stood there and aimed it, but stopped short of hitting the power button. The story on the screen had caught my attention.

It was another report on the same guy from the story I'd seen weeks before. The rich guy who'd made an out-of-court settlement with the actress from a television show, after being accused of unwanted sexual advances. The updated story claimed the man had settled cases with more women. They were running the same video clip used in the previous report, with the man trying to avoid being interviewed. But this time I saw something I hadn't noticed before. Or maybe I'd seen it, but at the time it had lacked significance. Standing in the background, by the SUV the man was fleeing toward, was another man. He was big and muscular, with a shaved head and red-framed eyeglasses. The rich guy's name was Damon Radburke. It took me a couple of minutes to remember where I'd seen or heard the name before. Then it came to me. Damon Radburke was the name I'd seen listed as the publisher of Joan Flaith's book.

Chapter Forty-Eight

No one was paying me to pursue this any further. Kasey Dylan had made it clear that she was done, moving on with her life, dealing as best she could with her feelings about her lost friend and wandering husband. But I couldn't quite bring myself to ignore what I'd seen, to stop digging a little deeper into something that was really no longer any of my business. The man in the red eyeglasses, whom I'd seen with Rutherford Dylan, was connected to Damon Radburke. Radburke was connected with Joan Flaith, who was controlling Melissa Adamson with an undetermined goal in mind. As far as I knew, there was no one else currently looking out for Melissa's well-being. It was summer. I had the time. There would be no harm in poking around a little more. My grandfather had taught me it was good to stay busy.

On Friday morning, I found Deputy Adele Carter sitting in her squad car, parked in front of the pharmacy on Main Street in Weston. I tapped on the glass on the passenger side, and she unlocked the door to let me in. She was slurping black coffee from a paper cup with a plastic lid and nibbling on a chocolate-frosted doughnut with rainbow sprinkles on top. I refrained from passing judgment. The coffee smelled good. An illusion I would not fall for. She offered me a doughnut, and I accepted. Unlike the coffee, it would taste as good as it smelled.

"Sheriff said you were looking for me," she said, before taking another tiny bite of her doughnut.

"Yeah. Got a question for you. You still in contact with any law enforcement from back when you worked in D.C.?"

"I am. From time to time. Got some people I talk to. Why? What's up?"

"I need to know who this guy is." I showed her a photo on my phone of the man with red eyeglasses.

"Hmm. Hard-looking dude. Never seen him around here."

"Me either. Snapped the photo in Fredericksburg. Had D.C. plates on his car."

"Okay. Anything else?"

"I'd also like anything they could give me on a wealthy guy named Damon Radburke. Especially any info that wouldn't already be out in the media."

"Okay. I know the right guy to ask," she said. "Send me all the photos you have of the big dude and another one of your business card. I'll forward them on. How soon you need this?"

"Next couple of days, if possible. As far as I can tell, it's not exactly urgent. But it may have some bearing on the future safety of a woman I've spent some time looking for."

"Copy that," she said. "Feels kind of like the good old days."

"How's that?" I said.

"Back in high school. You giving me a homework assignment. I miss solving all those algebra problems. I loved math."

"That's nice to hear," I said. "Usually I get the opposite."

* * *

Three hours later, I was back in Fredericksburg, parked on Lornewood Avenue, across the street from the home of attorney Karl Bassle. It was a modest, two-story brick structure on a corner lot, up on a small hill with a terraced yard and a matching brick walkway with steps up to the front door. Along with most of the surrounding houses, the place looked like it dated back to the sixties. All the lawns and shrubs were nicely trimmed. There weren't any *No Trespassing* or *Keep Off The Grass* signs. It looked like a nice neighborhood. I wondered about the people tucked away inside.

There were two vehicles parked in the driveway. Just off the front sidewalk was a green Range Rover. Behind it, closest to the detached garage, sat a late-model gray Mercedes sedan, most likely the one Noranne Dubart had stolen, and Phil Trunvid had returned.

The red-painted front door of the house was mostly open, with the full-panel glass storm door closed. There was a man inside, moving around, carrying a coffee mug, walking in and out of view.

Back at the meeting at the estate, Bassle's reaction to my bringing Tammy's name into the conversation had sounded a bit on the protective side. Something about the way he'd jumped on it had bothered me. It was more than a legal protest over her involvement. There had been a trace of something personal in his voice. Wendi and I had both noticed it.

After watching the place for ten minutes or so, I got out and ambled up to the front door. I knocked on the glass, and Bassle appeared. He was dressed in a Nike t-shirt and running shorts and shoes, carrying his mug in his right hand. It took a moment for a look of recognition to appear. He wasn't smiling when he flipped the latch and cracked the door open a few inches.

"What do you want, Mr. Barrow?" he said, sounding bothered, like I'd been there ten times before, trying to sell him a wet paper bag full of dogshit.

"I'd like to talk," I said. "Off the record. You mind if I come in?"

He shrugged and opened the door the rest of the way.

We stood in the living room. The furniture was modern and nice. The place was neat and clean. There were framed photos all over the walls, artfully arranged. A lot of them were printed in black and white. On a long narrow table by the front window was an expensive-looking camera with a long lens. He didn't invite me to sit or offer any coffee. I was okay with that. It wouldn't be that kind of visit.

"There were things that didn't come up at our little meeting the other day," I said. "Things that need to be clarified."

"I don't know what you're talking about," he said. "What more would there be to say?"

"How about the fact that a woman named Noranne Dubart, who was staying at the estate, took your Mercedes out there, and you never reported it stolen."

"It wasn't. She borrowed it. Another friend returned it. It's that simple."

"The cops don't think so. They found it peculiar that she admitted taking the car, but you never reported it stolen."

"The police? Why would…?" He stopped himself from saying more.

"And then there's the matter of your association with Kasey Dylan's husband. I noticed you didn't bother to mention that to Kasey."

"It wasn't relevant. The meeting was between the two women. Rutherford had nothing to do with it." He was starting to sound defensive and nervous.

"Hmm. I wonder if Kasey Dylan would agree with that?"

"I wouldn't know. Their marital affairs have nothing to do with me."

"How about Tammy Tydiss? She have anything to do with you? You seemed to get all bent out of shape when I mentioned her name. You care to tell me why that is? You know where she and the kid are now?"

"No. I do not," Bassle said. "I really don't know the woman."

He picked up his coffee and took a long, deep drink. When he resurfaced from behind the mug, his whole demeanor had changed. He was back to being a slick-talking, persuasive lawyer who thought he could talk his way out of anything.

"Look, Mr. Barrow. I'm sorry I've been…well…rude. Let's tone this down a bit. Shall we? Be more civil. Can I get you some coffee?" He waved his mug in the direction of the kitchen.

"Sure," I said. "Why not? Thank you. I'd love some."

"How do you like it?" he said. "Cream? Sugar?"

"Black is fine."

"Please, have a seat. I'll be right back."

"Thanks. But I could really stand to use your bathroom. You mind? Too much coffee already today."

"Of course. Down the hall. Second door on the left."

He went into the kitchen, and I plodded toward the bathroom. The walls lining the hallway were covered with more framed photographs of all kinds. Curious-looking people, exotic animals, and antique cars. I stopped to take a longer look when one in particular caught my eye. It was a photo of the greed of lawyers standing on a dock in front of a yacht with another man.

Damon Radburke.

Behind the closed bathroom door, I rooted around inside the medicine cabinet, where I found a child's toothbrush in an unopened package decorated with D.C. superheroes. In the trash can under the sink, I discovered a tangled wad of extra-long, light-brown hair. I flushed the toilet, washed my hands, and went back out to the living room, where my coffee was waiting for me on the table next to the sofa. Bassle was sitting in a chair by the front window, looking delighted to see me again. I sat down and picked up the mug. It smelled heavenly. I took a conservative sip and managed to suppress a shudder.

"You have an interesting hobby, Karl," I said. "Some of your pictures are very artfully done. I find it intriguing when a photographer manages to capture an image in a way that reveals a different aspect of the subject."

"Thank you," he said. "I enjoy the challenge. I find great satisfaction in the work. It's quite different from what I do to earn a living. A much more relaxing pursuit."

"I don't see any family photos around. You're not married, are you, Karl? No steady girlfriend? No kids yet?"

He hesitated, seeming flustered again. "No. I've not been—"

I held up a long single strand of hair, dangling it in the light.

"Then who's this belong to?" I said. "The only person I know with hair this long is Tammy. Put it together with the kid's toothbrush in your medicine cabinet, and that tells me you've had visitors. Are they still here?"

"You don't understand," he said. "The others don't know about us. If Fordy found out there'd be hell to pay."

"You're in a *relationship* with Tammy?"

"Yes."

"And she and the kid have been hiding out here with you?"

"She was scared. For herself and the boy. A man came to see her. He told her she'd better keep quiet about her dealings with Joan Flaith. That she shouldn't talk to the police, or you. He threatened her."

"You the one helped her fake the custody papers to get the kid into school?"

"It was the right thing to do for the boy. He needed to be in school. Be around other kids. The lawyer's name on the documents is a friend of mine. He owed me a favor. I figured he'd cover for me if anyone asked about it. I didn't think anyone would. Schools don't have the resources to check those things out. We could always hide behind attorney-client privilege."

"Any of your cohorts know whose kid he is?"

"What do you mean?"

"Come on, Karl. I already know he's Roma Coltrell's son. That she asked Tammy to take care of the boy for her. Only Roma didn't expect to turn up dead in the river. She expected to come back for him."

"When you said at the meeting that Roma was dead, that was the first I'd heard of it. You said she was found in the river? Did she drown?"

"That's not for me to say."

"Can you tell me *when* she died?"

"Couple of months ago. Her body was just recently identified. The family has been notified. Hasn't been out in the media yet. You *really* didn't know she was dead until I mentioned it?"

"No," he said. "I swear."

"You still haven't answered my question. Does anyone else know whose kid he is?"

"I don't think so, no."

"So, are they still here? Upstairs?"

"No. They've gone."

"Where?"

"I shouldn't tell you. They won't be safe."

"The man who threatened them? Big guy, shaved head, red eyeglasses?"

"Yes. You know who he is?"

"Not exactly. Yet. But I will."

"You can't tell anyone else where they are."

"I won't. I just want to talk with her."

"About what, exactly?"

"What she knows about what happens to the women after they leave Joan Flaith. About what Melissa Adamson is headed for?"

"She doesn't know anything about that. I don't know anything about that."

"Someone's paying out a lot of money, Karl. For what? How about I go directly to old Fordy Dylan and ask him? You think he knows?"

"You can't do that. You'll ruin everything."

"You mean the money that's coming to back your new law firm?"

"Money. And the clients we've been promised. Fordy's going to make it happen."

"With whose help? Damon Radburke?"

"I don't know who that is."

"Should we take a walk down the hall there and look at his picture, to jog your memory?"

"All right. Yes. He's involved."

"In exchange for what?"

"I don't know all of it. I've said too much already."

"One more time, Karl. Where's Tammy?"

"She's with the boy's uncle," he said. " His name is Riley Zerco. You're not going to say anything to Fordy?"

"Not if I don't have to. You're in some deep shit here on both sides, Karl. How deep remains to be seen. For now, I'd strongly advise you to keep your mouth shut."

I left with an awful taste in my mouth. Maybe it was the coffee.

Chapter Forty-Nine

"Do you know the name of the man who threatened you?" I said. We were in the living room of Riley Zerco's home in Hofflinsburg. Wendi was with me, sitting close on the sofa. Tammy and Riley sat in chairs across from us. Somewhere in a closed bedroom behind them, Riley's nephew, Bobby, was asleep. In the kitchen, a window air conditioner was straining to keep up with the evening heat and humidity. The odor of steamed broccoli and something that might have been pizza hung in the air.

"No," Tammy said. "Though I'd seen him out at the estate once. He was in a car with another man, leaving when I arrived. When I asked Joan who they were, she didn't answer."

I pulled out my phone and went across the room to show her a media photo of Damon Radburke.

"This the other guy?" I said.

"I'm not sure. Maybe."

"Anyone else, besides Karl Bassle, know you're here?"

"No. I haven't told anyone," she said.

"How about you, Riley?"

"No. No one," he said.

"Let's keep it that way," I said. "You have your phone, Tammy?"

"Yes."

"Turn it off now. And keep it off."

"I'm scared," she said, stroking at a long strand of hair that curled down to her lap.

"You're probably safe here. But if this guy who threatened you, or anyone else suspicious, shows up, call the police."

"All right," Riley said, choking back something that sounded a lot like fear.

"Tammy," I said. "Do you know what happens to the women when they leave the estate? Where they go? What they do? Did Roma tell you anything?"

"She didn't say much. She didn't know much. There was some talk of a wealthy man. A benefactor of some kind. A protector who would give them a nice place to live and guaranteed employment that paid big money."

"Doing what?" Wendi said. "It sounds too good to be true. Especially for a woman. Who wouldn't be suspicious of an offer like that?"

"A desperate woman in need of hope," Tammy said. "One who's been knocked around and beaten down in every imaginable way her whole life. One who wants to believe she'll be protected and valued. Unless you've been there, it's hard to understand why a woman wouldn't question what she might be asked to do in exchange for safety and security."

"But Roma never said if she knew what they would be doing?" I said.

"No. She tried to find out, but Joan didn't like people to ask questions. Roma said she was big on all the women demonstrating unwavering trust in her. She got angry when they didn't."

"Did you ever attempt to question Joan about where all this was leading?" Wendi said.

"No. I should have, but I didn't. She was paying me well to do what I did. To keep the women with me for a while. Until she decided if she wanted them to move on to the estate."

"And you don't know how she decided whether or not they were chosen to do so?" I said.

"No. I was told to find out as much as I could about them while they were with me, and to pass the information along to Joan."

"What kind of information?" Wendi asked.

"Personal stuff. How many people they kept in contact with. You know. What close ties they had. That sort of thing. It seemed like the fewer contacts they had, the better their chances of moving to the estate would be.

I don't think they wanted anyone with kids. Roma must've figured that out somehow. Probably why she kept Bobby a secret."

"Anything else?" I said. "Anything more personal than that?"

She closed her eyes for a long moment and sat completely still. When she opened them, she spoke in a quivering voice, deep and raw like an open wound.

"She wanted to know the details of the abuse they'd suffered. Exactly what had been done to them. All the gory details. Physical damage. Burns, cuts, broken bones. And the methods of mental and verbal abuse they'd suffered. Sexual abuse. Sick stuff. And especially if they'd been locked up or confined in some way."

"And the women confided in you?" Wendi said.

"Yes. Most did. I was good at drawing it out of them. Telling them my own horrible story usually got them to open up. I thought I was doing it to lift them up. No one had ever really tried to help *me*. I wanted to help *them*. Now, I'm not sure what I did."

"And what about Roma?" I said.

"Roma and I loved each other like sisters. Joan was paying me a lot of money. I was saving much of it. Roma and I were going to pool our money. When we had enough, go away somewhere and start over where no one could find us. When Roma left that night, after leaving Bobby with me, she wasn't sure what was going to happen when she went back to the estate. If Joan turned her away, she'd come back. We'd leave with what we had. When she didn't come back and wasn't at the estate, Joan told me she'd moved on to the next level in the program. She said Roma was happy and safe. I wanted to believe what Joan told me. I wanted to be patient and to keep our secret. Now she's dead, and it's all for nothing. Maybe it's all my fault. I should have seen I was being used."

"You did what you thought was right," Riley said. "No one can blame you for that. There's other people got you to do what you did. Her death isn't on you. And now I need your help to bury my sister. And to find a way to tell that little boy asleep back there that his momma's not ever coming home."

When we left the house, it was dark. The air was thick and heavy. Far away in the northern sky, there were intermittent flashes of lightning, too distant to hear the accompanying boom of thunder. We drove away toward the storm.

Chapter Fifty

On Saturday morning, Wendi drove the two of us to D.C. It was the Fourth of July, but the traffic seemed lighter than usual. I didn't like to drive in the city. I was okay in a smaller one like Fredericksburg, but driving in Washington was on a whole different level. Traffic was always thick and close, with cars and trucks and buses moving way too fast, or at the other extreme, inching along from one stoplight to the next. Throw a wannabe NASCAR driver into the mix, and you get more than one story for the evening news.

When we got there, we found the reserved spot where we'd been instructed to park near the cluster of Smithsonian buildings. On the dashboard, we left a parking pass printed from an email received the night before. Finding a parking spot on our own on the Fourth would've been nearly impossible. The area was crowded with holiday weekend tourists flocking to the museums, and out enjoying the clear, cooler weather that had arrived after the previous night's storms.

Deputy Adele Carter had called late Friday night to set up a meeting with her contact in law enforcement. His name was Tevin Danisk. She didn't say what agency he worked for. While I waited out front for him to appear, Wendi headed inside the Museum of American History to geek out on an Abraham Lincoln display and whatever else she could soak in. After no more than five minutes, a brown-skinned man approached me. He was average height with a strong build, dressed in running clothes with a tight shirt that accentuated his muscles. His hair was cut short, and his face was clean-shaven.

We exchanged greetings and walked across Constitution Avenue to a bench under the trees. Fast-walking people streamed past. City folks never seemed to amble. Tevin didn't ask to see my identification.

"You've known Adele a long time, I understand," he said.

"Since I taught her in high school," I said. "Along with most of her siblings."

"She said you ran a tight ship. But you were fair."

"Tried to be. I hear that a lot, so it might be true."

"She says you're honest. On the job to help people."

"I do what I can. Sometimes things work out."

"The man in the picture you sent. His name is Edik Levka. A real bad dude. Hires out only to people who can afford him. That narrows down his client list considerably. Has a minor arrest record. Managed to avoid major charges, though he's suspected of being into some serious stuff. Nobody's caught him yet."

"I know he scares people. He capable of killing?"

"That's the rumor. Unsubstantiated."

"Good to know."

"You got some dead people?"

"Two. Could be accidents. Overdose. Bump on the head."

"Wouldn't be inconsistent with events in his past. You'd best tread lightly when he's around."

"What about Damon Radburke?" I said. "Tell me something I can't find in the news."

"Dude's got a lot of money. Uses it to get out of precarious legal dilemmas. All the accusations in the media lately are from cases five years back or more. If it wasn't for the actress coming forward, I doubt he'd ever have been on the evening news. He seems to be less active these days. There are more women who won't come forward. Took the money and signed the papers before word got out. Others who've been scared off, without taking any money. There are people looking into his finances as we speak. Levka is believed to be working with Radburke. The two of them may be into other things I can't talk about."

"So Radburke has enough money to hire lots of guys like Levka?"

"He does, but that's not something he's inclined to do. He has trust issues with the hard-ass types. Been burned a couple of times in the past. Likes to keep his heavy workforce to a minimum. Lately, it's just Levka."

"You know anything about how Radburke got his money?"

"Inherited a fair amount of it from his daddy. Runs an investment company. My associates are pretty sure he's accumulated a good portion of his funds through less-than-legal means."

"Didn't earn it mowing lawns?" I said.

"Ha! Don't believe he's ever touched a lawnmower."

"You think any of the women who haven't come forward would be willing to talk with me? Off the record."

"I know who to ask about that. I've got your number. If that's possible, I'll let you know."

"Thanks for your help, Tevin."

We stood and shook hands.

"Watch yourself, Mr. Barrow. Levka's not one to play around. You got good backup down there in the country?"

"I've got an honest sheriff who looks out for me. And there's Adele."

"Knows how to handle herself. She's one of the good ones."

"She is, in fact."

"Been down to your neck of the woods to see her a couple of times. Lots of trees and water, cows and corn. Not a lot of people and traffic."

"We have our busy seasons. But it's a quiet life. Most of the time."

He handed me a card with his name and a phone number, but nothing else. "In case you come across anything that needs to be passed on."

"Will do," I said.

"You'll put in a good word for me with Adele?" he said.

"That important to you?"

"It is."

"Then I'll be sure to do that."

"Tell her I'll be down the country to see her soon."

* * *

Back home at the cabin that night, just after dark, we loaded up with bug repellent and sat out on the deck watching the annual fireworks display emanating from the cluster of marinas down shore, close to town. Across the water, somewhere along the Maryland coast, was a simultaneous, but less spectacular exhibition.

When it was over, Wendi decided to stay, and we went to bed early. The mass exodus of vacationers from the Northern Neck through Potomac County the next day would rival the urban traffic we'd navigated earlier that day. Sunday would best be spent here at home.

Chapter Fifty-One

At two o'clock on Monday afternoon, I was sitting in the corner booth in an old-style diner off US 301, just south of Clinton, Maryland. Seated across the table was a woman in her early thirties named Faith Calyce. Her straight, shoulder-length hair was a deep, natural shade of red, and her face was pale. She was wearing a tight-fitting white t-shirt and black jeans without any holes. Her left arm was covered with tattoos of amphibious creatures from her wrist to where they slithered beneath the tip of her short sleeve. Her right arm was free of any artwork. Symmetry wasn't her thing.

I'd been referred to her through a contact of Tevin Danisk. When I'd talked to her on the phone that morning, she'd agreed to meet with me, for a fee, as long as what she said was off the record. She'd balked at my request to bring along a female associate, saying she didn't need another woman around to judge her. I didn't debate the point and went alone.

We were having breakfast for lunch. No one was sitting nearby. The place wasn't busy. When I tasted the food, the reason for that became clear. The scrambled eggs were tasteless. The hashbrowns were yellow, and the bacon was floppy and dripping with grease. The toast was warmed-up bread.

Faith didn't seem to mind, eating fast and furious without talking, like she hadn't had a meal in days. When she finished, I pushed an envelope across the table. Inside was the cash she'd requested. She snatched it up, opened the flap, counted with her lips moving, then shoved it into the purse beside her on the bench.

"I signed one of those agreement things," she said. "Kind that says I'm not supposed to talk about Damon."

"An NDA," I said. "Non-disclosure agreement."

"Yeah, one of those," she said, pointing her finger at me. "Why you wanna know about him?"

"I'm trying to help a young woman. Keep her out of harm's way. She seems to be headed in his direction."

"Then you'll wanna turn her around. Damon Radburke is one sick motherfucker."

"In what way?"

"In every fucking way."

"Okay," I said, trying to summon my patience, already wishing I'd waited to pay her until after we'd talked. "Tell me about it."

"What part of it?"

"Your specific experience with him. What he did with you. In general, what he's done with other women he keeps. If you know."

"He hired two of us at the same time to work in his office. Girl named Patricia Palone was the other one. He set us up with nice clothes and jewelry to wear. We looked good, but we didn't really do much in the way of actual work."

"How did he find you?"

"We were both sent to him by our social worker. An old bat named Franny Lowell."

"Why you two?"

"I don't know. Patricia and me talked about that. We were both attractive. We had similar backgrounds. Fathers, boyfriends who beat the living crap out of us. "

"Anything else?"

"We'd both lived in slummy places our whole lives. Always wanted something better, I suppose."

"And he promised you both he could provide you with better accommodations?"

"He didn't just promise. He delivered. He moved us into his house in D.C. What a place. The best of everything. We didn't have to lift a finger. He had people to come in and do the cooking and cleaning and shit. Pretty soon, we didn't go into the office anymore."

"And what did he get in return?"

"We were both screwing him. If that's what you're getting at."

"Did that cause problems between you and Patricia?"

"Not at first. But after a while, it did. It started to feel like he was pitting the two of us against each other. Making us compete, like someone had to win."

"And how did the two of you react?"

"We went at it. With our mouths mostly, sometimes our fists. Usually, when he wasn't around. But the place had a lot of cameras, so he knew what was going on with us."

"So which of you won?"

"I guess I did. At least I thought so. One day, Patricia was gone. Damon said he'd paid her a lot of money to go away and leave us alone."

"You believe that?"

"At the time. Later, not so much. Not when I heard she was dead."

"When was that?"

"A few months after I got away from him."

"Why did you leave?"

"It was less leaving, more like escaping."

"That doesn't tell me why."

"He got controlling. I still had a lot of friends that I stayed in touch with. He didn't like that and started knocking me around. Locking me up in my room when he was gone. Took my phone away sometimes. And then the really weird stuff started."

"Weird? In what way?"

"There was a balcony at the top of the stairway at the front of the house. Up two floors. Really high. He'd make me climb over the railing and hang onto him by the hands. Dangling in the air. I'd beg for him to pull me up. I think that's the part he got off on. The begging him to save me."

"But he always did?"

"Yeah. But I didn't trust him. I was scared. Every time we did that, he'd make me hang there longer than the time before."

"So this odd behavior made you want to leave?"

"And he knew that. And he'd like…he'd push me into talking about wanting to leave. And then he'd fly into a rage. About how he'd saved me. Taken me away from an abusive life. Given me money and nice clothes to wear and a luxurious place to live. All without having to work. And then, when it looked like he'd calmed down, he'd start screaming again. That maybe he should just *let go of me*."

"Not *let you go*, but *let go of you?*"

"Yeah. That's why I got the hell out of there, first chance I got."

"But he found you?"

"His lawyer did. Guy named Laurelworth. Paid me a lot of money to keep my mouth shut. Not go to the cops or tell anybody what went on there. Sign the papers."

"And what about Patricia? You have any idea if she was offered a deal?"

"Mutual friends say she was. That she turned it down. Threatened to take Damon to court to try for more money than he was offering."

"You know anything about the circumstances of her death?"

"She was found at an illegal dump outside the city. Beaten to death. Just about every bone in her body was broken. Some drunk, mentally ill, homeless guy got tagged for it. Had her credit cards on him. Her underwear in his coat pocket."

"And no one pointed the finger at Damon?"

"A rich guy? You know how the system works. Even if someone did point to him, cops don't follow through, or the D.A. don't follow through. Someone gets some money along the way."

"And how long ago was all this?" I said.

"Three, four years ago," she said. "This is all off the record, like you said? Right? Damon's not gonna hear I talked?"

"Not from me," I said. "Here's my card. You think of anything else you'd like to share, give me a call."

Chapter Fifty-Two

A fter the hour-long drive back from Maryland, that included a stop for a pack of *Tums*, I spent a good part of the rest of the day sitting with my laptop at the kitchen counter. Looking deep into the nooks and crannies of every internet database to which I subscribed, for any information I'd previously missed on the subject of Damon Radburke. I didn't find much that seemed significant, beyond what I already knew.

I unearthed little things that you'd expect to find about people in general and wealthy people in particular. There were records of the various places he'd resided over the years. Property transfers for those homes. Old landline phone numbers, long since disconnected, no doubt. I found family information. Names of his parents, with birth and death dates for both in their obituaries. No record of any siblings. There were newspaper accounts of business mergers and acquisitions of buildings and properties near and far. Articles announcing new hirings in his investment company. There were photos and articles detailing generous donations he'd made to various local charities and worthy causes. Some were churches in and around the D.C. area.

On his own social front, there was little information. No records of marriage or divorce. No grand announcement of an engagement to a socially elite debutante, or any of lesser note. No gossip of being seen in public with anyone of importance. That is, nothing beyond his more recently publicized legal entanglements.

As far as I could tell, he'd appeared in court on a minor personal matter only once. Oddly enough, it had been here in Potomac County. A year ago, he'd been cited for speeding and driving in a reckless manner on a back road near a popular winery, out near the Rappahannock River side of the county. He'd passed a breathalyzer test, showed up for his court date, pled guilty, and paid the fine.

The only other thing I found out of the ordinary was an old, short article from a small-town newspaper in the western part of Virginia. The story gave a sparse description about two teenage witnesses to an accident involving a woman who'd fallen off a mountain trail in a state park. Damon Radburke had been reported as the one who stayed with the injured woman while his companion had gone for help. The other kid was named Noah Herzhaft. Both were identified as being from Washington, D.C. I couldn't find any kind of follow-up article that reported on the woman's condition or fate. The article read like it might have been heavily edited to fit into the available space. There was nothing in it that said whether or not the two teenage boys knew the injured woman.

In the middle of all that digging around, I put in a call to Murphy to update him on my recent activity. I told him about what I'd learned from Tevin Danisk and Faith Calyce. We set up a time to meet in his office the next day.

Wendi showed up at dusk, bearing a gift, a carton of organic strawberry ice cream imported from Oregon. It was too late in the day for me, but she retrieved the smallest bowl she could find from the kitchen cabinet and dug out a single scoop.

"You know," I said. "I don't think, in my entire life, I've ever eaten just one scoop of ice cream. How can you *do* that?"

"I've noticed," she said. "You're more of an eight-scoop guy. You have no willpower."

"Which you'll set me up to prove by leaving the rest of the carton here for me."

"Mmm. Oh my God. This is so good. You should try some now."

"I'm sure I will, tomorrow. And the next day. Until it's gone."

While she finished eating, I told her about my meeting with Faith Calyce.

"Dangling her off a balcony?" she said. "That's some sick shit."

"And that was three or four years ago. I think it's reasonable to assume that whatever his issues with women are, they haven't lessened with time."

"Yeah," she said. "People who don't get help with a problem tend to escalate. I'm no psychiatrist, but I'd be willing to bet that whatever he was into back then has probably gotten worse."

"And then there's the matter of Faith's friend and rival turning up dead."

"You think Damon Radburke killed her?"

"Maybe he had someone else do it. Could be the homeless guy really did do it."

"What about the guy with the red glasses?"

"Edik Levka. From what Tevin told me, it doesn't seem like he was in the picture at the time. He's a more recent acquaintance of Radburke. Doesn't mean there wasn't someone else working for Radburke back then."

"You do realize you're not obligated to pursue this any further? There are dangerous people hovering around here. Maybe it's time to step back. Tevin told you there are people looking into Radburke's affairs."

"Looking into the financial trail. Maybe other things. But who's looking out for Melissa Adamson? Even Kasey Dylan has given up on her."

"And that leaves you to look out for her? Even if she doesn't want it."

"Sometimes people are confused about what they want. They can't always see the danger in their choices."

"They can't solve their own problem, if they don't see the problem?"

"Exactly."

* * *

On Tuesday morning, I was sitting with Murphy in his office. There was a bottle of ketchup on his desk, but no food around. The lid was flipped open. I started to worry that he'd been shooting the stuff directly into his mouth. Maybe it was time for an intervention.

Our appointment was set for ten o'clock. I'd only been seven minutes late. I waited for him to point out my tardiness. He didn't. Maybe he was pondering an intervention for me. I would deny I had a problem. If I wasn't prompt, at least I was consistent.

"Got some news," Murphy said.

"Good news, I hope."

"In this business?"

"Okay."

"One of the names you gave me. Lexi Fincler. I tried different variations on the first name. Alexandria, Alexis, et cetera. We had the correct spelling of the last name. Turns out the first name was Alexa. She's dead. Her body was found in Paris."

"Paris, Virginia, or Paris, Texas?"

"No. *The* Paris. As in France."

"Yikes. How'd she get there?"

"On an airplane. Same one as Damon Radburke. Stayed in the same hotel. Adjacent rooms."

"How'd she die?"

"Beaten to death. Nearly every bone in her body was broken. Face was unrecognizable."

"I take it she didn't fall off the Eiffel Tower while sightseeing?"

"Doubtful."

"So, what was she beaten with?"

"The people in charge of the investigation are not releasing that particular detail."

"But you know?"

"Maybe. Maybe not."

"So that means it's something unique? Not just his fists. Something they might hope to find among the killer's possessions?"

"Maybe so."

"How'd they identify her?"

"Metal rod in her leg from a previous injury. Had a number on it. Traced it through the manufacturer back to the U.S."

"And Radburke was long gone by the time they figured out who she was and whose company she'd been keeping?"

"You got it. And the authorities have no proof whatsoever that he had anything at all to do with her death. No physical evidence. No DNA.

Nothing."

"They talk to Radburke?"

"Paris cops asked D.C. to question him. He claims they parted company in Paris. Came back without her. Claims he was no longer in touch with her. Says they parted on good terms."

"Not so good for her," I said. "You get a chance to look into the homeless guy accused of killing Patricia Palone up in D.C. a few years ago?"

"I did. Never went to trial. Hung himself in his cell shortly after his arrest. So they say."

"Adele's friend, Tevin Danisk, told me about the rough-looking guy with the red eyeglasses. Edik Levka is rumored to provide permanent solutions to temporary problems. You think Danisk didn't know about Radburke's connection with Lexi Fincler's case? Or Patricia Palone?"

"Wouldn't surprise me. Sometimes information doesn't get shared between law enforcement agencies the way it should. If they're focused on financial crimes, they might view the death of two women as less important. Or maybe that's one of the things he said he couldn't talk about. At least not in detail, or not yet. Who's he work for?"

"He didn't say."

"Oh. One of those."

"Seemed like an upright guy," I said. "I believe he might have a *thing* for your deputy."

"He can have all the *things* he can get. As long as he doesn't try to steal her from my posse. We're short-handed around here as it is."

I laughed out loud for a second.

"What?" he said.

"I've never heard you use the term *posse* before."

"What would you call a bunch of deputies?"

I thought for a moment.

"A posse it is," I said.

Chapter Fifty-Three

By midafternoon, I was thoroughly ensconced in an Adirondack chair out on my deck, trying to make some headway with *Chesapeake*. Through no fault of Michener's, the reading was going slow. I was back to having problems concentrating again, feeling guilty, thinking I should be spending my time trying to further my efforts to help Melissa Adamson find another pathway through life. When Adele Carter pulled up the driveway and got out of her cruiser, I marked my place and put down the book.

"You busy?" she said, climbing the steps.

"Not at all," I said. "Though it feels like I should be."

"Hard thing to do sometimes. Slow down."

"It is. What brings you out to the river?"

"Got a call, about half an hour ago. From Tevin. Asked me to pass along some information. I was close by, so I figured I'd do it in person."

"Glad you did. He didn't want to call me directly?"

"I think he was using it as an excuse to talk with me again," she said, trying but failing to suppress a smile.

"But you didn't mind. Did you?"

"Naw. I kind of like talking to him."

"Kind of reminds me of that guy you had a crush on back in high school. On the track team. What was his name?"

"Who? DeSean? Yeah, they do have a similar look. Sort of."

"Maybe you have a type."

"Well, Tevin and DeSean might be the same *physical* type. But that's where the similarity ends. DeSean is an idiot! You know, I had to arrest him once? About a year ago. Drunk and disorderly down at the Moon Tide Inn. Had to handcuff him and everything."

"I'll bet that was awkward."

"You know, it kind of was. Especially when he kept asking me for my number from the back seat of the cruiser, all the way to jail."

"He knew he'd missed out on something good. Trying to make up for lost time."

"And he kept asking Sheriff Murphy for my number. Right up until he got out on bail. Sheriff teased me about that for a month. Kept telling me he was going to call DeSean back in there, give him my number."

"Serves DeSean right for dumping you for that other girl."

"Cheryl Bookman? She did me a favor. The two of them deserved each other!"

"Things do happen for a reason," I said. "So what news do you bring from your special friend Tevin?"

"A name, with work and home addresses for a man he said might be able to give you some background on Damon Radburke. Feds interviewed the guy when they were looking into Radburke's past business dealings. Didn't get much from him. Felt like he was holding something back. They think it might be worthwhile for someone unofficial to take a run at him. Might have more to say, if it's off the record. Says the guy has known Radburke since they were kids. In high school."

Adele handed me a yellow sticky note with the information. The name printed on it in neatly formed letters was Noah Herzhaft. The other kid who'd been with Radburke at the scene of the accident with the woman on the mountain trail.

Chapter Fifty-Four

oah Herzhaft wasn't far away. He was living twenty miles up the road in the town of King's Crossing, not far from the naval base on the Potomac at Dahlgren, near the bridge that had recently carried me across the river to meet with Faith Calyce. He worked as a lawyer for a tech company with offices located in a brick building off US 301 near the entrance to the base. I'd found a picture of him online and was parked outside the building where he worked when he arrived at quarter to nine on Wednesday morning.

Herzhaft looked older than his mid-forties. His wavy hair and short-cropped beard were completely gray. His face was crisscrossed with deep lines and wrinkles, especially around the eyes and on his forehead. He was carrying a briefcase with a jacket draped across his other arm. A pack of cigarettes protruded from the pocket of his plaid, button-down, short-sleeve shirt. His work ID card hung from a blue lanyard draped around his neck.

Before he made it to the entrance, I stepped in front of him, introduced myself, and showed him my investigator's license. He seemed surprised, but not impressed. Maybe I should practice my delivery. When I asked if we could talk, he looked at his watch, said "Sure," and buzzed us in the front door. He escorted me down a narrow hallway to a tiny office with no windows. After closing the door behind us, he sat at his desk, and I parked myself in a metal and hard-plastic chair with minimal padding.

"What's this all about, Mr. Barrow?"

"I'm currently looking into the background of a man you know. I have reason to believe that a young woman with whom he is associated may be in danger."

"Damon Radburke," he sneered. "That's who you're talking about, right?"

"Didn't take you long to come up with his name," I said.

"I've known him a long time. Seen the way he acts with women. I've heard other things. From mutual friends. No one has ever accused him of being a gentleman. First, the cops come to talk to me about my business dealings with him, and now you show up asking questions."

"You seem irritated by that."

"I told them, and I'll tell you, I have nothing to do with Damon anymore."

"You mentioned *business dealings*. Did you do legal work for him?"

"A long time ago. Right after law school. Small matters. Nothing important."

"So you haven't worked for him recently?"

"Like I told the cops, no. Somehow, they knew he'd reached out to me about a year ago. He wanted to know if I would be interested in joining a legal team he was putting together."

"And you turned him down?"

"I did," he said.

"You mind if I ask why?"

"I do mind, but I'll tell you anyway. Frankly, I don't trust him. I'm an honest man with an honest source of income, and family and friends who respect me. I've heard about some of the questionable things he's into, and I want no part of it."

"What kind of things?"

"I would not feel comfortable making accusations that I couldn't back up with facts. Let's just say I've heard about acts that may be less than legal."

"Well, like what?"

"Look, Barrow. Damon has a lot of money. With money comes power and the ability to get away with things and put the screws to little people like me. I'm not about to say anything to you that he might end up suing me for. Or worse."

"You mean like getting you fired?"

"There are worse things than losing a job."

"You mean physical harm? To you, or your family?"

He didn't say anything. Just looked at me like I was stupid. I wanted to tell him I taught calculus.

After what seemed like a long minute of staring me down, he gave in and spoke again.

"You mentioned a woman," he said, sounding more conciliatory. "What's that got to do with me?"

"In my investigation, I came across an old newspaper article from when you and Damon were teenagers. The two of you were witnesses to an accident on a mountain trail that involved a woman. I'd like to know more about that."

"Why? You said you were concerned with someone he was associated with now."

"Because I'm looking to establish a pattern in Radburke's behavior toward women. Learning about his past may be relevant to the present. It might help me to convince a young woman that she may be placing herself in danger by getting involved with him."

"You're not interested in Damon's legal and financial affairs?"

"Only if it has bearing on his character issues. I'll leave dealing with those matters to the folks in law enforcement. So, the incident with the hiker? Can you tell me more? Off the record."

He stared at me for a moment, like maybe I wasn't a moron after all.

"Off the record?" he said. "Yeah. Maybe it's time I said something. I've never really talked to anyone about anything more than the facts about what happened that day. I had no right to accuse Damon of something I couldn't prove. Just a feeling."

"A feeling? About what?"

"About how maybe he could have saved that woman."

"Maybe it would be best for you to start from the beginning."

"Okay. Yeah. We were hiking the trail that day, going up the mountain. We hadn't gone very far. Maybe half a mile, or so, from the parking area. It was a steep climb. A woman was yelling for help. She'd fallen about twenty feet down a steep embankment off the side of the trail. Damon climbed down to her. She'd been hanging onto the roots of a tree. Damon grabbed hold of her arms, like he was ready to pull her up. To keep her from falling over the cliff.

"The woman kept begging Damon to save her. To pull her up. He kept telling her she'd be okay. That he had her. He would save her. Then he yelled up to me and told me to go back down the trail to the parking area to get help from the people we'd seen down there. So I did what I was told. When I was almost to the bottom, I met up with some other hikers headed up the trail. They had a rope and gear for rappelling. But when we all got back up to the site, the woman was gone. She'd fallen nearly a hundred feet to the rocks below. Damon was just sitting there. He looked like he was in shock. When the professional rescuers arrived and got down to her, the woman was still alive. Barely. She died two days later in the hospital."

"And you told all this to the authorities at the time?" I said.

"Yes, yes. Of course."

"And the part you didn't tell anyone?"

"Damon had her. All he had to do was pull her up. He was a strong guy. She wasn't a big woman."

"A lot of things could've gone wrong," I suggested. "The woman could have panicked. Struggled to climb up herself. Caused him to lose his grip."

"Sure. I thought about that possibility. And that's pretty much the way Damon laid it out to the cops. But on the ride back to D.C. in the car, I was driving, and he was just so animated and excited about the whole incident. He just kept talking about it, over and over again. He wasn't sad or upset about what had happened to that poor woman. It was like he was high on something. He wasn't upset with himself for losing his grip on her. Not concerned she was in bad shape and probably not going to make it. He was just *thrilled* from the whole incident. Like he got a big rush from it."

"You believe he might have let go of her, or even pushed her?"

"I don't know. He was a sick fuck. Sicker than anyone knew."

"Anything else?"

"Couple of days later, after we'd heard the woman had died. We were sitting around in his basement, drinking a couple of beers we'd pinched from his parents' fridge. And Damon starts talking about the whole thing again. And he's laughing hysterically about how maybe it would be *fun* for us to go to the funeral. Wondering if it would be an open casket."

"But you didn't go to the funeral. Did you?"

"I didn't," he said. "Him? I don't know. After that, I didn't hang out with him much for a while."

Chapter Fifty-Five

By eleven o'clock on Thursday morning, we were parked in the lot beside a ten-story office building in the District. The engine was still running, and the air conditioning was blowing hard and cold.

"You're sure you want to do this?" Wendi said.

"No. I'm not," I said. "But I figure it's worth a shot."

"Mostly because you can't think of anything else to do?"

"There's that."

"You think it'll do any good? For Melissa?"

"He turned Lettie Midland loose. When he thought the cops might be looking for her."

"Did he? You don't know that for sure. It could've been Joan Flaith who kicked her out. Could've been her decision. Not Damon Radburke himself. You don't know how much she tells him."

"Maybe so. He might not be a micromanager. But I get the feeling he's the one who decides which girls to keep. The one laying out the criteria for continuing in the program."

Inside the lobby, we checked the directory on the wall and took the otherwise unoccupied elevator to the third floor.

"Is there an elevator in all of Potomac County?" I asked on the way up.

Wendi pondered my question for a moment.

"I've never seen one," she said, as the doors opened. "Maybe in the Courthouse. And there are only two traffic lights. In case that was your next question."

We found the office with *Radburke Investments* etched on the frosted-glass door and went in. The secretary seated at the front desk was young and pretty. She was wearing a lime-green sleeveless dress with a plunging neckline. Her perfectly shaped lips were outlined in fire-engine-red lipstick.

"May I help you?" she said.

"We'd like to see Mr. Radburke, please," I said.

"Do you have an appointment?" she said.

"No. But it's important that we see him."

"I'm sorry. Mr. Radburke isn't in the office today."

"That's funny," Wendi said. "We saw him walk into the lobby about fifteen minutes ago."

She seemed flustered and shuffled the papers on her desk, looking for something to grab onto. She decided on a pen and turned over a piece of paper to write on.

"What are your names?" she said, trying her best to sound indignant.

I handed her my business card. Her eyebrows raised and arched. She looked at it, and her eyes widened. Maybe I'd finally managed to impress someone.

"My associate is Miss Wynston," I said.

"And what is the reason for your visit, Mr. Barrow?"

"We're here to discuss the safety of a woman named Melissa Adamson."

"And the police investigation looking into her whereabouts," Wendi added.

She picked up the phone on her desk and punched a button. Nothing happened. She looked confused and punched another one. I heard a faint male voice on the other end. She gave our names and repeated, more or less, what we'd said. I couldn't make out his response until he got to the last word. It came through loud and clear. "Security."

She hung up the phone. "I'm sorry. Mr. Radburke has a full schedule this morning and is not available to see you."

"How about this afternoon?" I said.

"I…I don't…"

"Or tomorrow?" Wendi said. "We don't have anything scheduled for Friday, do we, Mr. Barrow?"

She grimaced and picked up the phone again.

"You'll have to leave now," she said, deepening her shaky voice, trying to sound authoritative. "I'm...I'm calling Security."

By the time she started talking into the phone, we were on our way out the door.

* * *

That evening, we enjoyed a leisurely late meal at the restaurant in the popular but pricey Weston Inn. After dinner, we stayed to while away the hours seated at a booth in the soothingly dim light of the basement tavern. A flow of friends and acquaintances, including some former students and colleagues, past and present, stopped by for a quick *hello*, or to sit and chat for a while. Back in one corner, a rousing game of *Trivial Pursuit* was in progress. Up at the bar, a waitress was performing card tricks for a group of six tourists who barked out their amazement in what sounded like Chicago accents.

In our time alone, we managed to avoid the topic that undoubtedly occupied our thoughts. Opting instead for unresolved discussions of where and when we might travel when the unmentioned situation at hand reached its conclusion. One way or another.

To our waitress's disappointment, we sipped our drinks slowly all evening. Wendi's wine was a Petit Verdot from a local vineyard. I'd skipped all the fancy microbrew offerings, opting instead for the only domestic beer they had on tap. I stopped altogether an hour before we left. It was my turn to drive.

* * *

The clouds that night were thick and dark. The air was sticky, and the wind minimal. No moon was visible. Outside the cabin, there was little light. Far across the water on the opposite shore, distant twinkles of light hung on the horizon like fallen stars retreated from the ominous sky above.

We sat in the car and talked for a minute or so. About what, I don't remember. My porchlight wasn't working, and I hadn't left any lights on inside. I pulled out my phone and punched at the app that was programmed to control the lamp up in the loft. When I turned it on, adequate light spilled out onto the deck from inside, through the glass doors and windows above. Seconds later, still inside the car, we heard the muffled sound of shattering glass and saw the simultaneous spray of fragments burst from a window above the sliding doors.

I yelled at Wendi to stay down and get out to the ground behind the wall of landscaping stones. From there, lying on opposite sides of the vehicle, we heard two more shots, coming from somewhere out on the river. One hit the front fender of Wendi's car, parked ahead of us in the driveway. The second shot shattered a glass door.

Then it was over. And we heard the roaring retreat of a boat engine, trailing away in the darkness.

Chapter Fifty-Six

"I've notified the Coast Guard," Murphy said. "Gonna be hard to find any kind of witness. Not many people out on the water this late at night. Unless it's the weekend."

"Maybe a dedicated fisherman," I said. "Heavy-duty partiers."

"Or a couple out for a romantic night-sail," Wendi added.

We both gave her a look, but didn't comment.

"What?" she said. "It happens. Not that either of *you* would ever think of it."

It was past two o'clock in the morning. The deputies had finished their work and were heading out. I'd called a guy I knew who lived down the shore in Tusker's Beach. He worked construction and had what I needed to secure the cabin. We'd just finished nailing the last of the plywood over the shattered windows and door. The place looked like a Florida home battened down for a coming hurricane.

"You think this was a warning?" Murphy said. "Or an actual attempt on your lives?"

"Hard to say. Tough shot to make from a swaying boat," I said. "No matter how good you are."

"You think this was Radburke?" Murphy said.

"More likely the guy he's got working for him. We were at Radburke's office this morning. Attempting to scare him off Melissa Adamson."

"Looks like he might not have taken it too well. You piss anyone else off lately? Besides me."

"Not that I'm aware," I said.

"He's often not *aware* of who he's pissed off, Oscar," Wendi said.

"Your homeowner's insurance gonna cover this?"

"My agent once told me it covers damage from anything that comes out of the sky," I said. "Isn't that where the bullets came from?"

"You're not staying here tonight?" Murphy said.

"No. We'll be at Wendi's apartment."

"I'll post a deputy outside," he said. "Just in case."

"Be pretty dumb for someone to make another try at a place across the street from the Sheriff's office."

"Criminals these days are more bold than smart," he said.

** * **

When we left Wendi's building the next morning, Deputy Runyon Pugh was still outside on guard duty, leaning against his cruiser, sipping what I assumed was coffee from a tall, tapered travel mug. I waved and shouted a *thank you*. He acknowledged with a nod, then turned and started to trudge across the courthouse lawn toward the Sheriff's Department building. He didn't look all that happy about having spent the night in our defense. Maybe he was still brooding over that C-minus in Algebra.

Wendi and I had decided to switch cars for the day. She was off to spend most of the day with friends. We both had errands to run, though some of mine were, by far, more pressing. The shot to her front fender looked bad, but as far as I could tell, it hadn't done any serious damage to the vehicle's capacity to function. But then, what I knew about cars wasn't much. I'd need to consult a professional.

My first stop was the insurance company office. I told the agent about what had happened at the cabin, keeping the details on a need-to-know basis. When I came back out and crossed the street, there was a dark SUV with D.C. plates and tinted windows parked four spaces behind my car. The windows were too dark to get a good look at the driver. But from what I could see, he was wearing eyeglasses. The shape of his head suggested it might be Edik Levka behind the wheel. Maybe those eyeglasses were red.

From there, I drove a mile out of town to the local glass repair outfit. A couple of decades back, I'd taught the owner. Like Pugh, he'd been a C student. But as far as I remembered, he was always happy to see me, never being the type to harbor a grudge. He promised to get a crew out to my place right away and coordinate with the insurance company. When I headed back into town, I spotted the dark SUV, trailing two cars back.

My next stop was the barber shop. There was no one ahead of me. I got a trim that didn't take long. Truth be told, there's not that much left to cut.

Next was a stop at the Weston Market for a bag of food to take back to Wendi's. I went back to her apartment and put away the groceries. When I went out again, he was still there, parked up the street, out of view of the Sheriff's office. I didn't think the guy was stupid enough to take a shot at me in broad daylight in front of witnesses. If I thought that was a probability, I would've called Murphy. Like the shots fired in the night, I figured this was all about trying to scare me. And I had to admit, to some degree, it was working. At that point, I hoped I was wearing him down. Maybe my next two stops, at the bank and post office, would be enough to lull him off to sleep. Or better yet, bore him to death.

But of course, it didn't. He stuck with me through those stops and another at the pharmacy. After that, he followed me to the body shop at the car lot, out along the highway on the south side of town. The place was a full-service facility for all things automotive. They fixed engines, replaced tires, did body work, sold and rented cars. I was a frequent rental customer when sleuthing around, trying not to be noticed. But this time the tables had been turned. It was me being followed, and I didn't like it. I was starting to get irritated.

After a long chat with the owner of the place, Skip Partter, I swapped Wendi's vehicle for the same older model, gray Toyota Corolla, I'd rented before. When I pulled back out onto the highway and checked the rearview mirror, my tail was still with me.

I decided to make things a little more exciting and took him on a cruise down Durn Road, past Joan Flaith's house. Her kid, Alex, was outside with his shirt off, wearing a cowboy hat, riding a John Deere tractor, mowing the lawn. I honked and waved as I drove by. He didn't seem to notice. I made a few turns and looped back into town to Wendi's place to make a late lunch. When I parked the car, my shadow in the SUV was gone. Maybe I'd managed to bore him to death after all.

* * *

It was dark and close to eleven when I left the apartment. Hours before, I'd called Wendi and told her to stay at her friend's place until I called again. The air was still and humid, and the street was quiet. A single car rolled by and took a cautious turn at the next corner. Birds fluttered in the branches above, and a pair of squirrels scampered along the sidewalk.

I got behind the wheel of the Corolla and placed my grandfather's service revolver on the passenger seat beside me. I started up the car and headed out toward the south side of town. Another car pulled out behind me, moving slower, staying back. When I got to the car lot, the chain across the driveway entrance was up. I got out, unhooked the chain, and dropped it to the ground. It hadn't been locked. I drove in along the side of the building, further on to the open center of the lot, and looped around, aiming my headlights toward the entrance. I was surrounded on the other three sides by tightly packed rows of parked vehicles, mostly SUVs and pickups, arranged in a U-shape, facing inward. Their dormant headlights watching me like sleepy eyes, waiting for something to happen. Over on the corner wall of the building, next to an office window, was the night drop box for keys. The spotlights that usually illuminated the lot were off.

The dark SUV that had tailed me for most of the day crept along the building and into the lot with its headlights off, its dull orange parking lights on. I left my own headlights on but shut off the car. I picked up the gun from the seat beside me, tucking it into the waistband of my jeans as I rose from the car.

Edik Levka got out of the dark vehicle and stepped into the light. He adjusted his signature red-framed eyeglasses and squinted as he approached. I moved and stood angled sideways between the headlights of the Corolla.

The handle of my gun was clearly visible above my belt.

"Mr. Barrow," he said. "We must talk."

As he stepped closer toward me, I could make out the shape of a holstered gun mounted high on his waist under his untucked, half-buttoned shirt. He probably weighed close to twice as much as me and stood at least a foot taller. His shaved head glowed in the bright light, and the red frames of his eyeglasses looked like they were on fire. Continuing to move closer, he made no move for his gun but focused his skewed eyes on the handle of my weapon.

"I see you have a gun," he said. "Let me see it."

In one smooth motion, he closed the three-foot gap between us and snatched away the revolver with one hand while simultaneously stiff-arming me with the other, slamming me back and down onto the hood of the Corolla.

"Such a big gun for such a little man," he said, examining the revolver like a curiosity plucked from the shelf of an antique toy store. "And old like you. Does it even work?"

"It does," I said, still lying on the hood of the car, clutching at my back in pain.

"Good. Then maybe I kill you with it," he laughed. "But maybe not. If you promise to be nice, little old man. Leave Mr. Radburke's business with the women alone."

When he lowered the gun and pointed it in my direction, headlights flashed on from all three sides, and the floodlights on the side of the building came on.

"Police!" Murphy shouted, stepping into the light. "Drop the weapon now!"

At the same time, four deputies maneuvered out from between the parked vehicles with their long weapons pointed at Levka. Without hesitation, he released his grip on the gun and dropped it to the ground.

I got up from the hood of the car and kicked the gun away. Two of the deputies moved forward and instructed him to raise his hands behind his head and lower himself to the ground. Deputy Pugh removed the gun from the holster on Levka's belt. After cuffing him, it took three deputies to get him back on his feet and guide him toward the Sheriff's vehicle.

"I'll be out by morning!" he shouted. "I have good lawyer. You will see!"

"I wouldn't count on it, Mr. Levka," Murphy said. "You assaulted Mr. Barrow here and stole his gun. You threatened his life. We have it all on tape. Video and audio."

"This entrapment!"

"Not at all, Mr. Levka. We just happened to be parked here on a stakeout. Trying to catch some catalytic converter thieves plaguing the area. Got an anonymous tip they'd be here tonight. Mr. Barrow was just here to drop off his rental car."

"This bullshit!" he screamed, as the deputies wrestled him into the back seat.

"Read him his rights," Murphy ordered. "Make sure you record it. Then search his car. Let's see what else we can find."

Chapter Fifty-Seven

It was well past midnight by the time we got back to Murphy's office. I waited alone while he took care of business. Levka had made the call to his lawyer and was relaxing in the luxury of his cell, feeling calm and confident about his future. He was most likely counting on money to win out over justice. I wasn't so sure that would happen this time.

When Murphy joined me in his office, he was somewhat less than happy with me.

"How's your back?" he snarled.

"Hurts a little. But I'll live," I said. "Thanks for asking."

"You disobeyed my instructions," he said. "I told you not to bring the gun. He could've used his own weapon to shoot you as soon as he saw it. Tried to claim self-defense."

"You're not the boss of me," I said, doing my best impression of an insolent teenager.

"This isn't funny."

"I know. But it all worked out. He took it from me. Just like I figured he would."

"He could have shot you with your own gun before we had a chance to make our move. You consider that?"

"I did. That's why it wasn't loaded."

"God! You *really* piss me off sometimes."

"His taking the gun added another charge or two. Didn't it?"

"It did add to the many. We found other weapons in his vehicle. We're checking to see if any are illegal or stolen. Also found a bag of pills that looks to be an illegal substance. Preliminary search of the vehicle turned up some stains in the cargo area that could be blood. Been in touch already with the higher authorities. They're interested in tearing apart his vehicle. Using their well-funded resources to help out. Maybe take him off the county's hands, if they can dig up some federal charges."

"Looks like Mr. Levka got a little careless."

"No doubt he underestimated us country folk."

"A bumpkin sheriff," I said.

"And a schoolteacher P.I.," he said.

"Who'da thunk it?"

* * *

An hour later, I was across the street, alone at Wendi's apartment, trying to doze off to sleep. While at Murphy's office, I'd texted Wendi that she might as well spend the rest of the night with her friend, telling her all would be explained in the morning. She didn't respond, so I figured she was asleep.

When my phone startled me awake, I didn't feel like I'd been out that long. I rolled over and picked the phone off the nightstand, squinting at the screen to see who was calling at 3:11 A.M.

It was Kasey Dylan.

I sat up on the edge of the bed and rubbed at my face with my free hand.

"Kasey?" I said. "What's wrong?"

She was talking fast and loudly, almost hysterical. "Mr. Barrow, I've heard from Melissa. She asked if we could come and get her."

"Did she sound frightened?"

"We didn't talk. She texted. Said she couldn't risk being heard."

"Did she say what prompted this?"

"She heard cars arriving. Then voices in the library. When she went to the door to listen, she heard men arguing with Joan. She recognized one of the voices. It was Fordy. She asked why he would be there. I told her I wasn't sure, but didn't believe she was safe. That's when she asked if we could come for her."

"Look," I said, struggling to think. "I'll go over there to the estate as soon as I can. You're forty miles from here. Even further on over to Dominion County. You think you could find your way alone, meet me there?"

"Yes. I have the address from when we were there. I'll use GPS. But I won't be able to leave right away."

"That's okay. Get there when you can. You think she would trust me enough to leave with me alone?"

"I don't know. Maybe," she said. "I could text her back. Tell her I'm sending you."

"Do that," I said. "I'll see you when you get there. Keep in touch, if anything changes. I'll do the same."

It looked like I was back on the payroll. Sleep deprived, but once again, gainfully employed.

Chapter Fifty-Eight

By the time the sky was beginning to lighten, I was on the road that led to the Karruth estate. I made a quick call to Wendi to let her know what was happening. I hadn't called Murphy. Dominion County was out of his jurisdiction. Besides that, he was already pissed at me. Depriving him of sleep, just to let him know what I was up to, wouldn't get me back in his good graces.

I was still driving the rented Corolla. When I pulled up to the gate, it was closed. But this time, someone had taken an extra step to secure it. There was a rusted chain wrapped around the metal bars, and a padlock anchoring the two sides together. I got out of the car and rattled the gate. It wasn't going anywhere.

I drove the car on down the road and pulled into the rutted driveway that led to Willis Moleville's house. It was still mostly dark under the trees, and quiet except for the musical chatter of morning birds and the intermittent grating sound of the bottom of the car scraping against the ground.

His car was parked by the house, and the porchlight was on. I knocked on the door, but no one came. I tried the knob, and the door opened. Inside, I switched on the kitchen light and made my way to the living room. He was there on the couch, still dressed in his clothes, sound asleep, half-reclined with a game controller in hand. On the coffee table, there were bent empty beer cans and an open pizza box with two slices pulled apart. One had a bite out of it. Flies had gathered to dine on what remained.

When I turned on a lamp, he stirred, but didn't wake. I said his name a few times. His eyes half opened, and he turned on his side, facing away from me. He made a grumbling sound that resembled human speech. It took a moment for my brain to register that he'd whined, "Whata you waaaaant?"

I opened my wallet and started to toss bills of various denominations onto his face. Maybe the smell of money would revive him. I kept repeating, "Wake up, Willis. I need your help."

Twenty minutes later, he was fully revived, due mostly to coffee, but the smell of money hadn't hurt. After all that, it didn't take long for him to get the drone aloft. At his insistence, I'd had to guarantee to pay for the replacement of his equipment if it got blasted out of the sky again. I held onto my wallet and prayed.

After leaving the apartment that morning, I'd gone back to the cabin for a quick second look at the video footage Willis had sold me before. I knew the general layout of the estate. What I was looking for now was any change or movement around the place.

On the screen in front of us, we saw no cars parked near the house or in the driveway near the garage. It was still early, but no one seemed to be out and about.

"Buzz that thing closer to the house," I said. "Around the windows. Up and down."

"Okay," he said. "But if anything happens…"

"I know. I know. Just do it."

In the glare of the morning light, we could see nothing inside through some of the uncovered windows. In many of the rooms, the drapes had been drawn closed. No one was up for an early morning skinny-dip in the glass atrium-enclosed indoor pool. I knew Willis would be disappointed. At my instruction, he pulled the drone back away from the house, and we waited, half-expecting a provoked Phil Trunvid to come charging out of the house with his trusty shotgun. It didn't happen.

I had Willis maneuver the drone to survey the rest of the property, down to the beach beyond the trees, and back to the other end, to the garage near the gate. Nothing and no one.

I needed to get in there.

Chapter Fifty-Nine

Surrounding the entire Karruth estate was an eight-foot iron fence with thick, rounded spires spaced six inches apart and sharp-spiked finials on top. Here and there were signs warning potential trespassers that the fence was electrified. Climbing it was physically out of the question, not to mention beyond legal.

When I got Simon Wadsworth on the phone, he was still at home.

"What is it you want, Peter?" he said, sounding exasperated. "So early on a Saturday morning. You've interrupted my breakfast."

"I need your help to get permission to go onto a property owned by Charles Karruth, Senior."

"And just how do you expect me to help with that?"

"You said you know him. I need to talk with him."

"I said I *know* him. We're not *close*. I don't have his private number."

"But you know people who can get it for you?"

"You do know the man is in Europe?"

"Last time I checked, they still had phones over there."

"All right, all right," he said. "I'll make some calls."

"This *is* urgent," I said. "A woman's safety is at stake."

"Yes, yes. I get it. I'll do it now. You've ruined my appetite anyway."

Twenty minutes later, I was still parked outside the estate when Wadsworth called back with Karruth's number.

"You've made me late for my golf game, you know."

"Sorry about that," I said. "I do appreciate your help."

"Our working relationship needs to get back to its proper order. *You* working for *me*. Not the other way around."

"Be patient, Simon. We'll get there soon."

By the time I thanked him again for his help, he'd already hung up.

When I called Karruth's number, he didn't pick up. I left a message explaining who I was and how I'd obtained his number. I thought it worthwhile to add a comment naming his son as being a person of interest in my current investigation.

He called back ten minutes later, sounding cool and guarded. I tried to present the situation in as simple and tactful a way as possible.

"My son and I have a strained relationship," he explained. "Frankly, I've cut him off financially and otherwise. Now what's he got to do with your search for some woman?"

"It has to do with your estate in Dominion County, sir. You're paying a company called Old Dominion Services to manage the property for you. Your son is one of the owners of that company. So, in essence, part of the money you're paying is going to him."

"So that slimy little son of a bitch found a way to keep bleeding money from me!"

"It appears so," I said. "In your absence, the property is also being used by a group that claims to offer shelter and counseling for battered women."

"Battered women? My son wouldn't give a fuck about a cause like that. He's a narcissistic piece of shit who never gave two hoots for anyone but himself!"

"My investigation so far has led me to believe the situation is not what it appears to be."

"Then what the hell is it?"

"I have some ideas, but I'm not quite sure yet. The main reason I'm calling now is because a woman I was hired to locate sent a message to my client that she was on the property and wanted to leave. I need your permission to cut the chain off the front gate in order to enter the premises and retrieve the woman, if she's still there. I believe her to be in danger of physical harm."

"Chain on the front gate? What the fuck! You do anything you *goddamn* have to do to get in there! And I'm sending other people there as soon as I can to take over management. You tell anyone on the property that I said to get the hell out of there now!"

Before we ended the call, I convinced Karruth to get in contact with the Dominion County Sheriff's Department to let them know what was happening. If the place had an automatic alarm that notified authorities, the last thing I needed was a trespassing accusation slowing me down.

* * *

Newton Utt, the Dominion County sheriff, was not pleased to meet me when he and the deputy he neglected to introduce arrived in separate vehicles at the gate of the Karruth estate. He'd been ordered there by one of the county supervisors, a close friend of Charles Karruth, Sr.

I avoided mentioning my association with Oscar Murphy, Utt's deputy-stealing nemesis.

"This ain't really a legal matter," Utt grumbled. "This woman you're here for didn't call 911. A call to a friend for a ride ain't exactly an emergency."

"I appreciate your assistance, Sheriff," I said.

"I ain't doing it for you."

Wendi pulled up along the side of the road, just as the deputy was retrieving a set of twenty-four-inch bolt cutters from the trunk of his car.

"Where's Kasey?" she said.

"I don't know," I said. "She should've been here by now. I've called her a half-dozen times, left multiple messages. She's not answering."

Sheriff Utt reached up and snapped off the padlock with the bolt cutters. His deputy unwrapped the chain and dropped it on the ground off the driveway. Utt pulled a piece of paper from the shirt pocket of his uniform and punched a security code into the keypad mounted on a stone pillar. The gate slid open, and in we all went. Wendi rode with me, following the two official vehicles as they proceeded up the long driveway to the front of the house.

At the front door, Utt punched in another code, and we all entered. Inside, the place was quiet and cool. The four of us went in different directions, calling out as we moved along from one empty room to the next. No one was there.

Wendi found a bedroom with women's clothes in the drawers and hanging in the closet. She recognized the outfit that Melissa had been wearing on the day of our meeting with her, Joan Flaith, and Karl Bassle.

When the fruitless search was over, we all assembled in the foyer, ready to leave. Utt sent his deputy out to look over the grounds, while he fumbled with multiple tries at resetting the alarm. It was then that I spotted it. Lying on its side, on the floor next to a chair in a room just off the foyer. It was the purse that Kasey had given Melissa.

I walked over, picked it up, and pulled out the false bottom. Still nestled in its hiding place was the burner phone. I pulled it out. It wasn't locked, so I punched up the texts and read the last chain of messages sent. They were exactly as Kasey had described. A plea for help.

I slipped the phone into my pocket, and we left. All the way home, I wondered where Melissa was now and what had become of Kasey.

Chapter Sixty

Late in the afternoon, we were back at the cabin. I was on the phone with Tevin Danisk for the second time that day. I'd called him earlier to ask if he would check with his contacts on the current whereabouts of Damon Radburke.

"As far as anyone knows, he's not at his home in D.C. or at his office building," he said. They admitted to losing track of him. Having '*temporarily misplaced him*' was the way it was phrased."

"If their investigation is concentrated on his finances," I said, "then I suppose they don't care to know where he is every minute of the day."

"I know the guy in charge of the Radburke case. He's good at what he does, but just between you and me, he's pretty much a bullheaded asshole. Likes to be the man in charge. Resents interference."

"Especially from a small-town P.I.?"

"He was happy enough about you and the Potomac Sheriff's Department getting Levka locked up. Thought it was funny. I'm sorry, Mr. Barrow, but he and his people don't seem overly concerned about the safety of one woman. As callous as that might seem. They're building a case against his financial crimes. That's their priority. He strongly suggested that you stand back. Let them handle Radburke in their own way, on their own timeline."

"I'm betting they don't work nights and weekends."

"I know none of this is what you were hoping to hear."

"It's not. I believe Radburke has Melissa Adamson. That he intends to harm her, or worse. I need to find them. I suppose knowing where *not* to look helps. A little."

"You find yourself in urgent need of backup, call me."

I didn't bother to tell him that I couldn't get in touch with Kasey Dylan either.

***

By the time Wendi and I got to Fredericksburg, it was close to eight in the evening. We drove directly over to the Dylan house on Hawke Street. There were no cars in the driveway. I knocked long and hard on the door and rang the bell, but no one came. Once again, I was aware of the presence of the doorbell camera. This time, I wasn't trying to avoid it. I wanted Rutherford Dylan to know I was there. Looking for Kasey. Looking for him.

We drove over to Kasey's parents' house on the other side of town. She'd given me the address when she moved out of the house she'd shared with Fordy. The place was stately and old and reeked of money. There were security cameras all around, but no one appeared to be home there either. We peeked through the garage windows, looking for Kasey's car, but didn't see it.

Twenty minutes later, we'd made our way through the heavy Saturday night traffic, back across town to Lornewood Avenue. It was starting to get dark. We were parked across the street from Karl Bassle's place on its corner lot. The house was dark, and Bassle wasn't answering his phone. His Mercedes was in the driveway, but the Range Rover was gone.

I took a walk past the house and around the corner. As far as I could tell, there was only one security camera, down low enough above the back door for me to reach it if I stepped up on a bench. The camera looked old. I wondered if it was in working order, or just there to act as a deterrent to unscrupulous people like me.

I went back to the car, and we sat for a while with the windows down. The neighborhood was quiet. A heavy woman in a red tank top and too-short shorts waddled by with her tiny dog on a leash. Squirrels scampered among the trees, and rabbits nibbled on lawns.

Earlier in the day, I'd briefed Wendi on what had transpired on the previous night with Edik Levka at the car lot. She'd been peeved with me over putting myself in such a dangerous position. I got the silent treatment for a couple of hours, but after a while, she let it go. So far, she'd avoided bringing up the subject again.

We sat in the car for a while longer, waiting in silence for full darkness to set in. I needed to get inside Bassle's house to take another look at something I'd seen on my previous visit.

"Did you bring your gun with you?" she asked.

"*God no,*" I said. "Why would I do that?"

"Where is it?"

"Levka's locked up. I don't need it."

"Answer the question."

"Murphy has it. Said he needed to keep it for a while. It's evidence."

"So you have nothing to use to defend yourself?"

"I have you."

"You do."

"Wait. Don't tell me you brought *your* gun?"

"Okay. I won't tell you."

"Great. You *do* know we don't need it? No one will be shooting at us this evening. Levka's in jail. He's been taken out of the equation."

"But for how long? A good lawyer might get him out. For all we know, he could be out now."

"Murphy would've called me."

"And we don't know for sure that it was him who fired the shots out at the cabin."

"It was him."

"You're sure?"

"Educated guess."

"A bad education and a bullet could get you killed."

"Can we talk about this later? I'm about to perform my first *breaking and entering.* You know how nerve-wracking a first time can be."

She dropped the subject, and I figured it was time to move.

I told Wendi to stay in the car and watch for trouble. She didn't like the idea, but agreed it was best. After retrieving a plastic grocery bag from the trunk and slipping into a dark jacket, I made my way around to the rear of the house, staying close against the wall, hoping I was out of sight of the camera as I climbed the steps to the porch.

I'd spent most of my adult life carefully weighing the potential consequences before making a major decision. If I got caught here, the fallout was certain to include an abrupt retirement. The Potomac County School Board would not look favorably upon one of its teachers being arrested on a B & E charge. I could live with that. Maybe it was time anyway. My P.I. license would be yanked as well. I'd have a lot of free time on my hands. But Karl Bassle was likely involved in a multitude of illegal activities. I was fairly certain that pressing charges against someone who'd broken into his home, just to look around, would not rank as a high priority on his legal to-do list.

Behind the trees, the light from the street was minimal. I used my foot to reach out and snag the bench I'd spotted earlier, dragging it over to me against the wall by the door. I stepped up onto the bench and slid the bag over the camera. When I tied a knot in the bag to keep it in place, I felt something that could've been a loose wire. After all that trouble, the damn thing probably didn't even work.

I got down and tried the door. As expected, it was locked, but the handle was loose and rattled when I shook it. The door was old and flimsy. I pushed hard against it, and it moved a little. I slammed my shoulder into it, but it still held. I wasn't so sure about my shoulder.

I took off my jacket, wrapped it around my elbow, and slammed it against the pane of glass above the doorknob. It broke on the second try. After chipping away the shards of glass with the jacket, I reached inside and turned the knob. The door opened, and no alarm sounded.

Once inside, I made my way to the living room. Discovering the shades and curtains were already drawn closed, I turned on a lamp and tramped down the hallway towards the bathroom. I switched on the hall light and found the framed photograph I'd seen before.

It was the picture of Karl Bassle and the rest of the greed of lawyers, standing with Damon Radburke on a dock in front of a yacht. To my disappointment, the back of the boat with the name of the vessel was not visible. The hull identification number wasn't in the photo either.

I said "Shit" out loud to myself, and started looking around for more pictures of Radburke that might offer a clue as to where he might have made off to with Melissa Adamson in tow.

On a bedroom wall, I found two more framed photos with Radburke in them. But nothing of significance was included in the images. Upstairs, I checked the rest of the framed photos mounted all over the walls in the hallway and two other bedrooms. Nothing.

The last room on the second floor was his office. A small, adjacent bathroom had been converted into a darkroom. It was neat and organized, with all the chemicals and supplies put away in their proper places. A layer of dust made me think it hadn't been used in a while. Back out in the office, there was a table with storage boxes of photos stacked on top. The boxes looked like miniature filing cabinets. I pulled one open and found at least a hundred photos inside. There were a dozen boxes. It didn't take a calculus teacher to figure out how long it would take to go through all of them.

I pulled out my phone and called Wendi.

"Everything okay out there?" I said, in an unnecessary whisper.

"Yeah. No one around. I can see you have a light on inside, but nothing else. You find what you were looking for?"

"I did, but it didn't pan out. I found something else that needs to be looked through, but it'll take some time. Think you could come in and help?"

* * *

Nearly an hour later, we were still at it, having gone through most of the boxes of photos without finding anything that might lead us to the possible whereabouts of Damon Radburke. There were certainly enough photos of him. Many in the company of Rutherford Dylan. Most looked like they'd been snapped when Radburke wasn't looking. The pictures gave the impression that Bassle looked up to the man, wanted to capture as many images as he could of the *great man* in action. The term *hero worship* came to mind. Some of the photos had been shot in conference rooms and other business-like settings. But many had been captured at places outside, in casual settings like the picture in front of the boat.

Wendi got weary of searching and took a break. She stood up and stretched, then went over to Bassle's desk, sat down in the wheeled chair, and spun around. On the bookshelf behind the desk, against the wall, there were three cameras. She picked up the only digital one, powered it on, and began to scroll through the photos stored on its memory card.

She made an odd sound, and I turned my head in her direction, careful not to move my hands and lose my place.

"Pete," she said. "Come look at this."

The picture she'd found was that of an old church. A man who could've been Radburke was in the photo, turned away from the camera, his face in half-profile. Standing next to him was a woman wrapped in a green-plaid winter coat, accessorized with a matching knit hat and gloves. The trees in the photo seemed to be in the stages of an early-spring bloom. The digital time stamp on the screen indicated the picture was from late March of the current year. On the right side of the image was a cemetery. The headstones looked old, and some were tilted at an angle less than vertical.

"I know this place," she said. "It's in Potomac County!"

"You sure?" I said.

"Yes. I was there last year. In late spring, before the end of school. Mrs. Jones, one of the parents at my school, had asked for volunteers to help clear out the brush and high grass around the cemetery."

"Wouldn't that maintenance usually be done by the congregation?"

"The church had closed a while back, due to an aging, dying, dwindling congregation. They hadn't lured in enough young families to keep the place going, so it had gone out of business. It was up for sale at the time."

"So it hadn't been maintained in a while?"

"Yeah. It was a mess. The cemetery was there *before* the church. There was really no connection between the two. No one had been buried there in over a hundred years. At one time, Mrs. Jones' grandparents had attended services at the church, but no one she knew was related to any of the people buried there. She thought it was disrespectful to leave any cemetery unattended. She wanted to return it to being a place people could visit, in case there *was* anyone left out there who had a connection."

"And where is this place?"

"Out on Sandpoint Road. Past the winery. Not far from the public landing on the Rappahannock River."

"Radburke got a ticket out that way. For speeding and reckless driving. About a year ago."

Chapter Sixty-One

We were on our way back to Potomac County. Wendi was driving, freeing me to use my phone to pull up the notes I'd made on Radburke's activities. The traffic ticket he received had been issued by Deputy Runyon Pugh. I didn't know how to get in touch with him directly, so I called Murphy.

"It's late," he said. "I'm getting ready for bed."

When I told him what I wanted, it didn't make him any happier. He said Pugh was on duty. He'd contact him and have him call me. I didn't tell Murphy everything I was up to. There would be time for that later if this turned out to be something worth pursuing.

Six minutes later, my phone rang.

"Mr. Barrow," Pugh said. "Sheriff said you needed to talk with me about a traffic citation from back a year ago?"

"Yes," I said. "Thanks for calling. Guy's name is Damon Radburke. You snagged him out near the winery."

"I remember. Strange-acting city dude. From D.C. What about it?"

"Can you tell me the circumstances?"

"It was dark. Thought he was drunk or something. Way he was weaving around the road. Going real fast for a bit. Twenty over the limit when he went past me. Then he slowed down, almost stopped before hightailing it off again. I caught up to him, put on my lights, pulled him over."

"He offer a reason for the way he was driving?"

"Claimed he was looking for his dog. That she'd run off."

"He say from where?"

"Not that I remember. I didn't rightly believe him. When I asked what kind of dog it was, he stammered around, then said it weren't nothing but an ol' mutt of some kind. Black and brown. Sounded to me like he was making it up right then and there. Still thought he was drunk. Gave him the sobriety test and breathalyzer. But he passed. He seemed worked up about something other than me. Kept looking all around while we were going through the steps. There wasn't anything illegal in his car. No weapons or drugs. Just a funny-looking hammer on the front seat. That all you need?"

"Yeah," I said. "Thanks, Runyon. I owe you one."

"Sheriff says to call, I call," he said. "Gotta go."

After he hung up we were quiet for a while. Wendi was concentrating on her driving, staying alert for deer along the road. I went back on my phone and scrolled through the county property transfers listed in the Potomac News archives from more than a year ago. After a few minutes of squinting at the tiny screen, I found it. The church property had been sold to Old Dominion Services, Inc. in July of the previous year. You couldn't get a connection to Radburke much closer than that.

But the closer we got to the Potomac County line, the less confident I was that we were onto something of significance. Radburke owned property outright under his own name in a lot of places. He was a wealthy man who could travel anywhere he wanted. Maybe he'd be avoiding Paris these days, but the rest of the world was wide open. It was a long shot that he'd taken Melissa to the church. In my logical mind, I knew that. In my heart, I knew that. But going there was the only trail we had to follow. Even if it was a dead end.

Five miles past the county line, we made a right onto the road that would take us where we needed to go. Three miles later, up to the left, we could see the parallel rows of the vineyard, trailing up and over the hillside, silhouetted against the half-moonlit sky. Somewhere beyond, out of sight, were the winery buildings that included the recent addition of a huge tasting and event center. Less than a quarter mile farther, Wendi slowed the car to a crawl, then stopped at the end of a dirt road leading off into the trees on the right.

"I *think* this is it," she said. "I'm not sure. It's been more than a year. I know you can't see the church from out here on the road. They said back in the day, you could. But the trees have grown so much in recent years, they block the view."

Let's take a walk," I said. "We'll find out soon enough."

We parked the car across the road, down twenty yards farther, where there was room to pull off the pavement onto the gravel shoulder. I pulled a small flashlight from a storage cubby in the back of the vehicle and checked my phone.

"What the hell?" I said. "I'm not getting a signal."

"I forgot about that," Wendi said. "Service is spotty out this way. Pretty much a dead zone. Too far from the nearest tower. It's better back up the road. Out by the winery."

"Well, at least the damn things will be good for more light. I don't know how old the batteries in this flashlight might be. It could die on us any minute."

Wendi didn't seem to be listening. She was busy pulling her tiny twenty-two caliber pearl-handled revolver and shoulder holster out of her bag. She slipped it on and secured it. Then put on a denim blazer to cover it up.

"What are you doing?" I said.

"Protecting you."

"From what?"

"It's dark," she said. "We're going for a walk in the woods. We could encounter a rabid raccoon along the way."

"Is that thing loaded?"

"You bet your ass it is."

"How much ammo?"

"Just the five in it. One empty chamber."

"What if we stumble upon a whole pack of rabid raccoons?"

"It's not a pack. It's called a *gaze* of raccoons. And if we do, you better hope there's not more than five of the diseased little bastards."

We hurried across the pavement and started down the dirt road. About thirty yards in, there was a thick steel cable stretched across the lane, attached to wooden posts on both sides, one end secured with a padlock. Dangling from the center were two identical red-lettered signs that spelled out NO TRESPASSING. We stepped around the end of the barrier and continued on. Somewhere in the darkness in front of us, we could hear the rustling of animals. I worried more about skunks than raccoons.

The road made a sharp right, the trees parted, and before us stood the dark figure of the old church. As far as we could see, there were no vehicles around. Potomac County had a scattering of old churches, many still in use, others abandoned and neglected like this one. It was larger than expected, half again as big as similar structures I'd seen. Even in the dark, we could make out the peeling white paint on the clapboard siding. Long, bullet-shaped windows were hidden behind congruent, closed, dark wooden shutters. No light escaped from inside. Jutting out from the front of the building was a rectangular bell tower, at its base four steps leading up to closed double doors.

Extending across the peak of the steep roof was a structure that had to be a recent addition. I pointed the beam of the flashlight upward and swept the light over the rooftop. It looked like an extended walkway that ran all the way from the belltower to the rear of the building, where it ended at a deck-like platform. A strange variation of a widow's walk.

The front doors were locked, so we circled the building looking for another way in. We couldn't reach the shuttered windows to see if they were secure, and there wasn't anything around that could be used to stand on. At the back of the building, on the ground, was a pile of big rocks and broken chunks of concrete. Mixed in were a couple of old headstones from the cemetery, the names and dates, worn by weather and time, barely readable. The conical pile was about ten feet in diameter, nearly three feet high at the center. Above the pile, on the back wall was a single door with boards nailed across it.

I shone the light up the wall toward the peak of the roof. Directly above the pile of rocks was the rooftop platform. I didn't like what I was thinking.

I swept the light across the grounds surrounding the church. Grass and weeds had once again taken over the cemetery. There were broken tree branches scattered about and a cluster of rotting stumps towards the back of the open space.

Over next to a leaning shed was a stack of rotting firewood. Inside, we found a rusted shovel with half its handle broken off. There were rusted old rakes and a wooden box filled with ancient hand tools. Behind some wide boards leaning against a wall, Wendi found something that might prove useful. An old, rusted, but otherwise intact pickaxe.

Back outside at the front of the church, we rattled and pushed at the double doors again. I lifted my leg and kicked at the center a couple of times. It didn't budge. I considered trying again, but thought about how my shoulder still felt and decided against it. I was getting too old for this shit.

We stood in silence for a moment. Both of us likely thinking the same thing. Was there a valid reason to break in?

It was then that we both heard it. A muffled, distant sound from within. An indescribable animal-like scream that uttered no discernible words, only something guttural and pleading.

I raised the pickaxe and swung hard. After four strikes, the doors opened. Inside the vestibule, on both sides, were stairs leading up to the bell tower. Ten feet in front of us was another set of double doors. From the low ceiling, I guessed that there was most likely a choir loft above us as well. We opened the double doors and stepped into the nave, unprepared for what we saw.

Chapter Sixty-Two

J ust beyond where the low ceiling ended, four bare legs dangled in front and above us, like disembodied limbs, feet twisting and writhing with each scream growing louder and clearer. The feral sound finally forced into the desperate words, *"Help us!"*

When we rushed beneath them and turned with the light shining upward, their full figures and the extent of their predicament came into focus. Wearing only long white t-shirts and underwear, Melissa Adamson and Kasey Dylan dangled from the choir loft above. Their wrists were bound in metal handcuffs, the chains attached to something atop the half-wall at the front of the balcony.

"Keep the light on them," I shouted, thrusting the flashlight at Wendi.

I turned and ran, back out through the vestibule, feeling my way up the dark and narrow stairwell. When I reached the wall at the front of the balcony, I could feel the metal loops where the chains were attached. I told Wendi to move on down the aisle and direct the beam at a better angle, to the spot where my hands struggled to loosen the U-shaped bolts attached to the top of the wall. The light didn't help. I could see what I was doing, but the bolts wouldn't loosen.

I called for Wendi to come up and help me. She was there in an instant. When we slowed down enough to think things through, we realized that loosening the bolts was not the first thing that needed to be done. With each of us grasping an arm, we managed to pull Melissa up and over the wall. Kasey was next.

Out of breath, each of them collapsed into a fetal position against the wall, unable to move any farther. Their wrists were raw and bloody, the look in their eyes tired and distant. There were multiple bruises on their faces and arms. Long, deep scratches on their legs and feet.

The chains on the handcuffs were strong, but not thick or heavy. I hurried back down the stairs and retrieved the pickaxe from where I'd dropped it inside the shattered front doors.

Back upstairs, Wendi held the first chain tight across the top of the wall, while I took short chops at it with the dull chisel-end of the pickaxe. When I raised the axe higher and put more of my weight behind the thrusts, the chain finally split apart, freeing Melissa from the loop attached to the wall. The second one took a little longer. Exhaustion was setting in, and my arms and shoulder ached. When the chain broke, I collapsed to the floor, took in a deep breath, and let it out slowly. Both women were free, but the cuffs still encircled their bloody wrists, the broken chains dangling from each one like some kind of bizarre jewelry.

"We need to go," Wendi said, pulling on my arm to get me on my feet. "Right now!"

There was no time to look for the women's clothes or shoes. We needed to get out to the road to my vehicle, back to where we could get a signal to call 911.

We were halfway across the churchyard, headed for the lane, when we saw the lights of a car flickering low across the trees ahead. A vehicle had pulled in and stopped at the wire. The creak of a car door opening sent us scrambling into the woods. At the sound of the metal door slamming shut, we stopped. When the engine revved, and the lights continued down the lane, we held our place and crouched down low, waiting and watching for our chance to circle back around to the lane and head for the road.

When the vehicle reached the clearing, I could tell from its shape that it was a pickup truck. Its headlights swept across the churchyard to the front of the building, revealing the splintered, open front doors. The truck came to an abrupt stop, and a man got out and rushed inside. We started to move, but it was slow-going through the brush with two exhausted, shoeless women in tow.

We were ten yards from the softer terrain of the lane when we heard the slam of the truck door and saw the lights swivel in our direction. We hit the ground behind a fallen tree and waited. Kasey was shaking and whimpering. Melissa sounded on the verge of hyperventilating. None of that was going to help, but I didn't have the heart to tell them to shut up. Maybe because my heart was pounding faster than I'd ever remembered. I had the fleeting thought that my father's heart condition might've been hereditary. I saw Wendi check to make sure her gun was still in the shoulder holster. She seemed calm and collected. I was glad she hadn't wasted ammunition on any allegedly rabid raccoons.

The truck crept up the lane, close to the place we were hiding. The man inside was jerking the beam of a flashlight out through the open windows, scanning the woods on both sides of the lane. We waited and saw the light retreat. Then he was gone.

I could tell that he'd made it out to the paved road and stopped. But I couldn't see through the thick undergrowth enough to be able to tell what he was doing out there. There were sounds that I didn't recognize. We waited still longer, for what seemed an eternity, until the roar of his truck engine and his headlights trailed off in the direction of the vineyard.

Up and moving again, we stumbled out to the lane and hurried along the smooth dirt path. When we got to my SUV out on the road, I knew what he'd been doing out there. The feeling of relief we shared was instantly shattered by the discovery of four slashed tires.

There wasn't any time for self-pity and indecision. We turned and started to hurry along the pavement in the direction of the winery. Wendi and I kept checking our phones for a signal.

We were twenty yards from a dirt road leading up a hill through the vineyard when we saw the approaching headlights. We scrambled for the cover of the woods again and waited.

The truck stopped at the metal gate to the vineyard road, and the driver traced the beam of light up the pathway to the crest of the hill. He directed the light erratically from side to side into the rows of vines, then up the road again, before speeding away back in the direction of the church.

When he was out of sight, we were on the move again. We slipped between the horizontal timbers of the split rail fence that bordered the vineyard. I stopped and rattled the gate. It was locked. The guy in the truck couldn't follow us, unless he rammed his way through it. Progress up the hill was slow. I had an arm around Melissa's waist, with her own across my back, hanging onto my shoulder. Wendi and Kasey were likewise entangled.

When we reached a spot twenty feet from the top of the hill, the truck pulled up to the gate below. I turned to see the headlights go out, followed by the familiar sound of the truck door slamming shut. The beam of his flashlight caught us, and we made a sharp turn off the road and down an alley between the rows of vines.

We were running outright now. Moving in the general direction toward distant dim lights about three hundred yards away at the cluster of winery buildings. The two young women were ahead of us, adrenaline kicking in, pumping up their will to survive. The beam of the flashlight tagged us again, and a second later, at a break in the rows, we cut to the left and turned down the next alley. A moment later, the beam was on us again, and a shot rang out, whistling through the vines to my left. Kasey and Melissa screamed and hit the ground, scrambling on their bellies beneath the vines in opposite directions. Wendi and I did the same.

Struggling to my feet, I could see Kasey far ahead of me, her white shirt floating away like a specter in the light of the half-moon. A moment later, I stepped in a hole and went down hard. I was on the ground for a minute, trying to summon the strength to get up again and the will to ignore the throbbing pain in my ankle. Kasey was somewhere ahead of me, but out of sight.

When I got up, I heard something behind me and turned. With the moon high in the sky behind him, Damon Radburke stood twenty feet away, his arms extended in front of him. The gun in his hands leveled at me.

From somewhere behind him, Wendi shouted, "Hey!"

When Radburke pivoted, a shot rang out, and he went down.

He was on his back, clutching at his side with one hand where the bullet had hit. A dark puddle was forming on the ground beneath him. I hobbled over to him and stepped on the other hand, still holding the gun. He cried out in pain and let go. I picked up the weapon and stepped on his fingers again.

Despite a strong inclination to walk away and let Damon Radburke bleed to death, I rendered aid. Wendi took off her blazer, and I used it to stem the bleeding as best I could. In the meantime, she managed to get a signal and reach the 911 operator while heading on out across the rolling vine-covered hills, toward the lighted buildings two hundred yards beyond, hoping to round up Melissa and Kasey along the way. Meanwhile, I stayed behind, trying to keep an unconscious man alive. A man whom the world would be better off without.

* * *

Deputy Runyon Pugh was the first official on the scene, soon followed by a parade of lights and sirens, further disrupting the serenity of a summer night in the countryside. Before his arrival, two women who worked and lived on the grounds of the winery had hustled out on a four-wheeler with a first aid kit to help me with the wounded man.

Thirty minutes later, by the time the Potomac County Rescue Squad was on its way out with Radburke, Sheriff Oscar Murphy had arrived. He got our quick account of the whole mess, then left his deputies to secure the scene, while he followed the ambulances carrying Kasey and Melissa to the hospital.

Chapter Sixty-Three

Early on Monday afternoon, I was back in Murphy's office. He'd called me in to brief me on the progress that had been made on the whole Damon Radburke investigation. Either that, or to ream me a new one. At various times during the conversation, he would manage to do both.

Although my ankle was still sore, I was walking on it. Most of my other aches and pains had subsided to the point of tolerance.

"How you feeling?" Murphy said.

"Better," I said. "Thanks for asking."

"I'm the sheriff. I feel obliged to ask. Might need your vote next year."

"Always thinking ahead. A true politician."

"You know what you did was stupid, right?"

"I don't see it that way."

"If you thought there was a chance that Radburke had taken Melissa Adamson to the church, then you should've, at the very least, had Pugh go with you to check it out."

"It was a long shot. I didn't really believe we'd find her there."

"What made you think she might be at the old church?"

"We found a clue."

"What kind of clue?"

"A photograph. Taken by Karl Bassle. Radburke and a woman outside the church."

"Where'd you find this photo?"

"At Bassle's house."

"He show it to you?"

"Not exactly. I sort of…"

"Never mind," he said. "I don't need to know all the details."

"You find Bassle?" I said, trying to steer the conversation in a less self-incriminating direction.

"Right where you thought he might be. Hiding out at Riley Zerco's place with his girlfriend, Tammy what's-her-name."

"He complain about anything I did?"

"No. He seems grateful for the way you intervened. He and Tammy have agreed to testify against Radburke. Though Bassle knows a lot more than she does. First to make a deal with the Commonwealth's Attorney and the Feds. Says he and the other three lawyers were in deep with the financial crimes. The four of them were laundering dirty money for Radburke through the phony company they'd set up. Old Dominion Services. Also, on the personal business side, drawing up a boatload of NDAs and working hard at coercing a lot of women to sign them in exchange for a ton of money to keep their mouths shut about the abuse they'd suffered."

"He know what Radburke was doing to the women?"

"Says he didn't."

"But he knew it wasn't good?"

"Probably knew more than he's claiming. We'll leave all that for the good-guy lawyers to sort out."

"But Radburke himself will be going away for a long time?"

"The kidnapping charges alone would be enough. But there's a trail of dead bodies. Some of which he most likely did himself. Or hired them out to someone like Edik Levka. And we've already found at least two more women buried in the cemetery at the old church."

"You find out how Radburke got hold of Kasey Dylan?"

"She says her husband, Rutherford, handed her over to Radburke. She'd scheduled a meeting with Rutherford that Saturday morning to discuss their separation. That's why she was delayed in leaving to catch up with you at the Karruth estate. He told her you were on the wrong track. Convinced her that he was the only one who could take her to Melissa. Get her away from Radburke. When they got to the church, things went bad. Rutherford Dylan wanted Radburke to take care of his meddling wife for good. He left her there. We haven't located him yet, but we will."

"How are Kasey and Melissa doing?"

"They were released from the hospital this morning. They're going to be okay physically. But they went through a bad ordeal. They'll need a lot of therapy. Of the legitimate variety."

"And what about Joan Flaith?"

"Haven't found her yet either. It seems she has abandoned her partner, Phil Trunvid. He has also decided to cooperate with the investigation. From what you've told me, there's a good chance Joan might be hiding out somewhere with her paramour, Rutherford Dylan. She's in deep, too. Seems when she got hooked up with Radburke through Dylan, the bunch started up their little enterprise to supply Radburke with the women he wanted. Like you figured, Joan Flaith was grooming the women for him. You might say he sort of subcontracted that part out to her."

"And they ran the whole program out of the Karruth estate. A place that couldn't be directly linked to Radburke without some digging around."

"Which you did," he said.

"Among other things," I said.

"Some things best left to the professionals in law enforcement."

"Well, you *are* shorthanded around here. I like to help out when I can. It's my nature."

Chapter Sixty-Four

By ten o'clock on Wednesday morning, Wendi and I were packed and ready to go. The plan included a leisurely three-night stay at Colonial Williamsburg before heading north to Maryland for a long weekend with Bret and Breana and her family, at her place in Westminster.

We were out on the deck, sitting in the Adirondack chairs, looking out at the river, taking in the sun for a few minutes before our planned precise departure time of 10:30.

I'd talked to Murphy frequently and at length over the last couple of days, catching up on all the details as they trickled in from various sources.

"Murphy says they found the contractor who did the work on the old church," I said. "An outfit out of D.C. Probably didn't want anyone local to gossip about what he was doing with the place. Radburke told the contractor it was a platform for stargazing with a telescope."

"And instead, it was a dropping point to the rocks below," Wendi said. "How sick is that?"

"About as sick as it gets."

"And the whole thing with the program for the women at the estate?"

"Radburke wanted the women to break off all contact with everyone in their lives. So that when they disappeared, no one would know. At least not for a while."

"And Joan Flaith was the perfect instrument to carry that out," she said. "An opportunity for her to practice the theories in the book Radburke had published for her. She acted like a guru for them. Convincing the women to cast off everyone from their previously failed lives. To start fresh. To feel safe. Maybe for the first time in their lives."

"That's what Radburke wanted. Needed," I said. "For his victims to be certain that he would save them from a life of abuse. In his twisted mind, he needed them to feel that he was the only person who could save and protect them."

"When in reality he was their greatest nightmare," she said.

"And that probably added to the sick thrill he got. For them to feel psychologically and physically safe until the instant he turned on them."

"So he required women who had previously been abused to feel as though they'd been saved. But when things turned…"

"When things turned, he wanted women who would know what was coming."

"And they would, because they'd lived it before," she said. "They knew the horror that was coming."

"But maybe Radburke would've wanted it to be worse than anything they'd experienced before."

"Like falling onto a pile of rocks? Like the woman in the park did when he was a teenager."

"It's like he was trying to relive the thrill of that incident."

"Do the police think he killed all the women that way?"

"No. The setup at the church is relatively recent. It looks like the bodies they found out there were also beaten with a Piton hammer. The fall might not have killed them, so he used the hammer to finish the job. It's the kind rock climbers use. The same kind of hammer Pugh saw in Radburke's car the night he gave him the citation for speeding. That's what was used to kill the woman dumped near D.C. a few years back. And the woman in Paris. They think the platform thing at the church was some sort of recent evolution in his method."

"And what about the other killings? Roma Coltrell and Flo?"

"Those were most likely hired out to Edik Levka. The theory is that when Roma escaped from the estate that night and took the neighbor's boat, Levka and Phil Trunvid were chasing her in another boat that was docked at the estate. The cops found a boat there with a rifle hidden inside. Probably the one he used to shoot at us."

"And Flo?"

"Someone, probably Levka, got Harry from the Crisis Center to admit that he'd told me where to find her. They couldn't take the chance that she'd tell me more than they wanted me to know. The pills they found when they arrested Levka at the car lot that night matched what was found in Flo's system. And Levka was sloppy at Flo's trailer. Turns out he left a thumbprint on the underside of the coffee table. Tech guys missed it the first time. Caught it when they went back for another look. It also appears that Levka's been dipping into his own opioid supply. Showed symptoms of withdrawal at the jail. He's been transferred to the hospital over in Dominion County. And it turns out the lawyer he called was Bassle. Who never showed up. Now that Radburke's not paying his legal expenses, he's been assigned a public defender."

"And what about Harry and Margaret? You think they were killed, too?"

"Murphy said they turned themselves in to the cops in Fredericksburg when the news broke about Radburke's arrest and Rutherford Dylan's involvement. It seems Rutherford Dylan was a frequent donor to the Crisis Center. Cops figure neither of them knew enough about what was really going on for Radburke to send Levka to permanently remove them. Probably told them to just hide out for a while."

"And Fordy Dylan and Joan Flaith are still unaccounted for?"

"For now. You know what they always say. *You can run, but you can't hide.*"

"I thought it was the other way around. You *can hide*, but you *can't run.*"

"I'm pretty sure it's what I said. Either way, they'll turn up sooner or later."

"Let's hope so. I just hope they're not hiding out in Williamsburg at the same hotel where we're staying. It could be awkward if we ran into them at the pool. I might have to shoot them."

"It's probably best that Murphy's still holding your gun as evidence," I said. "But on a more serious note, how are you feeling now about having to shoot Damon Radburke?"

"I wish you'd stop asking me that! What's this, like the *tenth* time?"

"I wasn't counting. But you haven't answered the question."

"I'm *okay. Really*. It had to be done."

"It's not an easy thing to do. To shoot another human being."

"But it *was* him or us. I suppose it helps that he didn't die. Though it would've saved time and money for a lot of people if he had. Not to mention that someone who's inflicted so much pain on other human beings, women in particular, probably doesn't deserve to live. I guess I'm glad, though, that I wasn't the person who determined whether he lived or died."

When we'd temporarily satisfied our need to rehash the traumatic events of the previous days, it was close to time to leave. The two-hour drive would put us in Williamsburg in time for lunch. After that, we'd visit the colonial attractions for the rest of the afternoon and cap off the day with a nice dinner at the historic Christiana Campbell's Tavern. We were both looking forward to catching the dramatic witch trial reenactment one evening at the Capitol Hall of Burgesses. I had plans to spend some quality time in the cabinetmaker's shop, a place my grandfather and I had favored.

After one final sweep through the cabin to check for things forgotten, I was locking the door when my phone rang.

It was Oscar Murphy.

"Murph, what's up?" I said.

"I need you to come in to the office," he said.

"We're heading out for Williamsburg right now. Can it wait until next week?"

"No," he said with a firmness in his voice that I hadn't heard for a long time.

"What's this about? More on the Radburke thing?"

"We'll talk when you get here. This isn't something to do over the phone."

"You need both of us?"

"Just you."

"Okay. We'll stop on our way out of town. Wendi needed to stop at the apartment anyway, so it's no big deal. Be there in a few minutes."

He said, "Okay," and hung up.

Wendi rolled her eyes. *"Really?"* she said. *"Now?"*

Chapter Sixty-Five

When I got to the Sheriff's Department building in Weston, Deputies Adele Carter and Runyon Pugh were hustling out the door, headed for their official vehicles. Adele spared a second for a quick *hello* with a wave and a smile. Pugh managed a grimace and a half-raised hand. I wasn't sure if it was a greeting or if he was swatting away a fly.

Inside, a heavy gray-haired man in a khaki suit and a small thin woman, dressed in a blue t-shirt and jeans, shook hands with Sheriff Oscar Murphy and headed for the door. When we passed, the woman looked away, then down at her feet. The man smiled and nodded to me. I made my way over to the front desk, where Murphy stood watching them leave.

"Who was that?" I asked. "Or is that none of my business?"

"Guy in the suit's the woman's lawyer. She was here to report that she'd been abducted and beaten by Damon Radburke last year. She escaped."

"When?"

"The night Pugh gave Radburke the ticket. He was out looking for her then. When Pugh detained Radburke, it gave her the opportunity she needed."

"And she never reported it?"

"Not until now. Said she told her sister. Swore her to secrecy. She was hiding out, in fear for her life. Didn't know who to trust. She knew the man had money and power. Figured he'd get away with what he'd done to her. His word against hers. Afraid he'd come after her again or hurt someone in her family."

"She wasn't concerned he'd do the same to other women?"

"Fear is often a paralyzing force. Some people can't allow themselves to think that way. Self-preservation is all they can think about. It's not all that uncommon."

"Is this what you wanted to see me about?" I said.

"No," he said. "There's a man in my office you need to meet. His name is Vance Declan."

* * *

Declan was a guy of average height, with close-cropped white hair and a mustache and goatee to match. The skin on his puffy face was tight with a reddish glow, like he'd spent some time in the sun and wind. Behind frameless glasses, his eyes were dark and clear. His expression was solemn and businesslike. When Murphy introduced us, he stood to shake my hand, then we all sat down.

I wasn't all that surprised when Murphy announced that Declan was a retired Chief of Police. The unexpected part was where he was from. A place in North Carolina named Birch Creek. The same town where my grandfather, Pax Barrow, had once worked as a police officer.

"Chief Declan has been spending a fair portion of his retirement days working cold cases for the town of Birch Creek," Murphy said. "He came across some information related to an old case here in Potomac County that he wanted to share with us."

"I don't reckon, Mr. Barrow," Declan began, "that this will be the kind of thing you'd be expecting to hear. Especially after all these years. But the service revolver that belonged to your grandfather was used in a robbery in which an elderly store clerk named Hattie Block was shot and killed. The case was never solved. In my review of old records, I came across a file on the incident stuffed in the bottom of a box of documents relating to *solved* cases. Due to negligence, or downright deception, it appears the ballistics report from the Block woman's murder was never shared with any other law enforcement agency outside of Birch Creek. So, after recently taking care of that oversight, I found out the same gun had been used in the apparent suicide of Paxton Barrow, your grandfather."

He handed me a piece of paper that contained a summary of the details. I looked long and hard at the date of the robbery and murder. It was the day before my grandfather's death.

"You're not saying my grandfather had anything to do with killing that woman?"

"No, sir. I am not. I've learned from the information Sheriff Murphy has shared from the file on your grandfather's case that multiple witnesses placed Paxton Barrow here in Potomac County the day before his death. Nowhere near Birch Creek, North Carolina."

"So the gun was in someone else's possession the day before my grandfather supposedly killed himself with it?"

"And the person responsible for the murder, or someone else, transported the weapon up here by the next day."

"And gave it to my grandfather," I said. "Who then turns around and kills himself with the gun the very same day? I don't believe that."

"Frankly, sir, neither do I. Based on some interviews I've conducted and a bit of poking around in old records, I believe it's much more likely that Paxton Barrow was murdered with his own gun. A gun he hadn't possessed for more than ten years."

"Before his death, the last time I saw his gun was when I was just a nine-year-old kid. You're saying he got rid of it?"

"I am. I talked with a woman who was the daughter of the Chief of Police down there at the time. She used to hang around the headquarters on occasion when she was a little girl. She knew Paxton Barrow and liked him. He used to give her a lollipop every time she visited the offices. When she was a young woman, after your grandfather had retired, she started working there as an office assistant for a while. She remembered a time when your grandfather came back to visit. She claims she remembers seeing Paxton Barrow hand over a gun to one of the officers there. She was certain the two men didn't know that she'd seen the gun handed over to the officer."

"She remember who the officer was?" I said.

"She did. Says his name was Giles Burton."

"I don't remember ever hearing my grandfather mention that name."

"Mmm. Well, anyway, Giles Burton had a son. From what I hear tell, he was a right bad one. In trouble with the law off and on. At the very least, an embarrassment to his papa. The boy died of a drug overdose about five years after the killing of Hattie Block. After the kid died, some local tongues loosened up a might. There was no proof, but there were a lot of rumors swirling around after his death that he was the one who'd killed Hattie Block in that store robbery."

"With my grandfather's gun."

"Yes, sir. So I got to digging around deep into the records at the police headquarters. And I found out that Giles Burton had taken off work for a couple of days after the killing at the store."

"So you think Burton found out that his son had gotten hold of my grandfather's gun and shot the woman when he was robbing the store?"

"And Giles Burton wanted to keep his son from going to prison. He knew if that gun was identified as being the weapon that had belonged to your grandfather..."

"Then my grandfather was the only one who knew who was in possession of the gun at the time of the killing."

"And so, to save his son, I believe Burton traveled up here to Virginia and killed your grandfather. Made it look like a suicide and left the gun at the scene. And when he got back to Birch Creek, he's likely the one who made sure the ballistics report never got seen by anyone else or distributed."

"It's been more than four decades. I doubt we could ever find a record of Giles Burton having been here."

"Might not be anything to look for. Could have slept in his car. No hotel to have a record. Even if their records did go back that far."

"I'm assuming this Giles Burton is deceased now?"

"A long time ago," Vance Declan said. "I like to believe he's had his judgment day in the next world."

"It would be nice to think so," I said.

Chapter Sixty-Six

I can't say the news that someone other than me believed that my grandfather had not committed suicide made me *happy*. That wouldn't be the right word. It was an odd mixture of feelings. Relief. Anger. Vindication. Comfort. Satisfaction. Peace.

It would take more time, if ever, for the feeling of forgiveness to earn its way into the mix. It would be difficult to forgive the man who had ended Pax Barrow's incredible life in an effort to protect his own vile son from facing the consequences of his actions.

But at least the truth would come out. Word would get around Potomac County like it always did. But most of those who had known my grandfather were long gone. Perhaps, like me, they'd known the truth all along. That Pax Barrow was not the kind of man to take his own life and leave his only grandson behind. I like to believe that with our passing comes the knowledge of all truth. That all is somehow revealed to us as we pass into the next phase of being. At least it's nice to think so.

Wendi and I talked about it all while we were on the road to Williamsburg. But after that, over the next week or so, I managed not to dwell on the recent events and revelations. I kept those thoughts at bay for the most part, enjoying our time alone together, then uniting with my family. Reveling in the amazing joy of being with my own granddaughter, my own children.

Neither of my kids had known Pax Barrow. To them, he was a distant image in the old photographs they'd seen, an accumulation of the many repeated stories they'd heard. Over the years, I'd probably talked more of him than I had my own parents, their own grandparents. I would need to fix that. If they wanted to know more, I would tell them. The good with the not-so-good. But always the truth.

*   *   *

The day we returned to Potomac County, Wendi transferred her luggage to her patched-up SUV at Skip's repair shop and headed out for her apartment. Before parting, we made plans to meet for lunch the next day. On the way out of Weston, I stopped by Murphy's office long enough for him to fill me in on the events that had unfolded in our absence.

Rutherford Dylan and Joan Flaith had been found. Edik Levka had somehow escaped from the hospital where he was under guard. Vanished. Likely never to be found. Melissa Adamson and Kasey Dylan were getting the care they needed, and hoping that Wendi and I would visit soon. In a rare instance of judicial common sense, Riley Zerco had been granted custody of his nephew, Bobby Coltrell.

Back at the cabin, I stood alone for a while, watching the sunset, looking out over the wide darkening river, feeling the water lap against the shore between and over my naked toes. In the distance, sailboats glided peacefully along, reflecting the last of the day's light. I thought for a moment about the life hidden below the surface, and how the passing of another day meant little to those creatures.

Before the darkness chased away the light, I turned my back to the river and surveyed my home. The skeleton of the place was mostly as it had been when my grandfather built it. Over the years, especially after my divorce, I'd made improvements. New windows. A new deck. An extra bedroom with a bath added onto the back. I hoped that the current and future generations of Barrows would keep it in the family. Retain ownership. Maintain it as a place where they could come to gather and relax, take pleasure in each other's company. A place to think and plan. A place to dwell on the important things in life. Family and friends. Safety and truth.

Acknowledgments

Special thanks go to:

Janet Hutchings, past Editor of *Ellery Queen's Mystery Magazine*, for making me a published author with the debut of "Stray" in The Department of First Stories.

Linda Landrigan, Editor of *Alfred Hitchcock's Mystery Magazine*, for publishing the very first Pete Barrow short story and for keeping the series going.

To Shawn Reilly Simmons, Editor at Level Best Books, for your continuing guidance and support, and for giving an old math teacher a chance.

To all the members of the amazing Chestertown Writers Critique Group; Frances, Ronny, Rick, Linda, Joe2, Alice, and especially fellow Level Best Author, Wendy Sand Eckel, for all your suggestions, encouragement, and support. Each and every one of you made me a better writer.

To Joe O'Connor and Bill Frazier, two talented writers and funny guys from the Group, who left this world way too soon.

To all my past writing teachers, for their guidance and encouragement, especially Vincent Stewart and Joseph Nicholson from my time many years ago at Lock Haven State, and Robert Hilldrup of Richmond, Virginia, who back in the early 1980s encouraged me to keep going with my characters, Pete Barrow, Wendi Wynston, and Oscar Murphy. It took a few years, Bob, but I finally got there.

To Judi, the one and only love of my life, for believing in me as a writer, reveling in our shared quirky sense of humor, and putting up with me for all these many years, including back in the day when I spent too much time with my horse.

To Bethany and DJ, Mark and Anne Marie, for cheering me on every time I called to tell them I'd sold another story. And for giving me all those wonderful grandchildren; Adrienne, Collins, Graham, and Emma, who will all have to wait a few more years before being allowed to read anything that Grandpa has written.

About the Author

Ken Linn spent four decades teaching mathematics in both private and public high schools throughout the Chesapeake Bay region of Virginia and Maryland. His short mystery fiction has appeared in *Ellery Queen's Mystery Magazine* and *Alfred Hitchcock's Mystery Magazine*. He lives on the picturesque and peaceful upper Eastern Shore of Maryland.

AUTHOR WEBSITE:
  kenlinnauthor.com

SOCIAL MEDIA HANDLE:
  Ken Linn on Facebook

Also by Ken Linn

Short stories in *Ellery Queen's Mystery Magazine* and *Alfred Hitchcock's Mystery Magazine*

9 798889 820155